ii

The Gospel Truth

Tales from Ty Ty

Dedicated to Charlotte Elizabeth Robinson,
my first and best editor and so much more,
whose gift made this book possible.

ISBN-13: 978-0615850788
ISBN-10: 0615850782

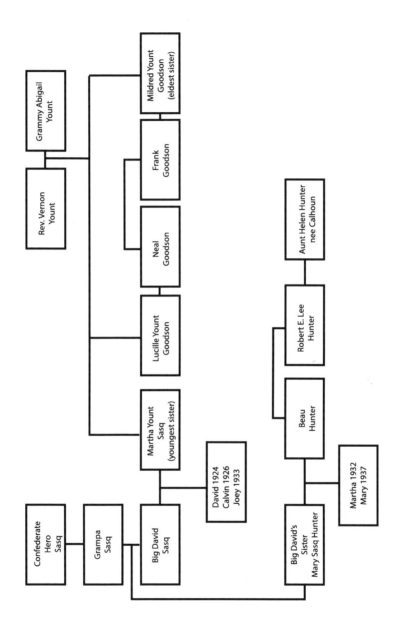

Rev. Vernon Yount — Grammy Abigail Yount

Mildred Yount Goodson (eldest sister)
Frank Goodson
Neal Goodson
Lucille Yount Goodson
Martha Yount Sasq (youngest sister)

David 1924
Calvin 1926
Joey 1933

Confederate Hero Sasq
Grampa Sasq
Big David Sasq

Aunt Helen Hunter nee Calhoun
Robert E. Lee Hunter
Beau Hunter
Big David's Sister Mary Sasq Hunter

Martha 1932
Mary 1937

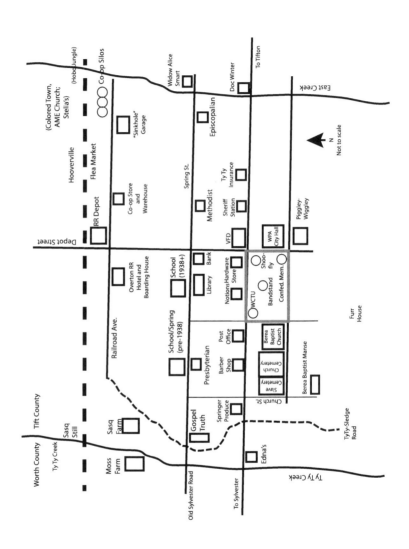

This is how I remember it. It's my truth, and no one else's.

—David Sasq

Table of Contents

September 1940
Funeral Casseroles

Joey was dead.

I sat with Mama and Calvin in the front pew. Daddy and Uncle Frank carried in Joey's little coffin and set it on sawhorses that had been covered with a sheet, and then sat beside Mama. Some of the women put wildflowers on top of the coffin. Aunt Helen added white sunflowers and purple amaranth from her garden. She hugged Mama then handed me her cardboard fan. "You're flushed, David. Please take this."

I was flushed partly because I was wearing a suit coat and a tie. Mama said since I was sixteen, I had to dress like a young man. I was flushed partly because I was angry—angry because Joey was dead, angry because Joey didn't have a chance to grow up, angry because in seven years he'd never learned to talk or been able to walk. I thought about what it might have been like to play hide-n-seek and tag with two little brothers instead of just Calvin and me, and bit my lip hard to keep from crying. I was too old to cry. I knew that as long as I didn't cry, Calvin, who was twelve, wouldn't either.

Deacon Clement stood from his chair behind the pulpit. Mrs. Clampert pumped up the organ and started playing *The Church in the Wildwood*. The voices of the congregation echoed from the wooden walls of the Gospel Truth Baptist Church and hid the wheezing of the organ's leaky bellows.

Mama pressed her handkerchief to her eyes. I knew what she was thinking. *Church in the Wildwood* was Joey's favorite song, even though he didn't know a word and couldn't sing a note. Memories flooded my mind: Joey, sitting slack-jawed and vacant-eyed, silent until the chorus began, and then his face lighting up as he crooned a tuneless creation from somewhere inside himself and waved his hands in time with the men's voices: "Oh, come, come, come, come . . . ."

I thought of Joey in his high-chair at the table with his hands deep in his mashed potatoes, squeezing them into shapes that we couldn't understand but which seemed to awaken something in him. I remembered Joey crawling across the kitchen floor and reaching for the fire in the stove and not understanding why Mama slapped his hands away. Telling him hadn't worked.

A deep sob shook Mama and jerked my attention back to the reality of my little brother's funeral.

"Jesus said, *suffer the little children to come unto me,*" Deacon Clement said. "An' he told us that no one shall enter the Kingdom of Heaven except as a child. Joey's sufferin' is over, and he is, this day, in the arms of Jesus."

He closed his Bible. "Let us pray."

After the service, Calvin and I stood with Mama and Daddy outside the church to receive the mumbled sympathy and the handshakes of the congregation. After three wet kisses from old ladies, I moved to stand behind Mama. Calvin followed me. For extra insurance, I picked up a pine needle and stuck it in my mouth like a toothpick. Calvin did the same thing.

Granny Meeks' eyes were dry. She wasn't anybody's grandma, but she'd midwifed in this part of Tift County for over thirty years and probably had seen more life and death than anyone in Ty Ty. If Joey's death had affected her, she didn't show it. She hugged Mama.

2

"Martha, I knowed each one of your boys was special the minute they was born," Granny said. "Joey was with us for seven years, and each one was a joy. Now, he's with Jesus." Granny must have seen my nostrils flare when she said that. I folded my arms across my chest. Calvin copied me.

Granny looked past Mama and caught my eye. "Davey-boy, you'll figure out some day that Joey was a blessin' to you and to all of us. You be happy for him." She turned away before I could think up something smart to say.

We didn't stay to see them put Joey in the ground and cover him with red Georgia clay. Mama chivvied Calvin and me ahead of her. "Got to get home," she said. "Folks'll be coming soon."

The funeral casseroles and desserts had started arriving at our house first thing that morning. Aunt Lucille was there in case people came early, but I think we all wanted to get away from the church, away from the graveyard. Even with four, the front seat of Daddy's pickup truck seemed empty without Joey.

Little Money, Little Dreams

The summer of 1932, the year before Joey was born, was maybe the worst of the Farm Crisis. Folks who had lost their farms were living in shacks put together from scraps of lumber, bits of tin roof, cardboard, and canvas from pup tents that were surplus after the Great War. It was called a "Hooverville," and Daddy forbade me from ever getting close to it. He didn't say how close was close, and I figured that the flea market across the railroad tracks from the Hooverville was far enough away.

It was Saturday, and we were in town for market.

J. Frank Goodson
Proprietor, Ty Ty Hardware

Daddy parked on the Town Square. Mama spread out a blanket for Calvin and herself to sell eggs and honey. Daddy walked to the barbershop and to Uncle Frank's hardware store. I wandered up Depot Street and then down Railroad Avenue to the flea market. Avery went with me. He was ten, two years older than me, but we got along right well. He was small for his age and crippled. Polio. We knew all about polio. Mr. Roosevelt had it, and he spent a lot of time across the state at Warm Springs. Mayor Hudson's

4

sister was a nurse there, and they said she was a favorite of Mr. Roosevelt.

The flea market wasn't much more than a bunch of tables cobbled together from sawhorses and scrap lumber with a bob-wire fence around them. Mr. Ebenezer Springer had set it up on a patch of ground by the railroad tracks. One of Mr. Springer's men sat at a table by the entrance.

"Buyin' or sellin'?" he asked. The man didn't seem to recognize Avery even though he was Mr. Springer's nephew. Either that, or the man didn't want to talk to a cripple.

I looked at Avery. He shrugged. "Just looking," I said. The man waved us in.

Avery and I stepped past the man and into a different world. Babies were squalling. Folks were calling out what they had to sell. Kids were running around everywhere, bumping into people and yelling. Most of the women's clothes had been washed so many times the color had gone out of them. A lot of the little kids wore flour sacks for clothes.

Avery tugged my arm and pointed to a collection of pocketknives. Maybe the fellow selling them thought I could afford one because Avery and I were dressed better than most of the folks. He handed me a truly righteous knife. The handle was smooth and white, and carved with a picture of a cowboy, galloping on a horse, about to lasso a calf. The blade was about three inches long, which would have been perfect for whittling but too short for hunting. I knew I couldn't afford it.

"Thank you, sir," I said kind of loud, so he could hear me over the noise.

I gave the knife back to him. "I don't think my daddy wants me to have a knife just yet. It's right nice, though."

He nodded and put the knife back in the case.

Avery put his mouth close to my ear and asked, "What are you lookin' for?"

I started to yell back when a shrill voice cut through the hubbub. "I have little money and little dreams, so I don't never have to worry I'll do without."

I felt like I'd been punched in the tummy. Something was wrong with thinking that way, but I didn't know what it was. My eyes jumped from one person to the next, wondering who had said it.

Was it the woman with the quilt draped over her table? I knew she'd never sell the quilt. The price was too high. But the quilt did attract folks, and a few of them bought a potholder or a towel. Despite her countrified ways, she was a shrewd bargainer. I watched her steer customers away from the potholders to the more expensive kitchen towels.

Avery saw it too, and giggled. "Them towels came from the mill in Sylvester," he said. "They's seconds. She picked off the labels and is sellin' them for three or four times what they's worth."

No, I thought, she isn't the one with little dreams.

At the next table, a woman was selling flatware. Could she be the one with little money and little dreams? On her table were a couple of serving spoons, a paring knife, and some mismatched table knives, forks, and spoons. It looked like she had emptied her kitchen drawers. Her face was slack; her hair, lank. The cloth of her dress was thin from too many washings. A baby wearing nothing but a dirty diaper sat in the dirt at her feet. The child's face was pinched, but its belly was sticking out. I didn't know that it meant the baby was starving, but I did know something wasn't right. The mother? She wouldn't have the energy to dream, even little dreams.

The next table held bluebird houses made from rough-sawn pine. No one stopped at that table, and the face of the

6

man behind it said he didn't expect anyone to. *He'll probably not make even the quarter he paid to rent the table,* I thought.

A new voice rose above the sounds of the crowd. A man stood behind a table with a purple and gold sign that read, "Dr. Justin Bartholomew's Patented Elixir." He was calling out to the crowd.

"If you're feelin' poorly, if you're feelin' sad,
If your kids got colic, an' especially if they're bad.
If you've got the sugar, if you've got the grip,
Dr. Justin's Elixir can save yourself a trip."

He held up a bottle of what was probably just coal tar, alcohol, and licorice. At a dollar a bottle, it was a lot more than most could afford. But folks bought it anyway. I suppose it was because the man was so good at what he did and because it gave them hope in a world that held little of that. Maybe because at over 100 proof it did make them feel good for a while, and it did put the children to sleep.

The woman across from the patent medicine man was wearing a short-sleeve dress that showed a little color. Her face was sharp, like her hair bun had pulled the skin of her cheeks back to her ears. On her table, a blue enameled pan with chipped and rusted edges sat on a rack over a can of Sterno. A crayon-lettered sign on a piece of corrugated cardboard torn from a box read, "brunswitch stu." My stomach tumbled every time the breeze brought the smell in my direction. She handed a Dixie cup to a man wearing ragged bib overalls, and said, "That'll be a nickel." It was the voice of the woman with little money and little dreams.

The man took the cup. He dug into his pocket and found a nickel, but he held it tightly in his fist. "Got a spoon?" he asked. The woman tore a paper-wrapped ice cream spoon from a string of spoons. "That ain't much for a nickel," he said as he gave her the coin.

"Come back afore closing," the woman said and then looked at the man's tattered shoes. "If they's any left, I'll give it you."

Little dreams but a big heart, I thought. I suppose I shouldn't be surprised how they go together. Maybe she's thinking about 'do unto others,' and maybe something good will happen for her.

I didn't have but a quarter to spend and didn't see anything worth spending it on. Mama had invited Avery to share our picnic lunch, so we looked around a little more and left before noon.

§ § § § §

The tight-fisted man in the ragged overalls and tattered shoes moved in with the woman with the big heart and the little dreams. She kept selling Brunswick stew at the Flea Market and started wearing long-sleeved dresses to cover her bruises. Her little dreams became a nightmare. When she died two years later, Doc Winter said at the inquest it was from a beating and it had been going on for a long time.

Dr. Bartholomew's elixir didn't cure little Alice Jenkins' cramp colic. By the time her appendix burst, the huckster who had sold it was all the way over to Waldo, Alabama, bribing the sheriff in that town and selling alcohol and hope to another batch of folks.

§ § § § §

It was more than 35 years later that I wrote about the woman with little dreams and the child with the distended belly. I was on assignment in Africa. The name of the place is not important—just one of several countries that had been part of the French colonial empire. Now it was a battleground in which most of the population was starving. Anything edible, anything that might be used for fuel to cook a handful of rice from the relief agencies, had been ripped from the ground. The landscape had become a wasteland in which nothing grew. With no vegetation to hold it, what little rain fell, ran off. The summer sun baked the ground like the hardpan that had surrounded the old farmhouses in Ty Ty.

Even though this country's government professed secularism and religious tolerance, the Sunni Muslim minority didn't. The war that I was covering was said to be about religion; however, it was fought over the diamonds that could be found under the ground. *Blood diamonds* they were being called. Religion was an excuse for war and the vehicle with which leaders on both sides drove their followers into battle.

I knelt by a body that lay on a patch of blood-soaked ground. Nothing I had seen before, nothing I had imagined, had prepared me for this. The body was that of a child, a boy, perhaps eight years old. He wore a camouflage shirt that was several sizes too large and gym shorts imprinted with the logo of a famous sportswear company. He was barefoot and bareheaded. His hands clasped a semi-automatic rifle that was longer than he was tall. It was an M-1, not unlike one I had carried twenty-five years before.

Flies danced on the boy's lips and eyelids, seeking moisture that was absent elsewhere. I nearly threw up when he opened his eyes and licked his lips. He wasn't dead!

I lifted the child's head and dribbled some water from my canteen on his lips.

"*Dieu vous benisse*," the child whispered. He took a deep breath. His eyes opened wide. Then, his entire body slumped. His eyes glazed, his chest collapsed, his limbs went limp. He was dead.

In a country of starving children with distended bellies, this one had been fed, only to die on an arid battlefield. What might have been his dreams? My own dreams were troubled that night, and the newspaper rejected the story I sent by wire from the capital the next day.

The Widow Alice's Shotgun

Jesse and I were friends. Still, it took a long time before he knew me well enough to tell me this story. We were both eight when it happened.

§ § § §

The Widow Alice Smart snapped the locks on her front and back doors and felt the latch of each window on the ground floor before climbing the stairs to her bedroom. She was the only person in Ty Ty who locked her doors, and she exercised enough vigilance to make up for all those who did not. Once upstairs, she walked across the darkened bedroom. Although Mr. Smart had been dead for fifteen years, Alice still undressed in her closet before pulling a nightgown over her head.

The bedroom windows were open to a summer night, and the hiss of a breeze through the pines competed with the staccato chirps of over-heated crickets and the croaking of over-sexed bullfrogs. Despite the breeze, the heat was oppressive and sleep came slowly to Alice.

In the half-world at the edge of sleep, Alice heard a sound—a mewling, faint but sharp. *Mrs. Brandon's cat is in season again,* she thought. *That cat ain't* natural! However, the expected din did not follow. The mewling continued. *A rabbit* was her next guess. *One of them boys hit a rabbit with his slingshot, and it's crawled into my roses to die. My* roses!

A very distinct "Ow!" sounded from below her window. Alice was sure a burglar, not a rabbit, was in her roses. She did not wonder why a burglar would mewl like a randy cat or a dying rabbit. She shivered in fear and perhaps a little excitement and then reached under her bed for the late Mr. Smart's shotgun.

"Jesse? Where in the blue blazes are you, boy?" a man's voice bellowed. Splashes followed. The bullfrogs went silent. Someone was wading across the creek behind her house. Alice got up and stood by the window, looking over her side yard.

A dog barked. Its dark shape ran across the yard followed by a man carrying a lantern held high. It illuminated his path and his face. Alice gasped. *It's that no good Silas Glover. He's livin' in the Hooverville across the tracks.* She took a deep breath. "Silas Glover, you get outta my yard!"

"Who's that?" The man looked up and shaded his eyes as if from the sun. He seemed to realize how foolish that gesture was, and lowered his hand.

"You know good and well who it is. Now you get out of my yard before I fill you with buckshot!"

"I ain't leavin' without my boy," Silas yelled.

"Your boy? What do you mean, your boy?"

"That's him right underneath your winder," Silas said. He had been looking up at the second-story window. Now, he lowered his gaze. His voice, which had been at a civil yell, lowered in pitch and became a snarl. "Come on out, boy, afore the dog gits you. Come on, you're due for a whaling."

Alice might have been a little bit paranoid, but she wasn't stupid. It hadn't been a cat or a rabbit or a burglar in her

12

roses. It was a child, and one that was hurting. She turned the switch of her reading light. "Silas, you see me and you see my shotgun. You take one step at my house or that child, and I will shoot you." She drew back both hammers. The click as they set in place was loud over the crickets.

Silas was a bully. Like many bullies, he was at heart a coward. He took a step back and snarled. "Boy, if you hide under a woman's skirts, don' even bother t' come home." He turned, whistled to the dog, and splashed across the creek.

Alice watched the lantern until it was a firefly spark. "Boy? You still there?"

"Yes'm."

"You hurt any?"

"No ma'am. Not much. 'Cept where he hit me. An' the thorns."

"Can you get out of the thorns?"

"Yes'm."

"Come around back. I'll let you in."

"Aw, ma'am, you don' have to," the boy said.

"Nonsense, boy. You were hurt on my roses, and I'm responsible. Now, get around back."

"Yes'm."

Five minutes later, Jesse was sitting at Alice's kitchen table drinking cold milk from the refrigerator and eating a peanut butter sandwich.

"I'm sorry I ain't got better food for you, Jesse. I don't rightly know what youngsters eat."

Alice studied the boy as she spoke. His wrists stuck out from a shirt too small and now tattered from its encounter with the roses. His face and hands were clean. She'd made him wash at the sink. His hair hung over his eyes and his collar.

The boy pushed his words out as fast as he pushed the sandwich into his mouth. "Eats what we can get, ma'am. Use to be better, 'fore Daddy started drinking. Sunday, I goes to the Gospel Truth Church picnic. Mama was a member 'fore she died, and I was baptized there. Most of them ain't any better off than we is, though." He took another bite of the sandwich.

"Tuesdays, the Presbyterians have bread and soup, if you get there 'fore it runs out. And Wednesdays, the Berea Baptist Church has their pound supper and prayer meetin'. You'd think they'd be something in the garbage after, but they wrap it all up and take it with 'em. *Charity begins at home*, I heard one of 'em say." He tilted up the glass of milk and drained it. Alice poured it full from the jug.

"Ain't nothin' on Thursday and Friday," the boy continued. "Saturday, the Sallie—uh, Salvation Army—sets up, but they is real preachy." He giggled. "They make you listen to a sermon and testimony 'fore they puts out the food.

"Sometimes, I go to the dump and sees what I can find. Mostly nothin'. Can I have another sammich?"

Jesse slept in the room off the back porch that had been the colored woman's room back when Alice had a maid. It wasn't that Alice was afraid of the boy or had any feelings against him. It was just that he stank. By noon the next day, however, the boy, his clothes, and the bedding he had used were clean.

"I always heard boys don't like to bathe," Alice said.

Jesse blushed. "That 'a been right 'fore we went to the Hooverville," he said. "But three months without any bath

14

'cept a splash in the creek with all my clothes on an' I come to 'preciate a bath."

§ § § § §

Dressed in next-to-Sunday-best, the women of the Rachael Circle of the First Methodist Church had finished their iced tea, oatmeal cookies, and their plans for the Labor Day picnic when Alice Smart spoke. She told them about the child now living at her house and how he'd gotten there. She told of the privations Jessie and others endured. "He hadn't had a real bath in weeks. If that wasn't bad enough, he's been rooting in the dump for food." Alice shuddered.

"They are white trash!" Mrs. Brewster snipped. Her pursed lips and narrowed eyes clearly indicated that no more was to be said on the subject.

"They are children, Mrs. Brewster," Alice replied. "They are living in that dreadful Hooverville—"

"Don't you dare dignify that shantytown with the name of the President of the United States," Mrs. Brewster interrupted. "It is a shantytown, pure and simple, and they are shantytown trash."

"Oh," Alice said. Her voice was soft, but now it had an edge. "Tell me, please, which is lower, white trash or shantytown trash? And which is less important in the eyes of God?"

"Why, Mrs. Smart, that was just hateful!" Mrs. Brewster said. "You're talking just like that Frances Perkins woman who's campaigning with Mr. Roosevelt. She'd take bread off our tables to feed the vagrants."

"Like when Jesus said, *I was hungry and you fed me*? Like Jesus said, you mean?" Alice's jaw was set. She knew she

15

wasn't going to win this argument, but she also knew she couldn't give up.

"Devil can quote Scripture," Mrs. Brewster snapped.

"Gladys," Alice said. There were gasps at this breach of their unwritten formality. Alice ignored the gasps and continued. "Didn't you learn to think any better at that school you went to?" Gladys Brewster was one of the few women in town other than some of the teachers and Doc Winter's nurse who had attended college, and Gladys was never reluctant to mention that.

Mrs. Davidson spoke up. "Mrs. Brewster is right. Anyone can quote Scripture. And Mrs. Smart is right. They are children, and they are precious to God. And we are His servants, aren't we?"

Although Mrs. Smart and Mrs. Brewster didn't address each other directly, the discussion that followed was a bit more civil and a great deal more productive. Future Thursday meetings of the Rachael Circle were held at the Hooverville, and the unspoken competition among the women changed from dresses and hats to the quantity of food they could pack into a picnic hamper.

§ § § § §

Jesse's daddy never took to losing his son, but after a showdown to which Alice brought the husbands of several of the Rachael Circle members, he hopped a freight train. They said he died in a fight in a hobo jungle outside of Birmingham. Jesse lived with Mrs. Smart until he joined the Army the day after Pearl Harbor. He got a medal and an artificial leg in the Normandy invasion.

16

Brothers' Keeper

Granny Meeks and I had a feudin' friendship. Mostly, it was because I lipped off to her. She always managed to smack me down, though. Never touched me; she just had a sharper tongue than I did. Still, we were friends, and she told me a lot, including what I didn't know about when Joey was born.

§ § § §

I helped Daddy move Calvin's bed into my room and haul the old crib from the barn loft into what had been Calvin's room. At eight, I wasn't sure I wanted to share a room with four-year-old Calvin, but Daddy said it was either Calvin or the baby that was about to be born. I voted for Calvin. Now, Daddy and Calvin and I sat in the kitchen, waiting. Calvin had his eyes on the casseroles that women from the church had brought over—Crowder peas and ham hocks, and macaroni and cheese. Daddy was sitting so he could see the stairs and hear what was happening up in his and Mama's bedroom.

The smack of Granny Meeks' hand on the newborn's bottom was not followed by the expected cry. Granny looked sharply at the tiny boy she held hanging by his ankles. He gasped and began breathing but still didn't cry.

"Granny, what's wrong? Why don't he cry?" Martha Sasq's voice was strong. This child was her third. She was a healthy woman, and the delivery had been easy. In fact, it had been a lot easier than Calvin's. Calvin hadn't wanted to come into the world and was still a mite shy. These thoughts and the midwife's words comforted her.

"Not a thing wrong. Maybe a little small," Granny Meeks said. She wrapped the tiny form in a blanket that had been warming on some hot bricks and handed the baby to his mother.

"Your name is Joseph," Martha said. "Your oldest brother David was named for a great king. Your other brother Calvin was named for a great preacher. You are named for a carpenter who just happened to be the daddy of Jesus. We'll probably call you Joey for a while, but don't you forget—Oh!" She delivered the placenta; it surprised her.

Granny Meeks finished cleaning up. "You'll not be needin' me for a while. I'll stop by tomorrow."

"Granny, he won't suck," Martha said.

"Maybe he ain't hungry, yet," the old woman replied. She was packing her carpetbag and didn't see the expression on Martha's face.

"No, Granny, there's somethin' wrong!"

Granny Meeks looked closely, now. The child was breathing. His eyes were closed. "Pshaw, woman, he's just asleep. He'll be hungry when he wakes up. If he won't suck, you just squeeze out a drop and put it on his lip. He'll get the idea. All men do." Granny laughed at her own wit and left the room.

She didn't have much to say when she came into the kitchen. She told Daddy he could go up. He asked if she would stay for lunch, but she said no thanks. Daddy told me to feed Calvin and then bring in a plate for him and Mama.

Once outside, Granny stuffed rabbit tobacco in her corncob pipe and lit it before beginning the walk home. The January afternoon was cold, but it was her thoughts that caused her to shiver. *I surely hope that baby will be all right. Ain't never seen a child who didn't squall the Devil outta him when he was born. Ain't never seen one quite so small, except that Stone baby, and she didn't live two minutes. An' I ain't never knowed one who wasn't hungry.*

Joey fed when he woke an hour later, but he suckled listlessly, as if he lacked energy.

A week later, Grampa and Grammy Yount came to see Joey. Grampa Yount was a preacher who had the biggest Baptist church in Athens and a radio program. Grammy had been to college and was a nurse. She figured out that something was wrong and talked Mama and Daddy into taking Joey to the children's hospital in Atlanta.

§ § § § §

Daddy sat on the couch. Calvin and I stood by the fireplace. Mama sat in the rocker, holding Joey. Her face was red and raw. Aunt Lucille, who had stayed with us while Grampa Yount took Mama and Daddy and Joey to Atlanta, stood in the corner twisting her hands in the cloth of her apron. Daddy's face was white. I was scared, but didn't know why.

Daddy took a deep breath. It looked like he was trying not to cry. "Little David? Calvin? Joey ain't right. There's somethin' wrong in his head. The doctors say he'll never talk and that he might not ever know who his family is. There's somethin' messed up inside him, too. He'll have to eat milk and mashed up stuff, and he'll always have to wear diapers. An—" Daddy's voice broke, and Mama started crying. "An' he'll like not live long enough to grow up."

Daddy sat still and waited for what he'd said to sink in, and then held out his hands. Calvin and I ran to him, and buried our heads in his shoulders. He let us cry for a while. When we calmed down a bit, we sat beside him.

"Grampa Yount told your mama and me that God has given this family a mission. He has given us a chance to show how strong our faith is." Grampa Yount talked that way, but Daddy didn't. I figured Daddy was just saying the words that had been said to him.

God gave us a mission? Does that mean God made Joey be born that way? Why would God do that? Why does Joey have to suffer? Are God and the Devil betting on us like they bet on Job? That's what Deacon Clement preached last Sunday. I didn't understand it, then, and I sure didn't understand it, now. I was getting really mad and wanted to ask Daddy about it, but he didn't give me time.

"You boys are gonna have to grow up real fast. You're gonna have to be responsible. You're gonna have to be your brother's keeper, and you're gonna have to help your mother an' me. Can I count on you?" Now Daddy was talking like himself and not Grampa.

I nodded. "Yes, sir," I said. I wiped my cheeks with my forefinger and flung the tears into the air, where they sparkled for an instant in the lamplight before falling to the floor.

"Yes, sir," Calvin said and wiped away his own tears the same way I had.

That night, after we were in bed, I heard Calvin crying. I walked across the room and sat on his bed.

20

"Why you crying, Calvin?"

"You ain't gonna make me leave . . . are you?" he said.

"What in tarnation you mean?"

"Mama told Daddy that Joey would be sleepin' in the crib in their room an' I could go back to my old room. Please don't make me. I don't want t' be by myself . . . ."

I guess I'm my two brothers' keeper, now, I thought. *I guess this is part of being responsible. I guess this is part of growing up.*

"No, Calvin, you an' me, we're gonna take care of Joey. And we're gonna be together for a long, long time."

It didn't snow most winters, and when it did, it was usually just a dusting that melted right quick. That's why we were surprised when we woke up the next morning to find at least two inches on the ground and more falling. Calvin saw it first and woke me up so I could see.

"Boy howdy! It's snowing! You gotta tell Joey!" Calvin said.

For once, I thought before I opened my mouth. "You go tell him, Calvin, you're a big brother, too."

Daddy had told us we'd have to take care of Joey. Mama showed me how to change his diapers but didn't ask me to do it. It took me a couple of days to figure out she was waiting to see if I'd do it on my own. The first time I did, she hugged me. The very next Saturday, she bought me a book with her butter and egg money. It was a dictionary and I read every word in it.

Calvin was too little to change Joey's diapers, but he got right good at feeding him and playing with him. Soon as Joey went on the bottle, Calvin would hold him and the bottle and hum softly while Joey sucked. Then Calvin would hand Joey to me, 'cause every time Joey ate, he pooped. I asked Mama about that. She told me the doctors said it was because Joey's brain—what there was of it—couldn't control his sphincter. I had to look that up in the dictionary.

Joey tested us, all right. Of course, we couldn't know how God would grade the test. I started thinking about that and wondered why Joey had been born, at all.

A New Slavery

*"Order is heaven's first law; and, this confessed,
Some are, and must be, greater than the rest."
—Alexander Pope, Essay on Man, 1733 C.E.*

I grew up thinking that slavery was a relic of the past. I didn't know about the debt slavery that kept tenants and share croppers in servitude. I didn't find it strange that the Coloreds deferred to the Whites, and that a colored man would step off the sidewalk and lift his hat when a white woman walked by. It took a few years after Jed told me this story before I started to understand.

§ § § § §

I was eight years old when Joey was born. Daddy sent me to the train depot to send a telegram to Grampa and Grammy Yount in Athens and to Aunt Mary and Uncle Beau in Valdosta. Jed Harmon was the telegraph operator. The only heat in the depot that afternoon was a pot-bellied stove in Jed's office. I took the note Daddy had written and pushed it through the window. Jed told me to come in and warm up while he sent the telegrams. Then he showed me how his telegraph worked.

"Sometimes, David," he said, "late at night, when things aren't busy, the telegraph operators talk to each other.

I've talked to Atlanta, New York, Chicago, Denver, and once all the way to San Francisco." The farthest from Ty Ty I'd ever been was to Athens, and what Jed said opened a lot more than my eyes. I resolved then and there that someday I'd visit all those places.

I got to know Jed over the years, and he told me about what Ty Ty had been like during the early days of the Great Depression, including something that happened in 1929 that set the stage for things that came later.

§ § § § §

The morning freight train hadn't stopped in Ty Ty, and Jed was free for a couple of hours. He sent a telegraph signal to the Sylvester station saying he was going to breakfast and would be back by ten o'clock. Sylvester acknowledged. The dispatcher there would hold messages for Ty Ty. Jed walked the mile to Edna's Diner.

"Jed Harmon, you get your feet off'n that seat. People gonna be settin' there come lunchtime." Edna slapped a plate of biscuits and sausage gravy in front of him.

Jed grumbled but put his feet on the floor. "Aw, Edna, don't talk like that. You ain't my mama."

"No, I ain't. But if your dear mama was still here, she'd tell you the same thing, an' you know it." Edna curled her lips into what she thought was a smile. "She was a good woman. You want anything else, hon?"

"No, thanks, Edna. Thank you for saying that about Mama . . . ." Jed's voice drifted off, and he turned his eyes to the plate of glistening milk, flour, and sausage grease that was already starting to congeal. Edna looked at the back of Jed's head for a minute and then went to her seat behind the counter.

When Edna heard Jed scraping his plate, she picked up a piece of apple pie and walked over to the booth. "Here, Jed," she said as she set the pie on the table. "It's yesterday's, but it's still good. No charge."

Jed looked up and mumbled his thanks. Edna slipped onto the bench seat across from him, the seat where his feet had been. "How's your pa?" she asked.

Jed chewed a couple of times and swallowed before answering. "He's taking it mighty hard, Miz Edna. Losing Ma and the baby, and now being foreclosed off the farm. I got a few dollars saved—but it ain't enough. And they cut my pay again."

Jed shifted in his seat and grimaced. "I can't complain, though. At least I've got a job."

"You still workin' the telegram at the train depot?"

"Yes'm, and selling tickets and checking bags and cleaning the toilets and sweeping. Old Mr. Rawlins got let go last week 'cause he couldn't lift the bags. I could, so I'm working from dawn till midnight most days."

"Oh, no!" Edna said. "What's he gonna do?"

"He's moved in with his sister. She's got that widow's pension."

Jed took another bite of pie.

"What's your pa gonna do, Jed?" Edna's voice was soft and lacked her usual rasp.

"I don't rightly know, and I don't think he does, either. Mr. Springer got the mortgage from the bank and said Pa can stay on as a sharecropper. That ain't right for a man who's owned his own farm. There's more room where I'm living, but

I don't know if Mrs. Jackson wants my pa and three young 'uns living in her basement with me, and I'm not sure Pa would like that, either."

He sighed. "Thanks, Miz Edna. Thank you for the pie. I, uh, I may not be coming in so much. Probably be eating day-old bread and peanut butter. Thank goodness we got enough of that!"

Jed put a quarter on the table to pay for his breakfast. Edna stood and pushed the quarter toward Jed. "Keep that quarter, Jed. It'll buy a whole mess of peanut butter for them young 'uns. I ain't hurting." *Yet,* she added silently.

"Thank you, Miz Edna. I'll tell Pa you asked after him."

"You do that," she replied. "An' come see me when you can—even if you're only visiting." She hurried through the door to the kitchen and grabbed a dishtowel to dry her tears.

§ § § § §

At six o'clock that evening, when most folks were at supper, Jed was on the telegraph at the train depot, copying orders from stationmasters up and down the line. Across town, five men sat at Mayor Hudson's dinner table. The mayor was there, of course, and Arpie Lee, one of the town councilmen. The other chairs were filled by Judge Leffler, the Reverend Thorn, and Ebenezer Springer. These five men were the real power in Ty Ty.

The stock market wouldn't crash for another six months, and when it did, it wouldn't mean much to the folks in Ty Ty. They'd been suffering from the Farm Crisis since about 1920. A lot of the Coloreds had gone up north, looking for factory jobs. A couple of the big landowners couldn't find enough folks to work the fields, especially cotton. And the government

26

was getting into everything, telling people what to grow and what not to grow, and how much cotton they could plant. A bunch of folks had lost their land and were coming into town looking for work, a handout, or a place to sleep.

"Gentlemen, we're getting entirely too many vagrants in town," Mayor Hudson cut right to the point of the meeting. "They're coming in on the train, and they're coming in from the farms."

The mayor's coffee cup clattered as he set it down hard. "I swan, every time a farm gets foreclosed, ten more people show up in town looking for a handout."

Reverend Thorn nodded. "Mayor Hudson's right. We fed bread and soup to nearly fifty people at lunch today. Many of them I didn't recognize. Men, women and children, too. It's costing a fortune. We're not going to be able to do it much longer."

"Deputy Donaldson caught two families sleeping on the Square—under the bandstand—night 'fore last," Arpie Lee said, mostly to be a part of the conversation. "He run 'em off, but they were back 'fore morning. Why can't Donaldson do something?"

"Now, Arpie," the judge said. "You know that Donaldson and the sheriff are related to half the families in this county, and Donaldson isn't going to run off or arrest someone he's related to. At least, not until he's checked with his uncle.

"However, you've given me an idea," the judge added. "Do you know how they used to run the steel mills in Birmingham?"

Eb Springer knew where the judge was going. So did Reverend Thorn. The others looked puzzled.

"Convict labor," the judge said. "It was the law most places. Mississippi even had a state commissioner for convict labor to make sure the state got their cut of the money. If you need workers, cheap, you get convicts. Doesn't cost much, and everybody gets a cut. You need more convicts, you arrest some Coloreds for vagrancy."

The judge saw interest in the eyes of the other men and continued describing his plan. Vagrants would be arrested, taken to the judge, and fined. To pay off their fine, they would be hired out to Ebenezer and Arpie. The vagrants' fines would never get paid off. Ebenezer and Arpie knew how to keep their tenants and share croppers in debt slavery—they'd been doing that for years, as their fathers had before them. The two men would pay a fee to be divided between the sheriff and the judge. Reverend Thorn couldn't see where he was going to benefit and didn't support the idea until Ebenezer agreed to sweeten his donation to the church's building fund. It was an open secret among these men that the building fund was the preacher's slush fund and had nothing at all to do with the church building.

Details had to be worked out, including the mayor's concern that three dollars per week for one convict wasn't enough. "Donaldson's going to want a cut. He'll need two, maybe three deputies to round up the vagrants."

Ebenezer protested. "Cotton prices are down," he said. "Three dollars a week's a lot to pay when I have to feed them, too."

"Don't forget your clerk, Judge," Mayor Hudson added. "If Bee is going to draw up all those warrants, she's going to want something."

"I'll take care of Bee from my share," the judge said. "And the sheriff can take care of Donaldson."

At 10:00 PM, Jed saw two vagrants jump off the train as it reached the yard limit. He had been told to call the sheriff when that happened. Tonight, he didn't bother to call. Deputy

28

Donaldson was probably at home or at Edna's Diner, and the sheriff would not send someone all the way from Tifton.

By 11:00 PM, the last train had left the station. Jed sent a "goodnight" to Sylvester and Tifton, where operators worked around the clock, and walked home. His stomach was uneasy from the sausage gravy.

Sean Cavanagh

Folks in Ty Ty didn't cotton much to Yankees, but there was one who managed to do what generations of carpetbaggers couldn't do—charm all the ladies in Ty Ty.

Sean Cavanagh arrived the first day of March 1933. He took a room at the Overton Railroad Hotel and Boarding House and spent the next two days wandering around town. He must have liked what he saw because on the third day, he rented what had been Baucomb's shoe repair, right next to Uncle Frank's hardware store. He paid cash: one month deposit and one month in advance. And then, he went back to the railroad depot and sent a telegram.

More than a couple of people, including the mayor, asked Jed Harmon what was in that telegram, but Jed said it would be against the law to tell. Nobody believed that, especially after Judge Leffler said there wasn't any such law. But Jed stuck to his guns.

Mr. Cavanagh hired some colored folks to clean out the store and haul away a couple of truckloads of trash. He visited the hardware store and left with more paint than Uncle Frank had sold in the past year.

Somehow, Mr. Cavanagh found the fellow who had lettered the signs on the bank window and hired him to do signs in the windows of the old shoe store. Lots of people walked by, hoping to find out what kind of store Mr. Cavanagh was going to open, but he'd covered the outside of the front windows with butcher paper, and nobody had the courage to pull it down. Nobody but C.W., that is.

If anybody was going to get in trouble, it would have been C.W. He and I were in the same grade, but we weren't friends. I knew about him and his brother, the one who kept getting sent to reform school. I guess that's where C.W. got his courage—or his stupidity. Mr. Cavanagh caught him before he had pulled more than a corner of the butcher paper from the window. C.W. was so scared when Mr. Cavanagh grabbed his arm that he pissed his pants. I know 'cause, I was standing in front of the hardware store, watching.

Just like he would do a couple of years later, C.W. came runnin' to me. I took him around back and filled a tub full of water to soak his overalls. He was still wet, but he was wet all over, and he didn't smell like pee.

The day was warm enough, but still C. W. was shivering. "*Not*," he said. "That's what the sign said. *Not*. How can anybody sell nothin' and make a livin'?"

I just shook my head. I didn't know, and I wasn't real sure C.W. knew, what he was talking about or what he'd seen.

Three days later, Mr. Cavanagh showed up at the train depot in time to meet the morning freight. There were a bunch of crates for him, and it took all day to tote them to the store. Everybody knew that Jed would have seen the bills of lading, but he refused to say where the crates came from or what was in them.

You'd have thought that somebody would have pulled the butcher paper off the windows or at least pulled a corner away to peep into the store, but folks just didn't seem to have the courage of their curiosity. Avery told me that he'd been walking by when the wind had pulled a corner of the paper away, and he's seen the word "Need" lettered on the window. Now we've got *Not* and *Need*, and I was beginning to think that C.W. was right. How can you sell nothing that nobody doesn't need?

On Monday, Ty Ty woke up to find Mr. Cavanagh's "Needles, Thread, Ribbon and Notions" open on the square. Mr. C was a hit with the women, who no longer had to go to Tifton for sewing supplies, even though on St. Patrick's Day he painted the nose on the Confederate statue green.

The Great Panic

Ebenezer Springer didn't drink often. When he did, it was something to behold. At least that's what Avery told me. Avery and his brother Lonnie lived awhile with their Uncle Ebenezer. When Mr. Springer drank, he told Avery things that he wouldn't likely have said when he was sober. I think he beat Avery sometimes, but Avery never would say. He did tell me some of the stories his uncle told him, though.

§ § § § §

Three years and five months after the Great Panic of 1929, six men sat in the parlor of the manse of the Berea Baptist Church. Reverend Thorn, Mayor Hudson, Judge Leffler, Ebenezer Springer, Arpie Lee, and Thomas Middleton drank coffee and ate slabs of Mrs. Thorn's cherry pie. Middleton had no illusions about why he had been invited. He was the Chief Teller at the Bank of Ty Ty, and he knew more about the operation and condition of the bank than did any of the members of the board, including the mayor and the judge. At any other time none of these men would have nodded at him in passing unless they were in a particularly expansive mood. Middleton knew that they wanted something, but he had no idea what it might be. So far, the conversation had rambled from weather to baseball. The men shook their heads at the idea that the Negro League would stage an all-star game and guessed at the Washington Senators' chances to reach the

World Series. Conspicuously missing from the conversation was any mention of the bank holiday Mr. Roosevelt had declared the week before, or of his first fireside chat the previous night.

During a lull in the conversation, Reverend Thorn set his cup and saucer on the table beside his chair and cleared his throat. *Here it comes*, Mr. Middleton thought.

"Thomas," the Reverend began, "it's pretty clear to me and the others here that you've been responsible for keeping the Bank of Ty Ty open during these troubling times. That has been the work of a powerful diligent man. I'm reminded of the time Jesus told the parable of the talents—"

Springer's cough cut off Reverend Thorn before he could start preaching.

Middleton knew that using his first name meant that these men wanted something from him and that they wanted it badly. He knew the extent of their wealth. He chose his words carefully to let them know that, while humbling himself. It was a pretty speech.

"That's mighty nice of you to say, Reverend," Middleton said. "But if you gentlemen hadn't kept your funds on deposit, there's nothing any mortal could have done—"

"By my funds, you mean the church's funds, of course," Reverend Thorn interjected.

"Oh, of course, Reverend," Middleton said. His voice was just shy of ingratiating. "I was thinking of you as the steward of your flock's accounts—the building fund, especially." Reverend Thorn had no idea that Middleton knew about the account the preacher had opened in the name of his nephew. Middleton thought it odd that a child would only use the night depository and that deposits were made regularly on Monday evenings. A little thought and a Monday night spent at the bank, and Middleton understood—the depositor was

34

Reverend Thorn, and he was probably skimming Sunday's collection plate.

Judge Leffler turned the conversation toward its real purpose. "It's clear that Mr. Roosevelt is going to pull us out of this thing." The preacher and the mayor nodded agreement. The judge caught Middleton's eye, and he nodded, too.

"Things are gonna be different," Ebenezer Springer added. Again, the others indicated their agreement.

"Where there is change, there is opportunity for men with vision," the judge said.

Middleton understood instantly. "Opportunity for men with vision, for men with power." He swept his gaze over his hosts. "And, for men with financing—seed money, so to speak."

§ § § § §

The arrangement was simple, its execution was complex. But no more complicated than what Middleton had already done to keep the bank solvent. Springer's goal was to own every farm in the western half of the county; the others, simply to make money. The plan was to offer loans with land as collateral. That more than half the loans would be used to buy sugar to make second-run moonshine was clearly understood but never said.

"Roosevelt's talking with some folks in Washington about an agricultural adjustment act. The government's going to pay as much as twenty dollars an acre to plow under most of this year's cotton crop. The money will come from Washington, but we'll be in charge of paying it out." Springer didn't need to say what he was talking about. All the men knew that Springer was right friendly with a certain Georgia representative and that the judge had the political connections to make sure the

35

right people were appointed to the Tift County Agricultural Board.

It was Reverend Thorn's job to get his flock to put back into the bank the money hidden under their mattresses and on the mantle in grandma's teapot. The following Sunday, he stood in the pulpit and shamelessly plagiarized and twisted the words of President Roosevelt's first fireside chat.

"More important than money, and more important than gold, is the confidence of the people themselves. You must have faith not only in the Lord God but also in the men who are his servants on this Earth. Let us unite in banishing fear. Together, we cannot fail." Mr. Roosevelt's words and the preacher's delivery convinced them. The people responded, and money began to flow back into the bank. Mr. Middleton started writing loans, and farmers who were accustomed to borrowing a hundred dollars for seed corn found that the bank wanted a lien on their farm, and that they'd have to plant cotton, too.

Mr. Middleton added a layer to the scheme that he kept to himself. He wired a few select bankers, asking to borrow money—not much, one or two thousand dollars. He offered a good rate of interest to be paid monthly. The telegrams were sent in the name of the bank. Middleton's name didn't appear on the telegrams or on the interest payment checks. He didn't have to send more than a few telegrams either. After the first couple of months, word quietly spread among friends as one banker told another. More and more money flowed into the Bank of Ty Ty. Wells Fargo men carrying green canvas bags arrived at the train station two or three times a week. Middleton no longer had to steal from the church building fund to pay interest to the initial investors.

Middleton didn't believe that he would be discovered. The interest rate he paid was high enough to be attractive without being suspicious. While only a few of the bankers had read Charles Dickens's description of the scheme in *Little Dorrit*, most of them had a passing memory of Mr. Charles

36

Ponzi. On the other hand, they weren't dealing with an individual but with a bank that had been declared solvent and allowed to open after the Bank Holiday. The government's approval of the Bank of Ty Ty and the new Federal Deposit Insurance Corporation's guarantee of deposits up to $10,000 was all the assurance they needed.

§ § § § §

Mr. Thomas Middleton closed the vault, said goodnight to the tellers, and then locked the doors of the bank. The next day was Thanksgiving. Friday would be a holiday. The bank wouldn't open until Monday. It was just about eight months since Mr. Thomas Middleton had sat in the manse of the Berea Baptist Church with the five men who ran the town. It had not escaped his notice that he had never again been invited into Reverend Thorn's home and that none of the men at the meeting had ever again sat down with him at coffee.

By Monday, Middleton would be far away. With him went more than two hundred thousand dollars, including most of Reverend Thorn's step-nephew's account. That had been the easiest part and had given Mr. Middleton the greatest satisfaction.

The Bank of Ty Ty opened on Monday without its head teller. Ten minutes later Myrtle McCoy, who had opened the vault, discovered that there were no bills larger than ones in the tellers' cash drawers. Three minutes after that, she found that there were no bills at all in the main cash repository. Myrtle wasn't as smart as Thomas Middleton, but she was no fool. She knew something was badly wrong. She called her sister to whisper the news and then called the sheriff's office.

§ § § § §

"They're going to take over the bank." Judge Leffler's words were greeted by sour looks.

"We're gonna lose a lot of money, if they do. Anything over ten thousand dollars, right?" Mayor Hudson looked at the judge.

"Yes, that's the way it works," the judge replied. "But we'd lose more if they didn't."

"The church's building fund—it's nearly $20,000. They'll make an exception for that, won't they?" the Reverend Thorn asked. He'd already figured on losing most of the money in his nephew's account—the one where he hid the money he took from the collection plates. In his mind it wasn't stealing— after all, stealing was a sin. It was money he was due ever since the deacons voted not to raise his salary. *God helps those who help themselves* was something the preacher believed as firmly as if it had been in the Bible.

"I don't think so, Adam," the judge replied to Thorn's question.

"The town's account?" the mayor asked. He knew the answer. His jowls and rheumy eyes looked like an old hound who'd lost the trail. The judge merely shook his head.

"Any word where that sumbitch went?" Ebenezer Springer really didn't care. His money was invested in land and mortgages. He wouldn't lose a cent.

"No," the judge said. "Jed Harmon said Middleton bought a ticket to Atlanta. Very particular, Jed said, about wanting to know when the train got in. Middleton said that family was going to meet him at the station. He bought a return ticket, too. For Sunday. Jed was there when the train arrived. Said nobody got off."

"Has the sheriff put out a bulletin on him?"

38

"Can't. We don't know it was Middleton—we have no proof, yet. You can't arrest a man for not showing up for work."

"But them bank examiners—they must 'a found something, didn't they?"

"Whatever they find will go to a federal grand jury," the judge said. "The federal attorney in Albany and I aren't on good terms. I won't find out any more than you until it's over."

"That's right, Reverend Thorn. Only $10,000 in the church's account. I'm sorry." The teller who gave this news was a stranger, one of several men brought in when a bank from Albany had taken over the Bank of Ty Ty. Mrs. McCoy and the other employees had been told maybe they'd get their jobs back after things had settled down.

"Um, my nephew has an account. Here, this letter says I can ask. Was it covered to $10,000, too?"

The teller looked at the letter and then went to a file cabinet. After shuffling through papers, he brought a ledger sheet back to the window. "Actually, Reverend, that account had only $1.50 in it, and that's all covered."

"A dollar and a half? That's impossible . . . I mean, his mama said . . . maybe I misunderstood." The Reverend Thorn was perspiring, even though the December cold swept into the bank each time the doors opened. "Uh, may I see?"

The teller turned the ledger around so that Thorn could see. There had been regular withdrawals of hundreds of dollars at a time since last March. *That conniving son-of-a-bitch!* Shaken, Thorn mumbled a "Thank you," and walked unsteadily from the bank. The new teller looked closely at the account sheet and then picked up the phone.

§ § § § §

Jed Harmon watched through the window from his chair at the telegraph machine. The noon train slowly chuffed and squealed to a stop. The conductor swung onto the platform, looked at his pocket watch, and then opened the door to the single passenger car. Jed looked at the automatic-update Western Union clock in his office: *twelve oh-two, only two minutes late.* Two men wearing matching brown trousers, khaki shirts, and short leather jackets stepped from the passenger car. Jed wondered, *Soldiers? No, those aren't soldiers' caps. They're wearing badges. Police?*

Jed's question was answered when the two men reached his counter. "United States Marshall's Service. You know your way around this town, son?"

The men left the station after warning Jed to say nothing to anyone.

Less than twenty minutes later, the senior of the two men said, "Reverend Thorn? I am a United States Marshall, and I have a warrant for your arrest on income tax evasion and federal bank fraud."

Reverend Thorn got off on the federal charges. It was just too hard to prove that he had been the one who was putting money into his nephew's account. They didn't charge the nephew 'cause he was only thirteen years old and nobody believed it was his account, anyway. The deacons figured out Reverend Thorn had been stealing from the collection plate and dismissed him. It was all supposed to be secret, so of course, everybody knew. Mayor Hudson barely won the next election and some said it was because of the town's money that had been lost. Mr. Thomas Middleton was never found.

40

§ § § § §

    In 1990, when I was about to retire from writing full-time for the paper, I was invited to invest in what was called the "Fifteen Percent Account." It was operated by some fellows who had a coin and stamp store in Camp Springs, Maryland. They were planning on investing in gold coins from estate sales and were promising a fifteen percent return. It sounded too good to be true, and it was. Five years later, when the store went bankrupt, nearly eight million dollars in investments had dwindled to less than $500,000. Several famous people lost a lot of money. I wasn't rich enough or famous enough to be mentioned in the press release by the Maryland Attorney General. I thanked the memory of Mr. Thomas Middleton that had kept me from putting more than a few thousand dollars into this particular investment.

Vagrants

I knew who Charlie Winter was. We had been in school at the same time, but he was four years older than me. He left town when I was fourteen, so we never got to be friends. It wasn't until he came back to Ty Ty in 1940 that I really had a chance to talk to him. Of course, I knew Deputy Donaldson, and my daddy knew what was going on at Ebenezer Springer's, so it wasn't hard to put the story together.

§ § § § §

Deputy Donaldson looked at the clock. Ten forty-five. He sighed and hitched up his belt. "Come on, fellers, it's time to get to work." Three deputies grabbed shotguns and handcuffs, and then followed Donaldson into the parched morning.

As he did three times a day and twice on Sunday, Donaldson drove the '28 Packard sedan along the railroad tracks near the depot, stopping every fifty yards or so to let out one of the deputies. The men concealed themselves in the trees and brush that grew a few yards from the track. When the third man was out, Donaldson drove back to the depot and parked behind the building. He had the easy job—checking out the vagrants who would jump from the train at the last minute. They were usually older, more cautious, and slower.

The *long-long-short-long* pattern of the whistle sounded as the train got near the crossing in Colored Town where it would start to slow. When it reached the yard limit, it would be going less than ten miles an hour—slowly enough that the vagrants riding in boxcars and on top of the coal in hopper cars could jump off.

The deputies watched as two vagrants, and then a third, jumped from the train. The first one ran into the trees and saw Danny Barringer holding a shotgun. The vagrant opened his mouth to yell. Before he could, Danny hit him across the temple with the butt of the shotgun. The man fell and skidded in the dry leaves. The other two vagrants followed the first like ducklings running after their mama and stopped when they saw Danny and his shotgun.

Just before the caboose went out of sight, the deputies saw a fourth vagrant jump from the train and head toward the station. Donaldson was watching from a doorway as the vagrant ran onto the platform. Donaldson stepped out and grabbed the back of the bum's overalls, bringing him up short. The vagrant lost his balance and fell hard on his back.

It's a kid, Donaldson thought when he looked at the motionless body.

Mrs. Ruthie Jones Hudson looked out the window of the telegraph office just as Donaldson grabbed the kid. She dropped her pencil and bustled onto the platform. Donaldson was bent over the body.

"Evan Donaldson, what do you mean by manhandling a child?"

Donaldson tipped his official deputy's cap to the President of the Berea Baptist Church Women's Bible Class, wife of the mayor of Ty Ty, and doyen of the town's society. "Not a child, ma'am, a vag—" As the deputy spoke, the vagrant, or child, opened his eyes and rolled off the platform onto the rail bed.

"Ow!"

Donaldson jumped off the platform. His boots narrowly missed the kid who lay motionless, holding his right hand against his chest with his left. Blood seeped between his fingers. More blood glistened on a piece of broken glass beside him.

"Deputy Donaldson," Mrs. Hudson snapped. "You stop scaring that child and help him up."

She saw the blood, and her voice softened. "Don't you be afraid of him, boy. Doc Winter will fix you right up. The deputy will take you."

A hundred yards from where Deputy Donaldson was quivering under Mrs. Hudson's glare, the deputy's men stood over their captives. The sun had heated the gravel of the rail bed, and the men were sweating. "Dang it, Danny-Boy! Why'd you have t' hit him so hard? He ain't gonna wake up 'til next Sunday."

"Dang it, yourself, Billy-Bob. I'm the one who's got t' carry him." Danny grabbed the man's wrists, careful not to twist his arms, and hauled him into a fireman's carry. He hadn't been careful once before and dislocated a man's shoulder. Doc Winter had given him what-for.

"Where in hail is Donaldson with the car?"

Donaldson was, at that moment, wilting under the ire of Mrs. Hudson. "Ma'am, I got deputies out along the track. I need to go pick 'em up . . . ."

"They're big boys and can take care of themselves, even that great ox, Danny Barringer," Mrs. Hudson said. "Now, you get that child to Doc Winter." A memory demanded her attention. *He's the age my little Andy would have been.* She pushed away the thought and followed Deputy Donaldson.

44

§ § § § §

"He's asleep," Doc Winter told Mrs. Hudson. "I sewed up his hand, and gave him a dose of laudanum. He said his name is Charlie. That's all I got out of him. What do you want me to do with him when he wakes up?"

Mrs. Hudson's eyebrows drew together. She frowned. Her initial outrage at seeing Deputy Donaldson hurt a child had given her the courage to defy the deputy. Now, the outrage was gone, and her courage had been replaced by confusion and uncertainty. *Oh, my. What will Mayor Hudson think? I'm sure Deputy Donaldson has told him by now.*

"I . . . I don't rightly know, Doctor. He can't be no more than fifteen. And he can't go—" She stopped before she said what everyone knew, but few dared to say. Vagrants caught by Donaldson were put on a chain gang and forced to work on a farm hoeing, weeding, chopping, or picking cotton—depending on the season. Ebenezer Springer, Arpie Lee, and three or four other men who had enough land to support this new form of slavery, paid off the sheriff and Judge Leffler. The sheriff paid Deputy Donaldson, the judge paid the county clerk, and everyone was happy. Except the vagrants.

"No, Mrs. Hudson, he can't go to Ebenezer Springer's farm on a chain gang, and that's exactly where he'll end up if Deputy Donaldson gets his hands on him again."

And that's how Charlie the Vagrant became Charlie Winter, the son of Doc Winter's brother no one had heard of before.

That afternoon, Mayor Hudson found his wife in the kitchen.

"Wife?" the mayor huffed. "Deputy Donaldson said you made him take a vagrant to Doc Winter. What in tarnation were you thinking?"

"What was I thinking? I want to know what Deputy Donaldson was thinking, beating up on a child." Mrs. Hudson glared at her husband with unaccustomed ferocity. Knowing she had probably saved a child's life had restored her courage. She crossed her arms over her bosom.

"My pa lost his job in the stamping mill in Gary. That's in Indiana," Charlie told Doc between bites. "Ma got a job in a diner. Didn't pay much, but she got to bring home food. Wasn't enough, though, especially when her sister and her husband and the baby moved in. Pa couldn't find a real job. The fellows all talked about jobs in the south, about getting in the Civilian Conservation Corps. I was oldest, and so . . . ." He shrugged.

"How long you been on the road?" Doc asked.

"Three years, I think," the boy replied.

§ § § § §

The last train of the day had passed through Ty Ty. Donaldson brought his men back to the station, and then collected their shotguns and handcuffs.

"Danny, you an' Billy-Bob go help Mr. Springer make three more sets of laig irons," Donaldson said. Ebenezer Springer's voice at the door interrupted him.

"Two. That redheaded feller you brought me the other day died. He didn't last half a week. Ain't paying for him." Ebenezer tossed a set of leg irons onto the deputy's desk.

46

"Well now, Mr. Springer, sir, I don't know what the sheriff's gonna think about that," Donaldson said.

"You tell that uncle of yours a deal's a deal. It's three dollars a week, and two days ain't a week. And these three men you got today? You'll get 'em to me right 'fore suppertime so's I gotta feed 'em without gettin' any work out of 'em."

Ebenezer stalked out, slamming the door as he did.

The three new men did not get supper, after all. One of Springer's overseers herded them with the other men into the sharecropper's shack that had been converted into a bunkhouse. The door needed no lock: the men slept in their leg irons. Sometime during the night, the baying of hounds broke into the men's restless sleep.

"Somebody's run," came a voice from the dark.

"He'll not get far," another voice said.

"Bet they catch him before breakfast," a third added.

The voices subsided, to be replaced with snores and gasps.

The next morning, before the sun had cleared the horizon, the men squatted on the ground, the luckier or stronger ones leaning against a tree. They all used their fingers to scoop corn mush from tin bowls that had come from Army mess kits, surplus after the Great War. The sky was already the steel-gray color of high summer, a color that promised an unbearably hot day.

Four of Mr. Springer's overseers rode into the clearing. Hounds milled in a pack, somehow managing not to be trodden by the horses. A rope led from one man's saddle to the bound hands of a man who stumbled and shambled behind.

"Caught him," the lead man said. "He was at the AME Church hiding in the outhouse." The man laughed. "I think he'd a jumped in if Fred, there, hadn't grabbed him."

"Shoot, he smells like he fell in," Fred said. He had gotten off his horse, and untied the man's hands. "You set right here."

"No breakfast, for you," Ebenezer added.

Ten minutes later, the man who had run and the rest of the workers were in the field, picking cotton and pulling behind them the huge sacks they filled with the soft fluff. The men worked to a steady pace. Too fast, and they'd miss some of the cotton, and get whipped. Too slow, and they'd not pick enough, and get whipped. They got water, but not enough, at the end of every second row.

As the sun and temperature rose, the pace slowed. Overseers strode among the men, prompting them with bullwhips. The man who had run the night before, fell farther and farther behind, earning repeated flicks across his back from the bullwhip. No one noticed the bloody footprints he left in the dust, and when he collapsed it was too late. Before they could carry him to the cabin, he convulsed and died.

§ § § § §

In farm country, schools started in the middle of August and then broke for a couple of weeks during harvest. Nothing important got done during the first couple of weeks. Everyone anticipated the harvest break—the kids who lived on farms, with dread, the kids who lived in the city, with delight. In any case, it was not until mid-September, after school started for the second time, that important things were done.

The girls gathered on one side of the playground for jump rope. Two girls swung the rope while others jumped in

48

and out, chanting, "First day white, next day red; third day from my birth, and then I'm dead."

On the other side of the playground, the boys gathered to settle who was going to be top boy for the year. For the past couple of years, the chief bully had been Milky Hudson, the mayor's son. Milky wasn't his real name. It was a nickname because one of his eyes was white where the other one was brown. It didn't take any time at all before he squared up to Charlie Winter.

"What's your name?" Milky asked.

"Charlie Winter."

"You're Doc's nephew, huh?" another boy said.

"You ain't from around here, are you?" Milky asserted. He stood toe-to-toe with the new boy. Jack and Lefty, the toadies who orbited Milky like ugly moons around a troubled planet, took their places beside Milky. Even in repose, their fists were clenched. Now, sensing a confrontation, their knuckles went white and their arms cocked.

"No, I'm from Memphis," Charlie said. That was the story he'd rehearsed with the doctor.

"What 'cha doing here?"

"Living with Doc, my uh, uncle."

"Your uh-uh-uncle, huh? You think 'cause you're Doc's kid you're better 'n us?"

"Huh? No—" Charlie began.

"No? Look around, kid. You see anybody else wearing knickers an' new shoes. You sure you don't think you're better than us?" His fist thumped Charlie hard, right below his sternum.

Charlie gasped as the nerves of his solar plexus fired and his diaphragm contracted violently. His eyes widened, and his mouth gaped as he struggled for breath. A rush of air, and he began breathing.

No one was quite sure what happened next, but when Charlie and Milky stopped moving, Charlie had Milky in a half nelson, and Milky was screaming cuss words that most of us had never heard before.

Milky's henchmen were too surprised to react. Before they could get over their surprise, Charlie told them, "I'll bust his arm. I done it afore, and I'll do it again."

Bobby Gordon started yelling, "Fight! Fight!" even though there was no fight, and as long as Charlie held Milky, it didn't look like there would be. A couple of other kids took up the chant. That was all Jack and Lefty needed. They rushed Charlie, fists wind-milling. If they thought at all, they probably thought that Charlie couldn't break Milky's arm.

Charlie could, and did, except that Milky twisted at the instant Charlie applied pressure, so instead of a clean break, Milky's arm broke in two places, and bone stuck out halfway between his wrist and his elbow. Charlie pushed Milky into Jack and turned to face Lefty. Two punches, and Lefty was on his knees, blood dripping from his nose. Charlie looked around. The chanting had stopped, and the kids stood, silent. They were looking over Charlie's shoulder, past him, at Mrs. Goodman.

Charlie turned and saw the teacher. His face went from red to white, and then he turned tail and ran.

They say a small town is one where everybody knows everybody else's business. At one time, Ty Ty was like that. Even before they got Milky to Doc Winter's place, someone had called Doc to say that Charlie had run. A minute later, Jed Harmon called Doc from the depot to tell him he'd seen Charlie hop a train. It didn't take Jed two minutes to have the

50

telegraphs at stations along the line chattering. Charlie, who was "ridin' the blinds" of a passenger car, got caught in Sylvester, and brought back to Ty Ty by two deputy sheriffs. Doc and Mrs. Hudson were waiting for him.

Nobody knows what Doc and Mrs. Hudson said to Charlie, and nobody knows what Mrs. Hudson said to her husband, or what the mayor said to Milky, but Charlie had no more trouble with Milky. Charlie graduated high school in 1936, and Doc sent him to college at the University of Georgia. He came back to Ty Ty about four years later, and that's when I really got to know him.

Saturday Market

"They're as poor as Job's turkey," Mrs. Jackson said. She pursed her lips in what I figured was disapproval as she watched the McBride family arrive for Saturday Market. Mrs. Jackson was the wife of the man who ran the Piggly Wiggly and was known for being stingy. Or, what was that word? Oh, yes, *parsimonious*. I'd reached the letter P in the dictionary Mama had given me. How would I use it in a sentence? *Scorn for the McBrides would have dripped from Mrs. Jackson's mouth except that she is too parsimonious to waste scorn on anyone.* I guess Mrs. Jackson didn't believe scorn was covered by the Ten Commandments or that 'love thy neighbor' applied to poor folks.

Aunt Helen Hunter

Mrs. Jackson and Aunt Helen were standing near Daddy's truck. He'd parked it on the square, across the street from Uncle Frank's hardware store. Mama had already laid out a blanket with her eggs, and Mason jars with the first of this year's honey. She'd given Calvin a piece of toast left over from breakfast, and he was chewing on it while he held Joey. On the far corner of the square, some kids I knew were chasing each other up the steps

52

of the shoofly, around the tree in its center, and down the steps on the other side. I was leaning against the truck wondering if at nine years old, I was too grown up, or if I should join them.

We all watched the McBrides. Their buckboard wagon might once have had a seat but was now no more than a platform of rough-sawn pine. The father, Ancel McBride, sat with his legs dangling over the front edge of the wagon. He held the traces of the mules that drew the wagon. Weekdays, the mules pulled the plow. Angus, the oldest boy, sat beside his pa, hand on the two-by-four bolted to the side of the wagon—it was the only brake the wagon had. Mrs. McBride sat at her husband's other side. She held tightly to the basket in her lap both to protect the eggs it held and to keep her calico dress from blowing immodestly above her knees. Of all the family, she alone wore shoes, although they were hardly more than wooden soles laced to her feet with strips of calico.

Ancel whoa'ed the mules at a spot near Daddy's truck. It wasn't shaded this early in the day, but would be when the sun was overhead. Angus swung the two-by-four brake against the rim of the right front wheel, and wedged it into place with a block of wood he pulled from between two sacks of onions. Brendan, the littlest child, jumped from the back of the wagon and shoved rocks under each of the rear wheels. Muriel, the oldest, had already gone around to the front of the wagon and was holding the precious egg basket while her mother stepped down. Claire, the middle girl, kept her eye on her little sister, Morna, and on Brendan. The family worked together like an orchestra, although probably none of them had ever seen one and wouldn't have recognized the word. Within minutes of arrival the mules had been given water from a wooden bucket and feed in nosebags, sacks and baskets of onions had been set out, and Mrs. McBride and Muriel had headed down the street to peddle eggs from door to door.

The market on the Town Square was quiet and genteel. The men wore their second-best clothes, and even the men in overalls usually had on long-sleeve white shirts, buttoned to the neck. Some of the men wore ties tucked in the bib of their overalls. Women walked around in flowered dresses and sunbonnets, carrying baskets. The better off had a colored woman carrying their baskets. They would go from farmer to farmer, buying a little of this and that.

"I'll come back, later," Mrs. Jackson said as she nodded *goodbye* to Aunt Helen. Aunt Helen spoke to Mama then walked toward me. I stopped leaning against the truck and stood up straight. Aunt Helen noticed that, and smiled. "Good morning, David."

"Good morning, Aunt Helen. How's Uncle Robert?" Aunt Helen's husband was a drummer who traveled all over Georgia selling hardware. He and Aunt Helen did right well. Even during the depression, people had to keep their farm equipment running. I didn't see him often.

"He's quite well, David and will be home on this afternoon's train. I'll tell him you asked." She turned her head and glanced at Mrs. Jackson's back. "I'm not as shrewd a buyer as she is, but there is something about her that disturbs me. Where do you draw the line between frugal and stingy?"

"You mean 'parsimonious'?" I asked.

Aunt Helen's eyebrows went up when I said that. "Yes, David, that's a good word for it. You know that Mrs. Jackson won't buy anything until late afternoon when the farmers will be anxious to sell whatever is left rather than tote it home. She'll get better prices."

I looked at the load of sweet onions in the McBride wagon. *Brought more than they can sell, for sure.*

Aunt Helen saw where I was looking. "I know I'll pay a few pennies more than Mrs. Jackson. Of course, I'm not buying for a whole store. Certainly I can afford it, and the McBrides could probably use the extra pennies."

"The Jackson's are pretty rich, aren't they?" I said.

"They are fairly well off—as far as money is concerned. But not so much in other things."

"What else is there?"

"Our new preacher, Reverend Fletcher gave his first sermon on that just last Sunday. *For where your treasure is, there will your heart be also,* was what he said. What do you think that means, David?"

I thought about that. My family wasn't rich, but we weren't dirt-poor, either. Daddy had gotten the farm free and clear from his daddy, and we always had enough to eat because we grew it. Mama bartered eggs and honey our bees made from the black and white ti ti trees that lined the creek. We didn't need much cash money, and what we needed, Daddy always seemed to find. It was a long time before I figured out why Daddy always had more money than most country folks.

"It means Mrs. Jackson is missing out on something," I said. "It means she's looking in the wrong place for happiness, I guess."

"That's a good start, David, but there's more, isn't there?"

I thought for some more. "Mrs. Jackson believes that earthly riches mean spiritual riches?"

"I believe you're right, David." Aunt Helen laughed, and then said, "It gives an entirely new meaning to *holier than thou.*"

Aunt Helen was my favorite aunt even though she was not really an aunt, but Daddy's sister's sister-in-law. She and Uncle Robert were members of the Berea Baptist Church, what the rest of us called the Big Baptist Church on the Square. She wasn't too preachy, but she asked questions that made me think, and she always told me when I came up with a good answer.

Bank Robbery

No car could travel far on the dirt roads around Ty Ty without getting a coat of dust. Add a summer shower, and there would be mud splashed over the running boards and halfway up the fenders. There was nothing strange about it when a car near covered with mud and dust drove into town and parked on the square. The six men who got out stood on the sidewalk, talking and looking around and pointing for a few minutes, and then split up.

It was Doc Winter who said later the car was a 1932 Cadillac and that the license plates, even covered with mud, were from Wisconsin. He hadn't wondered about that. The Civilian Conservation Corps camp west of Ty Ty had been bringing in people from all over the country, and somehow nobody was surprised that the bureaucrats who came from Washington to inspect things drove expensive cars.

Bee didn't think anything about it when one of the men went into the courthouse and asked to look at land records. The records were public, and the man wasn't the first Yankee to come to Ty Ty looking for cheap land. She said she knew he was a Yankee from the way he talked. And he did talk. Told her he was looking for a peaceful town to bring his family to, and asked about crime and how good the police department was. We didn't have a police department, and she told him the sheriff in Tifton didn't hire anybody who wasn't related to him. She didn't say whether that meant they weren't any good. She just raised her eyebrows and let him draw his own conclusions.

Two of the men wandered around, every once in a while asking somebody which road went to the Civilian Conservation Corps camp, and where did the other road go. One man went to the bank and spent a long time asking about opening an account and getting a safety deposit box. When Mrs. McCoy politely asked if he lived here, he told her he was going to be on the staff at the CCC camp. Another of the men walked into the bank and asked change for a twenty-dollar bill. Nobody at the bank had seen the men get out of the same car, and so nobody remarked that they didn't say anything to one another. The last man went to the hardware store and bought a box of 20-gauge shotgun shells. Nobody remarked on that, either. It wasn't anywhere near close to hunting season, but since the Farm Crisis began about fifteen years before, it was always poaching season.

At three o'clock in the afternoon, like they'd set their watches together, they all got back in the car and drove off. Nobody remarked that they took the road to Sylvester because that was the direction of the CCC camp.

§ § § § §

Anybody who knew all about the men's visit probably could have figured out that they were planning on robbing the bank, but nobody put it all together until later. It was a surprise when the muddy Cadillac stopped in front of the bank on Friday morning and five men got out. They went into the bank and pulled shotguns and Tommy guns from under their coats.

Mrs. McCoy said later they probably picked Friday morning because they thought the CCC payroll would be at the bank. It wasn't. The real superintendent had driven away— from the back door of the bank—about five minutes before the robbers got there. And that wasn't their only mistake. They had managed to scoop up a couple of hundred dollars from the tellers' drawers and were driving off when they cut the corner

58

on the Sylvester Road too close and ran over the petunias Aunt Mildred had set out in front of the hardware store. Her call to the sheriff's station came right after the call from the bank. Deputy Donaldson called Sylvester, and they set up a roadblock.

For Ty Ty, it was more exciting than Bonny and Clyde were down in Louisiana a month or so later. The deputies in Sylvester knew they'd be facing Tommy guns, and came prepared. Three of the robbers were killed on the spot. The others lived to be tried and sentenced to life in prison.

I was only ten when I saw the robbers drive over Aunt Mildred's petunias, I didn't know what was going on. It was the talk of the town, though, and I think I got the facts straight.

The Earth Cries Out

Folks told a lot of stories about Ebenezer Springer and his twin brother, Everett. Since folks called them "Eb" and "Ev," sometimes the stories got mixed up. I heard this one from the fellow who married Everett's widow, so I reckon it's true.

§ § § §

Rachael's sleep had been broken, but she welcomed the crow of the rooster. Beside her, Everett grunted and rolled onto his side. Rachael slipped her feet into old brogans and trudged into the kitchen. She laid a fire in the cast iron stove and left it to burn down a bit. She stood on the back steps, and frowned. "Red sky in the mornin'; that be a warnin'. There's gonna be a storm." The cat ignored her.

She took a deep breath and then stepped into the outhouse. She tried to hurry but couldn't hold her breath long enough. She breathed through her mouth, trying to avoid the stench, but it overpowered her. Her stomach tumbled and she retched. *Got to put down some lime*, she thought, *'cept we can't afford it. Wonder if Everett can borrow some.* She shut the door behind her and took a deep breath of the morning air. A cackle from the chicken coop caught her attention. She retrieved the egg—warm and slippery—and two others. *I'll scramble them up, and toast the last of the cornbread.* Though it wasn't much of a breakfast, she knew it was more than a lot of folks would be getting.

"Ev! I'm fixin' to fix breakfast," she called from the kitchen. "An' you gotta get some lime in the outhouse. See if you can't borrow some off'n your brother, won't you? An' maybe a dollar to buy some corn meal."

Everett clumped into the kitchen. "I ain't borrowing nothin' from my brother! Ain't nothin' he'd like better'n for me to come begging so's he can remind me how bad off we are." He reached through a rip in his cotton shirt and scratched his ribs. "How about chopping enough wood today so's I can get a bath?"

"We ain't got no wood to chop," Rachael said, pointing to the two sticks lying beside the stove. "That's the last of it. Oh, Ev, what are we gonna do?" Sobbing, Rachael let go the fork she was using to stir the eggs and covered her face with her hands.

Everett wrapped his arms around his wife. "Aw, hon, don't cry. Something's gonna turn up."

Rachael shrugged off Everett's hands. "You always say the same thing: something's gonna turn up. Something's gonna turn up. But it don't, and it won't unless you get out there and look for it. You remember what Deacon Clement said last Sunday 'bout pride going 'fore the fall? You swallow your pride and go ask your brother for help. And ask him to put you to work, too!"

"It ain't pride," Everett said. "You know what he'll say. He'll say I got all that was coming to me when Pa set me up with the garage and this house. That was the deal. I got the garage, and Eb got the farm. He'll say I got no more coming to me."

The smell of smoke alerted Rachael and stopped the conversation. She rescued the corn bread before it burned, but the eggs were ruined.

Everett cut a piece of hickory bark and slid it into his shoe to cover the hole in the sole. He folded his knife, and was about to put it in his pocket when he mumbled, "I can pawn this. Maybe get a dollar. It'll buy meal and a little cracked corn for the chickens. It'll keep us going." He sighed, and started walking toward Ebenezer's place. Of all the tools his father had given him, the knife was all that was left. The other tools had been pawned, a few at a time, over the past years.

The pecan trees that lined the road were already heavy with nuts. Beyond them, corn and sorghum stood tall in the late summer sun. Bile rose in Everett's throat thinking about how hard life had been on him and how good it had been to Ebenezer. Everett muttered to himself, "Of course, it helps that he's as crooked as a snake."

Everett heard rhythmic pounding coming from the barn, and turned in that direction. Ebenezer was standing at the forge, his back to the door.

"Hey, Eb," Everett called between the hammer blows that rang in his ears.

"What do you want?" Ebenezer replied. He continued pounding a metal strap, drowning out Everett's reply.

Ebenezer stuck the metal work piece back into the coals. Everett shouted to make himself heard over the hiss of the bellows and the roar of the fire. "Nothin'. Just come to say, *howdy*."

Ebenezer laid the work piece back on the anvil. "Liar. You always was a liar." He resumed pounding. Everett leaned against the doorframe and waited.

Ebenezer quenched the metal and covered the forge. "Come on." He gestured, and led Everett out the door and to the well. Ebenezer pumped a dipper of water and offered it to Everett, who shook his head.

"No, thanks." He took a deep breath. "An' you're right. I didn't come just to say, *howdy*. I know you don't owe me nothing, so I won't ask something for nothing. But, would you at least put me to work? I deserve that much—deserve it more than any of them Coloreds you got working for you." Everett looked again at the fields that surrounded Ebenezer's house and barn, fields full of maturing crops being worked even now by Ebenezer's tenants.

Ebenezer drank from the dipper. "You don't deserve nothing. And the Coloreds who work for me, they earn their keep. You wouldn't. I seen the tools Pa gave you, I seen 'em at the pawnshop in Sylvester. I got back Pa's favorite hammer and some others when you couldn't redeem them. You'll never amount to nothing. And that's why you're gonna lose the garage and the house. What you gonna do then? At least you and that woman didn't have kids. I might feel obliged to care for them, and I wouldn't like that."

"That woman is my wife. Her name's Rachael," Everett said. His face had flushed.

"That woman is a piece of trash you picked up at the roadhouse," Ebenezer said. He turned back toward the smithy.

Everett didn't know how the knife got in his hand nor how the blade got opened. He lunged at Ebenezer's back. Blinded by his rage, he plunged the knife into Ebenezer's left shoulder. Ebenezer stumbled and fell. He grabbed a stone and got to his feet. Ebenezer swung the stone and struck Everett's temple. Everett's eyes dimmed. His body fell heavily and twitched a couple of times. Ebenezer shrugged, spat in the dirt beside Everett's body, and walked to the house to phone the sheriff.

Ebenezer was not only rich, but also good friends with about everybody in Tift County who mattered, including the sheriff and the coroner. The coroner's inquest ruled justified self-defense. There was never any doubt about it.

Boilin' Sorghum

School was out for two weeks, but we weren't celebrating. We were too busy harvesting. For a lot of folks, cane for sorghum molasses was about the most important crop after peanuts—and corn for moonshine.

§ § § § §

Ebenezer Springer pounded one last time to tighten the staves of the bucket. He dipped the bucket in a trough and filled it with water. The water would make the wood swell so the bucket wouldn't leak when he started pressing sorghum. Pressing would start on Wednesday and keep going day and night until the job was finished. He owned the only sorghum mill in western Tift County. He also owned a lot of acreage. Most was sharecropped by Coloreds. He would get his twenty-five percent for running the mill and the boiling and fifty percent from his sharecroppers. He would also get the interest on the money he'd lent his tenants so they could buy flour, sugar, and shoes. He was very careful to leave them enough to live on and to buy an occasional jug of moonshine, and he was always polite to their women.

§ § § § §

The first time Daddy let me work the pressing was when I was ten years old. "Mr. Springer's going to offer you two dollars a day," Daddy said. My eyes must have gotten wide because he chuckled. "But that's going to be in scrip, what he pays his tenants with. The only place you can spend it is at Mr. Springer's store. You ever been to Mr. Springer's store?"

"No, sir," I said. "I didn't know he had a store."

"It's on the other side of Colored Town. I wouldn't want you going there, anyway. Now, you thank him for the offer, but ask for a dollar a day, in cash. Make sure he agrees. He keeps his word—in little things."

It was still dark when Daddy dropped me off at Mr. Springer's. Wagons and trucks were already lined up. They were full of cane, stripped of seed heads and leaves. The seed heads would be dried and some saved for next year's planting. What was left would help feed hogs during the winter. The first people in line were folks who had started out way before dawn. As the day went on, more wagons, most driven by Mr. Springer's tenants, would arrive.

Ten gallons of juice pressed from the cane and then boiled for hours would make one gallon of sorghum. The boilin' shed was a brick firebox about three feet high and six feet on a side. Poles at the corners held up a roof. There weren't any walls. Square holes along the sides of the firebox were for throwing in wood and shoveling out ashes. The boilin' pan rested on top of the brick walls. It was steel, and about two feet deep. Nearby, wood for the fire was stacked six feet high and fifty feet long.

The press that squeezed the juice out of the cane wasn't much to look at. It was a cast iron contraption about the size of a big apple crate, bolted to an oak stump. One side of the box was open, and you could see the gear teeth that pulled in the

66

sorghum stalks and crushed them. The side opposite was open, too. It was where the crushed stalks were pushed out. There were spouts on both of the other sides, and hooks for the buckets that collected the juice. A T-handle stuck out of the top. It was bolted to a pole, about 25 feet long, called the sweep. A mule at the other end of the sweep walked round and round all day, turning the mill.

The sweep was about five feet off the ground. The folks who fed stalks into the mill and took the crushed stalks away had to duck every time it came around. The ones who toted the buckets of juice to the boilin' shed would hurry in and out between passes of the sweep. It wasn't hard to miss the sweep because the mule was slow. My friend Avery, Mr. Springer's nephew, rode the mule because that's about all he could do, being crippled.

Mr. Springer and one of his men sat at a table under a shade tree. Boys took every bucket of juice to Mr. Springer who recorded the number of gallons that came from each person's cane. It was all mixed up in the boiling shed, but everybody accepted the tally as being fair.

Houston, who supervised the boiling, was a colored man who had worked for Mr. Springer for thirty years and for Mr. Springer's father before that. Houston's father had been a slave, owned by Mr. Springer's grandfather, who had stayed on as a Freedman after the Civil War. Houston had a paddle on a long pole that he used to stir and scrape the pan. Houston's son was his apprentice. He handled the skimmer, pulling the foam off the boiling liquid.

There were at least fifty people doing different jobs. There were people unloading cane and stacking it near the press. Men and boys fed the press two or three stalks at a time, others took the stalks away, and a brigade of boys toted buckets back and forth. At the boilin' shed, men and older boys threw logs into the fire and shoveled out the ashes.

The whole thing was orchestrated by long custom and practice. It happened only once a year, but it had happened every year for a hundred years, maybe longer. A lot of the jobs were passed from father to son. My daddy had carried buckets when he was a boy, and Houston's father had run the boilin' shed until he was ninety years old.

I saw plenty of folks I knew, including Junior Lind. I was kind of surprised to see him. He was a little persnickety about getting dirty. We hadn't been totin' buckets more than a couple of hours before Junior's hands blistered and bled, and he dropped a bucket. I was right behind him at Mr. Springer's table.

"Sir, I . . . ." Junior couldn't finish what he needed to say.

"I saw it," Mr. Springer said. "It's all right. I'll take it out of my tally. Just don't do it, again."

Junior ducked his head and mumbled his thanks. I caught up with him, and wrapped my bandana around his hand. "Here," I said. "You ain't done any really hard work before, have you?"

"No, I ain't much."

"You keep this between you and the bucket handle, and you'll be fine. You hear?"

Junior nodded.

I didn't know that if a boy tripped and spilled a bucket, Mr. Springer would take it out of his own share. I thought it was mighty decent of him. I remembered what Daddy had said about Mr. Springer keeping his word in the little things, and wondered—is he just being generous in a little thing so people would think he was generous in big things?

I thought on what Deacon Clement had said about jots and tittles, and how important even the smallest things were. Joey was the smallest thing in our family. And he was important. But I still didn't understand why God was testing us, and why Joey had been born only to suffer.

Mr. Springer's tenants treated the boilin' like a covered-dish supper at the church, except that there was music and dancing. The music wasn't a bit like the hymns we sang and of course, no one at our church would dance. A bunch of us boys were standing around the schoolyard once when one of the older boys asked why Baptists wouldn't have sex standing up. I didn't know what he was talking about, much less the answer. He said it was because people might think they were dancing. All the older boys laughed. I did, too, but it was a couple of years before I figured out what the joke was.

By lunchtime, the colored folks had set up trestle tables under the trees and loaded them down with cornbread, collard greens, field peas with pig knuckles, and chit'lins boiled in big pots and then fried in hot grease. Mama gave me a sandwich and a bunch of carrots for my lunch, but I must have looked hungry, 'cause one of the colored women came over to the tree where I was sitting with Junior and offered us a plate of chit'lins to share. Junior turned up his nose, at first, but when he saw that I didn't die from eating colored food, he tried some and said he liked them.

Mr. Springer was burning a lot of pine under the boilin' pan. Every once in a while, there would be a loud pop and sparks would fly from under the pan. Most folks paid it no nevermind—it was just sap exploding from a knot in the wood. While I was waiting for the sweep to pass, I watched Darrell Fletcher throwing split wood onto the fire. Darrell was the son of the new preacher at the Big Baptist Church. I wondered since he was new how he got that job and if I could get it next year. It was hard and hot work, but it paid a lot better than toting buckets.

I had picked up an empty bucket and was walking toward the press when I saw Darrell reach into his pocket and throw something that wasn't wood onto the fire. He and Tommy Babb looked at one another and then walked over to the big woodpile like they were going for more wood. They were halfway there when there was a loud bang, and fire flew out of both sides of the shed and, if you believed what Houston said later, lifted the boilin' pan a foot off the fire.

The fire that spit out hit Houston's son, setting his overalls on fire. He dropped the skimmer and was beating at the fire with his hands when Mr. McCorkle knocked him down and started rolling him in the dirt. Mr. McCorkle was a volunteer fireman and knew stuff like that.

I was watching the fire so hard, I didn't see the sweep until it knocked me in the head. They said Avery yelled at me, but there was a lot of yelling going on, and I didn't hear him. When I opened my eyes, Granny Meeks was standing over me.

"Git up real slow, Davey-boy. Stop if you get dizzy."

I did what she said.

"Now, look at me." She peeled my eyelids up and looked hard. "You're fine, boy. So's the sweep." She laughed at her own joke. "Come on, Davey-boy. Get out t' way so they can start pressin' again."

The shouting had died down while I was knocked out, so I heard right clearly what Mr. McCorkle said.

"Boy howdy! That was one heck of a pine knot, Eb. You burning lightered pine or something?"

"That ain't it," I said to Granny Meeks. "Darrell Fletcher threw something into the fire, whatever it was that blew up, and then walked away, just before—"

70

She put her finger on my lips. "Is anybody else sayin' that? You see that boy still workin'? What does that tell you?" Granny Meeks asked. Her voice was soft.

It didn't take long for me to figure out where she was going. "Nobody else saw him," I said. "They don't know he did it."

"Be careful how you pick your friends, Davey-boy. Be more careful how you pick your enemies," she said. "Darrell Fletcher's daddy, and the mayor, and Eb Springer, they run this town. An' they run the Klan, and not one of them would give a hoot if a colored man got hurt."

She squinted her eyes and looked around. "I'd appreciate it if you didn't tell anybody I said that."

I nodded. "Yes'm."

"Sure," Granny said. "They's people who'd believe you. I do." She nodded. "But the ones that have power? They won't believe you, an' nothin' would happen 'cept you'd make a powerful enemy."

"But Houston's son was burned! It ain't right!"

"No, Davey-boy, it ain't right. But it's the way things are. Some secrets are best kept."

§ § § § §

It was a few days later after school started again that we heard somebody had stolen blasting caps from the railroad. I figured that's what Darrell had thrown into the fire. But Granny Meeks was right, and I never told anybody, not even my daddy.

Christmas

Even during the worst of the depression, Christmas was a special time. Calvin and I would be up at dawn to see what Santa Claus had brought. About mid-morning, aunts and uncles would arrive with casseroles and desserts—and more presents.

When I was eight, Daddy's sister Mary had her first baby. She named her Martha, after Mama, who was godmother to the baby. Mama took the train to Valdosta for the Christening. Two years later, we all went to Valdosta to have Christmas with Aunt Mary, Uncle Beau, and Little Martha. I had a hard time explaining to Calvin, who was six, how Santa Claus knew where we'd be.

After supper on Christmas Eve, we went to service at Aunt Mary and Uncle Beau's church. There wasn't much preaching. Everybody got a candle. The preacher lit this big candle in the front of the church. Then the deacons lit their candles from the big one. The deacons went down the aisle, lighting the candle of the person on the end of the pew. The flame was passed down the pew until everybody's candles were burning. Mama tried to hold Joey and a candle, too, but Joey kept reaching for the fire, so Daddy held Mama's candle.

After everybody's candle was lit, we sang *Oh, Little Town of Bethlehem* and *Silent Night.* When we got to the part about "Holy infant so tender and mild," Mama started crying. I knew she was thinking about Joey and not Jesus.

Afterwards, we sat in the living room while Aunt Mary served eggnog and cookies. Then, she handed me a book. "This book has been in the family for a long time, David. Would you read it to us?"

Shucks, I didn't need the book. I knew the story, even had it memorized. Then I figured out it wasn't about the story; it was about the book. So I read.

"T'was the night before Christmas . . . ."

"Why did Santa Claus put his finger beside his nose?" Calvin asked. We were sleeping on pallets in Aunt Mary's sewing room and whispering in the dark.

"He was telling the kid who was watching him not to tell anybody," I said.

"Huh?"

"Putting his finger beside his nose means they shared a secret."

"And what's sugar-plums," Calvin asked.

"Some kind of candy is all I know. Now you'd better get to sleep or Santa won't come."

Christmas afternoon, Uncle Beau was rooting around in a candy jar. He pulled out his hand, empty, and asked, "Now who could have eaten all the peppermints?"

Calvin and I looked at one another. Calvin put his finger beside his nose. I did, too. I don't think Uncle Beau noticed.

Charlie Winter's Dog

Doc Winter woke to the siren on Deputy Donaldson's patrol car. The siren sounded the same as it always did going down the Tifton-Sylvester Road; but, somehow, Doc knew Donaldson was bringing someone to him. He was dressed and halfway down the stairs when the siren died. He heard the crunch of tires on the gravel apron in front of his house and flipped on the porch light in time to keep Donaldson from hollering and blowing his horn and waking up any of the neighbors who might still be asleep.

The soft thump of bare feet on the stairs and a whisper told him that Charlie was awake. "Doc? Can I help?"

"Sure, Charlie. Wash your hands really good with the green soap, and then put a clean sheet on the exam table. I'll be in—"

The front door burst open. Donaldson stood in the doorway holding the body of a child. *No,* Doc thought, *it's not a child. It's a dog.*

"Doc, I'm sorry. I know you ain't a vet, but I hit this dog and I just can't stand to see him suffer . . ." Donaldson's voice dropped to a ragged whisper. "Can you help him?"

"Sure," Doc said. *I'm already awake.* "I'll do what I can. Bring him in." He gestured toward the exam room.

The dog whimpered when Donaldson laid him on the table and again as Doc examined him. Charlie reached toward

74

the dog. The dog raised his head and curled his lips but couldn't muster the energy to growl. He dropped his head back onto the exam table and closed his eyes. Charlie softly stroked the dog's head. The boy's touch quieted the dog as Doc moved each leg and prodded its body.

"Left foreleg's broken," Doc said. "I can splint it. Don't know how well it'll heal unless he's kept off it. Can't tell about internal injuries. Whose dog is he?"

"Never seen him before," Donaldson replied. "He ran in front of me on the Sledge Road."

"He don't belong to anybody," Charlie said. "And if he did, they don't deserve him."

The two men looked at the boy. "Look at his coat. It's full of burrs. You can see his ribs—he ain't bein' fed. An' his eyes are all rheumy."

Perhaps understanding the tone of concern in Charlie's voice, perhaps simply relieved at not being poked and prodded, the dog licked Charlie's hand.

"Can I keep him, Doc? Please?" Charlie asked.

Doc never did say yes or no, and Donaldson never did find out who the dog might have belonged to. Whether it was Doc's splint or Charlie's tending, the dog came to walk without a limp. When the splint came off, it was too late to send him away. Charlie had already named the dog *Achilles*. *Achilles* became Doc's dog when Charlie went off to the University of Georgia, but seemed to know when Charlie was coming home for holidays and would be waiting for him at the train depot.

Decoration Day

If you had an ancestor who fought in the War Between the States—what the old ladies called "the recent unpleasantness"—you were eligible to join the Sons of Confederate Veterans, the United Daughters of the Confederacy, or for kids, the Children of the Confederacy. The grown-up women in the UDC were mighty particular about who could join their group and the children's group. Membership was by invite only. The Daughters were mostly the same as the Berea Baptist Church Women's Bible Class, and the Children were mostly their kids.

That's probably why Mama and Daddy seemed surprised when I got invited to join the Children of the Confederacy. Folks in the Berea Baptist Church tended to look down their noses at us members of the Gospel Truth Baptist Church—which they called the "Clapboard Church of Christ." Mama figured I had been asked because of her father, the rich preacher who had the biggest Baptist Church in Athens and his own radio program. Daddy thought it was because his grandfather had been a decorated Confederate hero in a South Carolina regiment. I figured it might have been because Aunt Helen was a member of the Berea Baptist Church and the Daughters of the Confederacy.

After supper the day the letter came, Daddy and I sat on the porch. He was in the swing holding the letter, and I was on the floor with my legs hanging off the side of the porch.

"Southern heritage is all well and good. So's pride in your roots. Come here," Daddy said.

I got up and sat in the swing next to him.

Daddy sighed. "Problems come when folks get involved in heritage and roots, and forget history. Lots of people will tell you lots of reasons for that war. Some will say *states' rights*; some will say *slavery*. I don't reckon anyone knows for sure. It might just have been people getting caught up in something bigger than they were."

We swung for a minute like Daddy wanted me to think on what he said.

"People's opinions are mighty strong, and their attachment to their heritage is powerful. You be listening and not saying anything when people get to talking about the war and slavery and the Confederacy. You come to me after, and we'll talk about it, you hear?"

"Yes, sir," I said.

"Do you want to join?" Daddy waved the letter.

Mama came out in time to hear Daddy's question, and my answer. "I'm not sure," I said.

Mama said it would do me good to make some different friends. Heck, I already knew all of them from school, but I let her talk me into it. About the only thing we did was decorate graves once a year and then get fed punch and cookies. The first time I went, I was eleven-going-on-twelve.

In some places, it was *Confederate Memorial Day* to distinguish it from Memorial Day. In Ty Ty, it was called *Decoration Day.* Following the custom begun in Macon before the War Between the States was even over, the Daughters of the Confederacy decorated the graves of the Hallowed Confederate Dead. Flowers planted by the phases of the Easter moon were cut, tied into bundles, placed in baskets, and carried in white-gloved hands to the southwestern corner of the Berea Baptist Church cemetery.

A black, wrought iron fence, freshly painted a week before by men from the Sons of Confederate Veterans, surrounded a plot holding the graves of ten soldiers who had been wounded in a skirmish near Ty Ty, then brought here where they died. The battle wasn't big enough or important enough to have a name and was remembered only by the people of Ty Ty. Scattered throughout the rest of the cemetery, small Confederate Battle Flags marked the graves of Confederate Veterans buried in family plots. In a couple of weeks, the American Legion would put flags on the graves of men killed in the Spanish-American war and World War I.

My Confederate grandfather, the hero, was buried in the cemetery behind our church. Once, there had been a wooden marker, but it wasn't there anymore. Mama said she knew where his grave was, and she would put flowers on it, but not today. She'd do it on Sunday.

A gaggle of children stood at the gate, waiting for the UDC ladies. We all were dressed in our Sunday clothes. Decoration Day wasn't an official school holiday, but none of us would be marked absent on this Friday.

Mr. Shackleford, the sexton, unlocked the gate and bowed slightly as the ladies and children filed in. I wondered if anyone but me grasped the irony of a colored man, born into slavery before the Emancipation Proclamation, being custodian of the keys to the Confederate graveyard.

Women and children moved among the graves. There was no ceremony and little talking. Now and again, a woman would stop and call softly to one of the children. She would

78

hand the child a bouquet from her basket, and point to a gravestone.

I hesitated at one grave, and whispered to Aunt Helen. "This gravestone says *IND*. That means Indiana, right? He's a Yankee."

"This is your first year, David."

"Yes, ma'am."

"He may be a Yankee, but . . . ," she lifted her eyes and swept them over the cemetery. "They're all equal in the eyes of God." Her gaze paused at the forsythia hedge, and she opened her mouth as if to say something but seemed to think better of it. "Here. Here's a bouquet for this one."

"Aunt Helen? You keep looking at the forsythia. Do we need more flowers? It's about done blooming, but I might find some."

"No, David. Thank you, but that's not it." She took a deep breath and asked, "Do you know what's behind the forsythia?"

"No, ma'am."

"It's an old slave cemetery. People who lived in town used to bury their house servants there, instead of the graveyard at the African-Methodist-Episcopal Church. About the only flowers there, besides the forsythia, are kudzu in the spring, and thistle in the fall. Last year, somebody in the church said the land ought to be cleaned up. Somebody else said it ought to be sold. But Reverend Fletcher reminded us that it was an old slave cemetery, and nobody would want it for anything, and that it was easier to plant forsythia to hide it than it was to clean it up."

She looked at her basket, now empty. "Come, David. You'll be late for punch and cookies."

After decorating the graves, we were herded to the manse of the Berea Baptist Church. It was a block south of the cemetery, on Church Street. I don't know why it was called, "Church Street." All the churches except the Berea Baptist and the AME were on Spring Street.

I walked with Junior Lind. As soon as we got out of the cemetery, I started talking. "Do you know what's back there?" I asked, pointing to the forsythia hedge.

Junior shook his head.

"It is an old slave cemetery, and it's haunted!" I told him. Junior was a little bit of a sissy, and I figured I'd scare him some.

"Ain't so," he said, but his eyes got wide, and his voice sounded like he wasn't quite sure of what he was saying.

"Yep," I said. "Slaves . . . and murderers! They say one of the slaves killed an overseer. They hung him, cut his head off, and buried him in two different places. At night, he comes out of his grave, looking for his head." We had turned the corner, and the slave cemetery was behind us.

"Really?" Junior asked, and I knew I had him hooked.

"Yep, I can't tell you who told me, but it was one of the women. You can't tell anybody, you hear?"

Junior nodded his head and crossed his heart.

There were more flowers at the manse. We came in through the kitchen, and stood in line to wash our hands at the sink before we went into the dining room and parlor. There were double doors between the rooms, but they were open to make one big room. We stood in line and got a cup of punch. We stood in another line to pick up a paper napkin with one cookie on it. There were a dozen women, wearing pretty

80

dresses and hats and white gloves like it was Easter. They watched us really carefully and made sure we didn't wander away—or take more than one cookie.

Incident at Edna's Diner

Deputy Donaldson walked with a limp. There were lots of stories about how he got it, including a pitched battle between revenuers and 'shiners. Bobby Gordon's daddy was there when it happened, and the story Bobby told me is more likely the right one.

§ § § § §

Edna's Diner was about the only place in Ty Ty open after 9:00 PM. The sheriff's station, a branch of the main office in Tifton, closed up about suppertime. Jed would be dozing over the telegraph until the last train came through around eleven o'clock, and there might be a few fellows playing pinochle and sharing a jug at the volunteer fire station. On Saturday night, bingo at the American Legion sometimes ran until ten, but after dark, most everything that happened in Ty Ty happened at Edna's. Deputy Donaldson knew that "everything" meant just about anything, and if there was going to be trouble in Ty Ty, it was going to start at Edna's.

The folks who ate at Edna's didn't mind that the cooks were all Coloreds. No one could see much of the cooks except for a hand pushing a plate through the slot back of the counter that connected with the kitchen. There weren't many Coloreds who had the money to eat at Edna's. Those who had the money went to the back door where their food would be handed to them in brown paper bags or wrapped in newspaper. It was an arrangement that had worked since Edna's great grandmother had started selling meatloaf sandwiches and fried pies out of her kitchen in 1875.

That was sixty years ago. Now, hard times had brought new folks to Ty Ty. They said that the Great Depression had hit the North harder than the South mainly because folks around here could at least grow food—the ones who hadn't been foreclosed off their land, that is.

Some of the new folks were Coloreds who had lost their jobs in factories up north and had come to live with relatives in the sharecropper shacks that dotted the county. Some of the new folks were white trash come looking for farm jobs that didn't exist, hoping to get hired by the CCC to plant pine trees, or just looking for a warmer place to pitch their bedroll.

On this particular night, business at Edna's was slow. Barney Bonds sat at one end of the counter, hunched over a soup bowl. Deputy Donaldson sat at the other end of the counter, sugaring his coffee. Darlene, the night waitress, stood by the cash register, leaning her be-hind on the counter, trying to take some of her considerable weight off her feet. A squeak announced the front door opening. Darlene gasped. Donaldson looked at Darlene and then turned to see what she was staring at. He choked when he sucked a mouthful of coffee down his windpipe. Two young colored men were sitting at the table right inside the door. Barney turned his head when the deputy coughed, but he didn't turn far enough to see the Coloreds.

"Darlene, gimme some more saltines, won't 'cha?" Barney whined.

"No!" Darlene answered. Then she whispered to Donaldson. "You gotta get them outta here! The boys from the fire station will be here any minute now, looking for coffee to sober 'em up 'fore they go home."

Donaldson wiped his finger across a spot of coffee spit that had landed on his uniform trousers. They were Army surplus, heavy wool, shiny with wear. He hitched up his belt, mostly to reassure himself by the weight of his .38-caliber revolver, and stepped to the table.

"You boys need to go 'round back," he said. "Knock on the kitchen door. They'll take care of you."

"I do not understand," one of the colored men said. "The sign in the window indicates that the establishment is open." The precision and cadence of his speech was like nothing Donaldson had heard before.

"Oh, I 'spect you understand, all right," Donaldson said. "You ain't from around here, but you been down here long enough to know better 'n what you done. Now, you want to eat, go 'round back. Else," he lowered his voice, "get your black asses outta here."

One of the colored men, not the one who had spoken, put his hands on the edge of the table as if to push back his chair. Instead, the table—lighter than the man and his chair—skidded forward and hit Deputy Donaldson's legs just below his crotch. Off balance, the deputy fell. His revolver dropped from the holster and bounced across the floor. Behind the counter, Darlene raised Edna's shotgun.

The second colored man, the one who had answered the deputy, saw the shotgun and dropped to the floor. Darlene, figuring he was going for the deputy's gun, fired the shotgun—first one barrel, and then the second. The first shot hit Donaldson. The second hit the colored man who had run the table into the deputy.

Barney looked up from his soup. "Darlene, what in tarnation's goin' on?" Outside, the crunch of pickup truck tires on gravel announced the arrival of the men from the fire station.

84

"What the hail?" George McCorkle took one step into the diner before he stopped. Danny Barringer wasn't so quick to stop and bumped into George.

"Them colored boys . . . ." Deputy Donaldson gasped.

"This one's dead," Barringer said, pointing to the colored man who had been shot.

"And this one's gonna be," Jim Horton said. He and Nate Gordon had grabbed the arms of the surviving colored man.

"What? No!" the man said. "We did nothing! It was the woman—the shotgun . . . ."

"How's the deputy?" George asked. Ronnie Babb had taken off his shirt and tied it around Donaldson's right leg, where the shot had torn away a chunk of flesh. Blood oozed from the other leg, where a stray pellet had hit.

"He'll be fine," Babb said. "I'll take him to Doc Winter's place." He helped Donaldson to his feet. "Here, lean on me."

"Darlene, gimme that shotgun," George ordered. "You wait five minutes then call Matty at the exchange, and tell her to ring the sheriff in Tifton. Tell him there's a dead Colored, and that Deputy Donaldson was wounded, but not bad. Then you don't say nothing to nobody. Nobody!" George turned. "Barney, you better come with us."

"I ain't stayin' here by myself with a dead man—" Darlene began.

"You ain't by yourself, woman. Who's cook tonight?" George asked.

"Eddie is," Darlene answered. "Eddie?" she called through the slot that led to the kitchen. There was no answer. The kitchen was empty.

§ § § § §

    They found the colored man, the one who'd ducked when he saw Darlene with the shotgun, hanging from an oak tree about a mile out of town on the Sylvester road. The next night, men in hooded white robes burned a cross in the yard of the sharecropper's shack where Eddie lived with his aunt and six cousins. Eddie hopped a freight the next morning and left Tift County. Even though Darlene had wounded Deputy Donaldson so that he walked with a limp and pain for the rest of his life, she was hailed as a hero for killing the man who had grabbed for Donaldson's gun. The flaws in the story were smoothed out in the telling until they were forgotten by everyone but Darlene and the deputy.

Death and Retribution

Other than an occasional lynching by the Klan, the only murder in Ty Ty when I was growing up happened right at the Gospel Truth Church. Maybe not in the church, but that's where they found the body. As it turned out, the murder was part of a much bigger story.

§ § § § §

Esther Watkins stepped to her back door and tossed a pan of dishwater onto the parched earth.

"Ain't no sense in pourin' it on the t'maters," she said. "They's long dead. Maybe the beans will 'mount to somethin', but they don't want water now."

She sighed and turned back to the kitchen, stepping by long habit over the place in the floor where two boards were missing. They'd been broken out when Mr. Springer had come to get the cast iron stove Esther had bought on installment. She'd been working for Mrs. Hudson, then. Now Esther was unemployed and cooked over a fire in the back yard. She didn't know what she would do when winter came.

The tramp spooked Esther. His face was so dark from sun and dirt she couldn't tell if he was white or colored until he got close. She picked up her pitchfork when he came into the yard. His lips, nose, and voice told her he was a white man.

"Ma'am, can I have a drink of water . . . and maybe a bite to eat?"

"Draw yourself water from the well," she said. "But I ain't got no food to spare." *Must be a northerner,* she thought. *Not nobody from around here calls a colored woman, ma'am.*

"I'll trade you for a meal," the man said after he drank. "I got this locket on a chain. See? It's real gold."

"Can't eat gold," Esther said. "An' I tol' you, I ain't got food to spare. Now drink your water and git, 'fore my husband comes out and whups us both."

After drinking another dipper of water, the man walked toward the railroad tracks. Esther watched until he was out of sight. Before she went to sleep that night, she stuck a kitchen chair under the knob of her bedroom door.

§ § § § §

The late summer sun beat on the roof of the Gospel Truth Church. The smell of the asphalt shingles competed with the resinous pines that surrounded but did not shade the clapboard building. It was Tuesday. The windows and doors that were opened to catch the breeze during Sunday service were closed. The smell inside was neither asphalt nor pine, but corruption and decay. Two dead flies lay on the floor. The eggs they had laid in the mouth of the child whose body lay on the floor next to them would hatch into maggots by Wednesday. The man who had violated the child and then killed her sat beside a small fire in a hobo jungle east of the Ty Ty train depot. He felt safe. No one had seen him carry the child's body into the church, and he had read the signboard—there would be

88

no Wednesday night prayer meeting. The body wouldn't be found until Sunday.

§ § § § §

A mile or so south of the hobo jungle, the Honorable Charles Howard Leffler, judge of the Superior Court and Grand Dragon of the Knights of the Ku Klux Klan, sipped moonshine from a glass that had begun life as a jelly jar. Had he been in his own home, he would have drunk barrel-aged bourbon from crystal. But, he never would have allowed this bunch into his house. The men who know his position in the Klan were sworn to secrecy. To break that oath was a death sentence. The subject of this night's meeting was a chicken processing plant that had opened west of town.

"They's payin' in cash at the end of every shift," Willie Lorton said.

George McCorkle added, "They's hirin' Coloreds and the worst kind of white trash from that hobo jungle, an' they's workin' side by side debeakin' chickens."

Judge Leffler smiled to himself when he heard this. He considered most of the Klansmen to be white trash, cannon fodder in the war to preserve the White Race and White Power. What interested the judge was that his chief political rival owned the chicken plant and that the man was getting rich from it. Using the Klan to cripple the labor supply would kill two birds with one stone. The judge smiled openly this time.

Two nights later, thirty men in hooded white robes assembled at the old roadhouse. They knew one another. Their voices were as distinctive as their pickup trucks and battered sedans. They carried mauls, baseball bats, and bullwhips. A few carried shotguns. The shells in the guns were loaded with rock salt, but the extra shells in the men's pockets held buckshot. Hoods were lifted as a jug of 'shine passed from mouth to mouth. The first jug was replaced by a second, and Ebenezer Springer was thinking about opening a third jug when the sound of a trumpet playing "Dixie" announced the arrival of the Grand Dragon.

Judge Leffler stepped onto a crate in the bed of a pickup truck and held up his hands. The cheering and singing that had begun when he arrived faded into silence. The judge's robe and hood were satin. Bright red crosses adorned the chest and back. He offered a prayer to Almighty God to bless their undertaking. He called the night's targets *animals* and reminded the assembly that God had given men dominion over the animals. He reminded them that Adam was white and that the Negro was created when God turned Cain's flesh black after he slew his brother. He reminded them that Jesus was white and called to mind the pictures in their Bibles and in their churches—pictures of a white Christ with blue eyes and blond hair. He exhorted them to rid the county of the Coloreds and the white trash. He led them in singing *Onward Christian Soldiers*. Then, the men crowded into the seats of sedans and climbed into the backs of pickup trucks. The license plates had been smeared with mud. Men in the lead truck carried the Christian Flag and the Confederate Battle Flag. The judge watched them drive out of sight and smiled. He nodded to Ebenezer Springer. The two of them left in Eb's truck, heading in the opposite direction.

George McCorkle swung a maul with both hands. He wasn't trying to kill, but the blow ruptured a hobo's liver. The man would live for a while and then die in exquisite pain. Three Klansmen walked slowly following the flames. They had set torches to the brush upwind of the hobo jungle. The advancing flames and a few blasts of rock salt drove the tramps into the path of the other Klansmen. Only two hobos, drunk on Sterno, burned to death.

Willy Lorton held a baseball bat. He was not trying to kill either, but the hobo stumbled and the bat connected not with his shoulder but with his skull. The bat struck the hobo's temple. Blood and brains squirted from his ear. He dropped. *Just like a cow that's been pole-axed*, Willy thought. He shrugged. *The Dragon said they was animals.*

Billy-Bob Furman saw the glint of gold at a hobo's throat. He rammed his maul into the man's stomach. The hobo folded, and Billy-Bob laid a blow on the back of his head. Billy-Bob bent down. His thick fingers fumbled with the clasp. The task was not made easier by the flickering light of the approaching flames or the moving shadows of the Klansmen. Billy-Bob looked around. No one had seen him. He stuffed the chain and locket into his pocket.

§ § § § §

Sheriff Smith drummed his fingers on the desk. His damn deputy from Ty Ty was bringing a man and woman who said their little girl had gone missing. The sheriff turned his head and spat. A slick, brown glob dropped into the spittoon. *If that damn boy weren't my sister's stepson, I'd fire his ass.*

"Judy! Put on another pot of coffee and then get me a scrambled egg sammich from the diner." Judy hurried to obey. Judy's late husband had been one of the sheriff's nephews. With her husband dead, she was no longer kin to the sheriff. She knew that she would keep her job only as long as she pleased him—or until he found a closer relative to hire.

"Sheriff? Deputy Donaldson is here." Judy's voice was low. She knew the sheriff was angry. The sheriff often took out his anger on her.

The sheriff put the second half of his sandwich on the desk. "Hell and damnation, Judy, tell him to get his ass in here. And bring me another cup." Judy took the coffee cup and hurried to the door.

"Hello, Uncle Bob." The deputy walked in.

"I ain't your uncle when you're on duty! Close the door. Sit. What in tarnation's goin' on?"

"Sorry, Sheriff. Uh, I got these people, Mr. and Mrs. Higden. They got a little girl. Twelve year old. They ain't seen her since Sunday afternoon."

The door opened. Judy put the sheriff's coffee cup on the desk and scurried away. The deputy looked at the coffee cup and cleared his throat. The sheriff ignored him.

"Dammit, boy, today's Tuesday. Why ain't they said nothin' till now?"

"Said they thought she was spending time with cousins. Didn't find out 'till today she wasn't. Took me most of the mornin' to check all the cousins. Nobody's seen her, so I called you."

"You're not entirely stupid," the sheriff said. "Bring 'em in."

A few minutes later, the Higdens were sitting in front of the sheriff's desk. Mr. Higden wore bib overalls. Under them was a white shirt, buttoned to the collar and soaked in sweat. Mrs. Higden wore a faded calico dress. Her eyes were red, and her hands moved constantly, twisting a white handkerchief as if looking for a dry corner.

"Mr. and Mrs. Higden, I want you to know how sorry I am and to assure you that the full resources of the Sheriff's Office will be put to work on finding your dear, precious child. Now, when did you last see her, and what was she wearing?"

92

He looked at the deputy. "Write this down."

As soon as Deputy Donaldson left with Mr. and Mrs. Higden, the sheriff picked up the telephone. He made two calls. The first was to the editor of the Tifton *Times*; the second was to his chief deputy. When the Sheriff reached the square in Ty Ty at dawn, he would be met by ten uniformed deputies, a newspaper reporter, and a photographer.

§ § § § §

Myrtle Carson had been a member of the Gospel Truth Church since she found Jesus at the age of seven. At seventy-seven, she had lost her hearing, but not her faith. She went to preaching every Sunday and to prayer meeting every Wednesday, even though she couldn't hear a word that Deacon Clement said. She didn't hear Deacon Clement announce that he would be away for a week. When she arrived for Wednesday night prayer meeting, she was puzzled to find no one else there. *Must be early,* she thought, and pushed open the door of the church.

The smell that greeted her would have felled a lesser person, but Myrtle had gutted deer, hogs, and chickens all her life. She frowned, and then walked far enough to see what was causing the stench.

Oh! It's a little girl.

§ § § § §

It didn't take long for news of the murdered little girl to spread through western Tift County. Esther Watkins trudged to the sheriff's station in Ty Ty. She had heard that the little girl had been wearing a gold locket that had gone missing. She remembered the hobo who offered to trade a locket for food. She shivered despite the heat. There had been a murderer drinking at her well.

Sheriff Smith had two choices. He could solve the case quickly and get a burst of publicity, or he could let it drag on for a while, milking it when nothing else was newsworthy. With an election coming up in another month, the decision was easy. Deputies delivered flyers describing the hobo and the locket to sheriffs' stations, newspapers, pawnshops, and churches for three counties around.

Billy-Bob had heard about the little girl's death. He couldn't read the papers, though, so he didn't know the details. He couldn't even read the initials on the locket he took from the hobo. He was smart enough to take the locket to Sylvester, but the pawnshop owner there had read the flyer from the Tift County sheriff. When the District Attorney threatened to charge Billy-Bob with rape and murder, he was eager to tell where he'd gotten the locket.

Judge Leffler and Ebenezer Springer had made many enemies. Two of them sat in the waiting room of the District Attorney in Tifton. Neither knew it, but they had both come on the same errand: to tell that they had seen Ebenezer and the judge, together and in Klan robes, on the night of the raid.

§ § § § §

It was easy to get a change in venue when every judge in the county knew the defendants. A jury in Albany convicted Ebenezer Springer and Judge Leffler of seven counts of inciting to murder. Eb's sorghum mill disappeared from his farm the day after he was sentenced to life in prison. No one reported it missing. Imprisoned in the state penitentiary in

94

Valdosta, the judge no longer drank either 'shine or bourbon and died when a colored man drove a six-inch shank into the judge's ear.

Haunted House

Everybody knew that the Furr House was haunted. It had sat empty at the end of an overgrown track ever since the whole family died of the influenza in 1918.

§ § § § §

I was eleven the first time I went to the Furr House. It had to be a Saturday because it was a market day. Daddy had gone to the barbershop and hardware store like he usually did. Calvin was playing Cowboys and Indians with some of his friends—running around the shoofly yelling *kerpow, kerpow* and pointing their fingers at one another, then falling down dead. Mama was watching Joey and talking to one of her women friends, and I was about to fall asleep when Daniel Sikes and Junior Lind came up. They said *Howdy* and flopped down on the brown grass beside me. I said *Howdy* back and was trying to doze off when one of them—I recall it was Daniel—said something about the Furr House. I opened my eyes and said, "Huh?"

"It's haunted," Junior said.

"No such thing as ghosts," I said, forgetting that I'd once teased Junior about a ghost in the old slave cemetery behind the Berea Baptist Church.

"Yeah," I said. "The Holy Ghost. It don't count."

"If they's a Holy Ghost, then they can be unholy ones," Junior said.

"Don't matter," I said. "Ain't no ghosts, and the Furr place ain't haunted."

Daddy had explained that the Will-of-the-Wisp that some people thought was a ghost was just swamp gas. Deacon Clement had preached that since ghosts weren't in the Bible, they weren't real. Granny Meeks sometimes would tell ghost stories, but she always told them like they were made up.

"I know how to find out," Daniel said. "We'll go look."

I couldn't come up with an excuse, so I got up. "Mama! We're going to play for a bit, all right?" Mama waved her hand and went back to talking with her friend.

It would have been a half-hour walk to the Furr House, but before we'd left the square Daniel smacked my shoulder and hollered, "You're it!" and took off running. I ran after him and Junior came behind me. I caught up with Daniel and smacked him. He turned and smacked Junior and the three of us were running down the path hitting one another and yelling *You're it!* and laughing and scaring the squirrels and blue jays until Daniel stopped real fast and we were there.

It might not have been so scary in the spring when the trees were green and the bougainvillea was blooming, but this was October and it had been a dry summer. The trees were bare, except for the pines, and they were more gray than green. The bougainvillea was a crispy brown, and even the kudzu that covered one of the chimneys and part of the porch was so dark green it was almost black. The paint had worn off the clapboard, and the wood underneath was dingy gray.

"They was all dead," Daniel whispered. "They was all dead of the influenza, except the baby. They say the baby starved to death in its crib, and the rats ate—"

"Don't you say it!" Junior said. "I told you, I don't want to hear that part again!" Now I remembered teasing Junior about the ghost in the slave cemetery.

"Don't matter," I said. "They ain't here, now. If they was good, they's gone to Heaven. If they was bad, they's gone to Hell." This was before Joey died, and I believed stuff like that.

"They say the mama's still here, tryin' to protect her baby from the rats," Daniel asserted. "The baby's here, too, but it ain't got a face—just a skull."

Right then, a cloud crossed the sun and it got dark.

"Ain't no ghosts," I said, although I wasn't quite as sure as I had been when we were back in the square with Mama and the sun was shining.

"If you're so sure, David Sasq," Daniel said, "I dare you to go in there."

I had said that there were no such things as ghosts, but I wasn't sure I believed it. I'd gotten myself into a fix but didn't realize it until Junior said, "I double dare you."

"Yeah," Daniel said. "An' you gotta bring something back. Something to prove you been in there."

I figured, then, that I'd been set up.

The steps were so rotten my foot almost went through one of the boards. The porch looked solid, but I set my feet down real gently. The door was half open. I pushed it, but it was stuck.

98

"Go on!" Daniel hollered. I heard Junior giggle. I'd been set up, all right.

The parlor stretched to the left, and what must have been the dining room was to the right. Rain had gotten in, and the table and chairs that remained were rotten and falling apart. In front of me, stairs led to the second floor. A window on the landing let in a little light. I wasn't going up the stairs, though.

Something caught my eye, then my imagination. I reached out and pulled it loose. I grinned.

I crept back to the front door and peeped through until I saw where Daniel and Junior were standing, elbowing one another and grinning. I leaned back against the wall, and waited.

"David?" It was Junior.

"Come on," Daniel hollered. "We ain't got all day!"

I grinned, stepped toward the door and yelled, "It's the baby! It's alive!" And then, I threw the thing I'd grabbed, the newel post cap, a white ball about the size of a softball—or a baby's head—straight at Junior's feet.

I wish I had been close enough to see their eyes, but all I saw was their backsides disappearing down the lane.

Klan Revival

It was an open secret who was in the Klan. Boys overheard their daddies talking about it and shared it with each other in schoolyard whispers. I was a listener, and never a talker, and no one ever said that my daddy was in the Klan. No one ever remarked that he wasn't, either. It was a while before I learned enough about him to understand why he wasn't.

§ § § § §

"It was the Klu Klux Klan!" Avery drew out the last word, giving it an extra syllable. He was so excited, he squeaked. He was thirteen, and his voice was changing.

"Aw, you don' know what you're talkin' about," C.W. said. "Ain't been any Klan hereabouts since the Grand Dragon went to jail—for murder." He whispered the last two words. A couple of the other boys nodded their heads with the absolute certainty of fifth-grade wisdom. A couple sneaked a look at Avery. What nobody said was that Avery's uncle, Ebenezer Springer, was in jail on the same charge as the judge. Avery and his brother, Lonnie, had been living with Ebenezer, but had to move into a sharecropper's shack with their father. Something else nobody said was that Avery's father was a no-good drunk.

100

"It was the Klan," Avery asserted. "Lonnie told me it was the Klan what lynched them two colored men!"

"Shoot, boy, what does Lonnie know about the Klan?"

I shivered, but it wasn't from the November cold. I had seen them that morning. I had seen the two men hanging from an oak tree beside the Ty Ty-Sledge Road.

Mama had given me two loaves of bread to take to the Widow Springer's produce stand. Mrs. Springer was having a rough go of things. Ebenezer Springer had killed her husband—his own brother, Everett—last year, but he didn't go to jail for that. Mrs. Springer was trying to make a living bartering chickens, pigs, produce, and whatever else she could.

It was dark when I left home. The sun wouldn't come up until 7:30 or so. A breeze was blowing from the south. I trotted down the road, mostly to keep warm but also so I wouldn't be late to school. I was almost to Mrs. Springer's place when I saw something moving off to my right. There shouldn't have been anything moving. There was nothing but woods.

I probably should have been afraid. It was only three months before that a vagrant had murdered a little girl and left her body in the church. Daddy said he'd seen a coyote as big as a wolf a little ways up the creek from our house. I guess I was more curious than afraid because I slowed, and then walked toward what was moving. And I saw them.

I stood there, stock still with my mouth hanging open. The sun was rising behind me. It got bright enough to see their faces, and the gashes that whips had opened on their chests and backs. I didn't realize how long I'd been standing there until I started shivering. It wasn't just from the cold.

In downtown Ty Ty, at Horton's Barbershop, the conversation was nearly the same as the one in the schoolyard.

Jim Horton stropped the razor. "Looks like the Klan had a big weekend," he said. He exchanged a glance with Danny Barringer who sat in a corner with the Atlanta newspaper. The paper came on the train and was always a day late.

Deputy Donaldson, who sat in the barber's chair with his face covered with warm lather, moved his lips carefully. "Ain't no more Klan, not since Judge Leffler and Eb Springer went to jail."

"There's Klan in Tifton," Jim said, and exchanged another look with Danny. "An' over in Worth County. Some of the boys from around here likely hooked up with them."

"Shoot, man, what you know about the Klan?" Donaldson spat out along with a blob of lather.

The conversation that counted, however, happened that afternoon in the mayor's office behind a locked door. "What do those boys from Tifton mean, comin' over here an' lynchin' two of our Coloreds?" Mayor Hudson asked and slammed his hand on his desk.

"Now, Mr. Mayor, don't get your dander up," Reverend Fletcher said. After Reverend Thorn was disgraced and left town, Reverend Fletcher took his place at the Berea Baptist Church. In no time at all, he'd rebuilt the sacred-secular link that was the real power in Ty Ty.

The mayor ignored the preacher, and snarled at Deputy Donaldson. "What did that uncle of yours say, anyhow?"

"He's investigating, Mayor. But there ain't much to go on."

102

"Damn it, Donaldson," Hudson snorted. "He knows who done it, leastways who had to order it. Them boys didn't jump into the nooses by themselves."

Reverend Fletcher drummed his fingers on the arms of his chair. When Ty Ty lost Judge Leffler, they lost a lot of political clout in Tift County. They also lost the local Klan, the most effective control they had over the Coloreds. It wouldn't be long before the Coloreds figured out there was no Klan in Ty Ty, and that would mean trouble.

"Gentlemen," Reverend Fletcher said. "We need the Klan to control the Coloreds, but we can't be beholden to the Tifton crowd. Without Judge Leffler and Eb Springer, we have little influence over the sheriff."

"We have to keep the white trash under control, too," Hudson added. "Including the rejects from the CCC camp. I wish they'd ship 'em back home when they kick 'em out."

"Mr. Mayor," Reverend Fletcher said. "You've given me an idea. I do believe it's time for a pastoral visit to CCC Camp Oglethorp."

§ § § § §

The Army man who was camp commandant welcomed Reverend Fletcher's visit. "We're supposed to have a chaplain, but one won't be assigned until after Christmas. I don't suppose . . . ?"

Fletcher nodded. "Perhaps an early service? Say eight o'clock on Sunday mornings?"

The commandant nodded. He agreed that Fletcher might wander around and meet the men, and he invited the preacher to join him in the officers' mess for lunch.

Fletcher didn't spend much time with the young Enrollees but talked extensively with the older men, the *local experienced men* who trained the CCC boys in lumbering, carpentry, and other skills.

Occasionally, he would ask one of them, "Do you know Mr. Ayak?" He had received puzzled looks and "No, sir," from three men before getting the answer he wanted.

"No, but I know Mr. Akai," Bubba Woods said. He narrowed his eyes, thought for a minute, and then added, "And I know the Great Titan of Worth County."

It didn't take long to convince the Great Titan to elevate Reverend Fletcher to Grand Dragon for Ty Ty, the position once held by Judge Leffler. It was harder for Fletcher to convince the Mayor that he should take a lower position as Imperial Wizard, but it was easy to recruit the right people to be Fletcher's deputies in the Klan: the Hydras. Fletcher made one visit to Tifton, and must have come to some accommodation with the Klan there. We never had any more trouble that couldn't be blamed on the local men.

It must have been the late 1940s before I learned who Mr. Ayak and Mr. Akai were. Mr. Ayak means "Are You A Klansman." Mr. Akai means "A Klansman Am I."

Civilian Conservation Corps Camp Oglethorp

Mama was never happy that Daddy made moonshine, but she put up with it because that's what bought us shoes and medicine for Joey. She didn't get any happier when Daddy started trading moonshine for beef cows, butchering them in the barn and selling the meat to the Civilian Conservation Corps camp that had set up across the line in Worth County. Most people made do by bartering, but Joey's medicine cost cash money, and the CCC people were about the only folks who had real money to spend.

Daddy hired a couple of men to help with the butchering. They were paid in hides and parts of the cow that Daddy couldn't sell and Mama didn't want. Daddy would hang the meat for a couple of days before loading it onto the truck and delivering it to the camp. If Calvin and I had finished our chores, especially tending the corn in the bottomland, he'd take us along. That's how I met Sam Brown.

Sam had broken his leg when a tree fell on it. While he was in a cast and on crutches, they'd made him the quartermaster's clerk. He inspected the meat, watched it being weighed, and then paid Daddy. Sometimes, we'd have to wait a while until Sam could hobble over to the warehouse, so I usually took a book to read. One day, Sam saw me reading *Robinson Crusoe* and asked me if I knew where the story had come from. I told him I figured it came from Mr. Defoe's imagination. Sam told me that Mr. Defoe had probably been inspired by both a book written almost a thousand years ago by a fellow named Ibn Tufail, and a true story about a Scottish buccaneer who'd been a real castaway on a Pacific island in the 18th century.

The next day, I went to the library. Mrs. Purcell helped me find out about Mr. Tufail and the Scottish fellow (his name was Alexander Selkirk) and the next time we delivered a cow, I told Sam all about what I'd learned. Sam told me he was impressed. That day we began a friendship that would last for nearly 50 years.

In the winter of '36, Sam quit the CCC and took a job with Everett Springer's widow running her produce stand. A couple of years later, they got married. By the time the next war started, Sam and his wife had turned that roadside stand into the Ty Ty Produce Company. Mama used to send me with eggs and honey for Mrs. Brown to sell on consignment, and I hung around, talking books and stuff with Sam. He told me a lot of stories about the camp, including one he asked me to swear not to tell until he and Mrs. Brown were dead. I had to wait a long time before I could tell this.

§ § § § §

There was little to distinguish them from any other bunch of workmen. Most wore hobnailed boots, denim overalls, cotton shirts, and hats that had once seen duty on Sunday mornings, back when these men had the time and inclination to go to church. Now, however, the men had neither time nor energy for church. They worked five days a week from dawn to dusk. They were the LEMs, the Local Experienced Men who supervised the 17-to-25 year-old boys and men who had joined the Civilian Conservation Corps. Together, they cleared land, planted trees, built log cabins, and cut trails and roads in what would someday be a state park. Saturdays were spent standing in line to wash clothes and bathe. Sundays were for sleeping and writing a letter home—or looking for someone to write a letter for them. A few of the men attended what was called an interdenominational chapel—but which was suspiciously Baptist. There was no way to distinguish the LEMs of Barracks 16 from any other bunch of workmen, and there was no way to have predicted what happened.

Saul Bloom had been born in Passaic, New Jersey, but grew up in Manhattan. At eight days of age, he underwent ritual circumcision; at thirteen, Saul was Bar Mitzvah'd. In 1929, when Saul was twenty-two, his father jumped from the tenth floor of his Wall Street office. Saul hopped a freight train going south. He hadn't been on the road long before he changed his name to Sam Brown. He eventually found a job with the Civilian Conservation Corps by convincing a recruiter he was older than he was and knew more about forestry than he did. It didn't take long for him to melt into the ranks of faceless men toiling in the Georgia woods.

Sam had changed his name, but he couldn't change his appearance. Heavy black hair matted his body. Although he shaved as closely as he could in cold water, his face was perpetually black with whiskers. Black eyebrows met over a beakish nose. And, of the twenty men in Barracks 16, only two were circumcised. The other was Caleb Stone.

Sam overheard one of the men ask Caleb, "How come your pecker ain't pointed, like everybody else?"

Caleb's reply had been muffled, but the first man's voice brought it to everyone's attention. "Hey fellows, we got us a Jew boy, here."

Sam was especially glad that the *mohel* who had circumcised him was short-sighted and more cautious than he might otherwise have been. Most of his foreskin was left, and his pecker was nearly as pointed as those of the uncircumcised men.

§ § § §

Sam was strong, and found his place at one end of a five-foot long, two-man, crosscut saw. Bubba Woods was at the other end. It wasn't the easiest job on the crew, and Bubba could have had any job he wanted, but he took a perverse pride in felling trees and showing his strength and endurance. He'd gone through two partners that Sam knew of before settling on him. At first, Sam had appreciated, even enjoyed the distinction of being Bubba's partner. Bubba stood in front of the line at the chow hall. After the first day on the saw, Sam realized that the others were standing aside, waiting for him to take second place. Sam's position as number two man in the barracks was cemented when Bubba gestured for Sam to sit at the table with him.

Sam had been Bubba's partner on the two-man saw for six weeks. They hadn't become friends, but they were something more than two men on opposite ends of a saw. Sam wasn't too surprised when Bubba pulled him aside one afternoon and spoke to him privately.

"One of the fellows got a jug. We're gonna meet behind the tool shed after supper."

Sam nodded. "Thanks." Sam figured Bubba's words were more of a command than an invitation.

There were a dozen men present when Sam and Bubba arrived. "Who's that?" someone challenged.

"It's me, you idjit," Bubba said. "This here's Sam, my partner on the saw."

"Yo, Bubba . . . Hey, Sam," a couple of men muttered.

"Corky here?" Bubba asked.

"Right behind you." Corky had a real name, but nobody knew it, except maybe the paymaster. The last person who had asked had gotten a fist in his stomach.

§ § § §

Bubba had an almost new deck of cards. Six men sat around a table at the end of the barracks playing poker. They played for toothpicks.

"We got a problem." That was Corky's voice.

"What kind of problem?" Bubba asked.

"Them Coloreds they put in the barracks by the creek," Corky said. "And who's eating at the same chow hall as us."

"They had to do that. Didn't you hear? Washington threatened to cut off money to Georgia unless they recruited some Coloreds," Sam said.

Corky fanned his cards. "That don't make it right," he said.

The men sitting around the table nodded and mumbled agreement.

"See your two, and call," Sam said. There were twenty-four toothpicks in the pot. They had always played for toothpicks, but now Bubba was the bank, and the toothpicks represented pennies. The winners would settle up with Bubba—less his handling fee—in private after the game. There weren't many winners. Most of the men who played dropped out after they'd lost their four bits—the fifty-cent minimum Bubba had set. But there were plenty of new players ready to join the game, men eager to lose a little money to Bubba to show that they were worthy of his protection.

Sam looked around the table and spotted the current sucker. Sam's Uncle Hiram had taught him a lot, including poker odds and how to read men's faces. Uncle Hiram had also told Sam, "If you don't know who the sucker at the table is, it's you."

Sam could easily have beaten Bubba—his bluff was always accompanied by a wiggle of his jaw. If Bubba believed he held a winning hand, he'd squint at it through his right eye. But Sam knew better. He always let Bubba win, but Sam usually managed to win more than he lost, and was able to send home an extra few dollars every week.

"What 'cha think needs doing?" Bubba asked. He picked up a toothpick from his pile and stuck it in his mouth. It was an ostentatious gesture that said *this penny doesn't mean anything to me.*

"Then, I'll say it," Corky said. His voice held no fear of Bubba, nor was there any respect in it. "Somebody needs to put the fear of God Almighty into them uppity Coloreds. Some right-minded people need to get off their butts and do something." He crossed his arms, leaned back in his chair, and stared at Bubba.

Bubba reached for his cards but drew his hand back. He crossed his arms across his chest and looked at Corky. "I do believe you're right, Brother Corky. I do believe you're right."

Two other men at the table exchanged glances. The sucker picked up his cards and sorted them, and the game resumed. *Something just happened,* Sam thought. *Something passed between Bubba and Corky, and those other two know what. What was it?*

§ § § § §

"Them Coloreds stick together, and there's only a dozen of us," Bubba said. "We need some more men." He and Corky were standing behind the barracks with a couple of other men.

"How about your partner, that Brown guy?" someone asked. "He's big—"

"I don't know 'bout him," Corky said. "He's too smart."

"Hail, Corky, if you didn't like anybody who was smarter than you, you wouldn't have any friends a'tall," Bubba said.

Corky glared. There wasn't anyone in the camp except Bubba who could have said that and gotten away with it. "Kiss my butt," he replied.

Bubba grinned. There wasn't anyone in the camp but Corky who could have said that and gotten away with it. Inside, Bubba seethed. *One of these days, I'm gonna have to take him down a peg or two*, he thought.

§ § § § §

That night, Sam dreamed he was suffocating and couldn't move. He woke to find the dream was true. Someone's hand was pressed hard over his mouth. Other hands held his arms and legs immobile.

A hoarse voice whispered, "Take it easy, Bud. We ain't gonna hurt ya." It was a voice Sam didn't recognize and, under the circumstances, wasn't inclined to believe.

"Hit's all right," said a second voice. Sam recognized it as Bubba's.

"We're gonna put a sack over your head. Keep quiet, and go where we take you, ya hear?" This was the first voice. The hand was removed from his mouth.

Sam gasped cold air into his lungs, and nodded. He realized how useless that gesture was in the dark, and whispered, "Yeah, sure."

Somebody pulled a flour sack over Sam's head. The sack smelled of wood smoke and pine resin. He fought not to sneeze. Hands, one on each arm, guided him as he walked barefoot across the icy floor of the barracks.

"Steps," said a new voice, and Sam cautiously descended the steps onto the ground outside the barracks.

Glad I wore pants and shirt to bed, or I'd really be cold, he thought. Realizing how stupid the thought was, he almost laughed, but sneezed, instead. He winced as he stepped with bare feet on pebbles and twigs that littered the ground between barracks.

His guides pulled him to a halt. "Reach out in front a' you." Sam obeyed and felt a wooden platform.

"Turn around and set." The platform tilted with Sam's weight, and then righted itself. Sam realized that he was seated on the back edge of one of the hand carts used to shuttle supplies within the camp.

"Stay here. Don't touch the hood. Somebody'll be watchin' ya. Here, put on your boots." Sam was sure, now that it was Bubba's voice. He grabbed the boots that were thrust into his lap.

After some time, Sam heard shuffling steps. A new voice ordered someone to sit beside him. The cart jiggled, and someone jostled Sam.

"Sorry," the person beside Sam mumbled.

112

"It's all right," Sam replied. The instructions to wait and not touch the hood were repeated, and footsteps faded away. Sam began to count, "One Yankee Doodle, two Yankee Doodle, three . . ." He lost count at 500 seconds, and gave up. He listened carefully but heard nothing but the wind passing through the tops of the pines. Twice more, people were brought to the cart.

"You two, on the yoke." That was Bubba's voice, again.

The cart moved. Sam figured from the men's chatter and the cry of loons that they were on one of the fire roads that led from the camp toward the lake. The cart stopped. Hands urged him to step down, then led him away. A bonfire made bright orange dots in the mesh of the flour sack hood. Shadows of men passing between him and the fire blocked the dots. Sam yearned for the light's return and breathed more easily when it did.

The hands pulled him to a stop. He was close enough to the fire to feel its warmth.

"Everybody, get where you belong." It was a bass voice. Its timbre and tone spoke of power and control. Sam nicknamed him *Boss*. There was some shuffling.

"Are we righteously assembled?" Boss asked.

"We are righteously assembled," replied a chorus of male voices.

"Are any among us strangers?" Boss asked.

"There are eight strangers among us," replied a higher pitched voice. Sam nicknamed him, *Deputy.*

"Who will vouch for these strangers?" Boss asked.

"I vouch for Sam Brown."

Sam recognized Corky's voice and wondered if Corky would have said that if he'd known Sam was a Jew named Saul Bloom.

"I vouch for Ed Entwhistle." That was Bubba's voice. The affirmation was given six more times in voices and for other names Sam didn't recognize.

Boss spoke, "Do you eight strangers swear never to reveal what you may see, hear, or learn this night? Do you swear this before Almighty God and on pain of your life? Sam Brown, do you swear?"

"I swear," Sam said, realizing he had no choice. Uncle Hiram said that an oath taken under compulsion is not binding and I am under compulsion as sure as my name isn't Sam Brown.

After the other men swore the oath, a ritual began. It was a perversion of the rabbi's instructions that preceded Sam's Bar Mitzvah.

"Who made the white man?" Boss asked.

"God Almighty made the white man," the male chorus replied.

"Who made the colored man?"

"God Almighty made the colored man when he cursed Ham, the son of Noah, and all his children, forever."

Sam's astonishment of this version of the story in the Torah almost caused him to miss the next question.

"Why did God Almighty make the colored man?"

"To work by the sweat of his brow in service and servitude to the white man."

"What charge did God Almighty give to the white man?"

114

"To have dominion over the beasts of the field and the colored man."

Sam's head began to spin as the ritual continued. He learned that Jews were no better than Coloreds, since they had killed Jesus Christ; that Jesus Christ was a white man; and that only the white race was pure and deserving of heaven. *This is absolute insanity*, he thought. He'd spent four years in a very progressive yeshiva, studying history, philosophy, logic, and literature. He knew something of the New Testament and of the Christian religion, but this was unlike anything he'd ever heard.

It was at this point that Sam had an epiphany: *This is an initiation, and they want me to join them in this insanity. Kaken!* He scarcely heard another word until his name was called.

"Sam Brown, do you swear that you are a pure member of the white race? Do you swear to Almighty God to keep the secrets of the Knights of the White Magnolia? Do you swear these things on pain of death?"

If I say no, they'll kill me. Sam had never been more sure of anything in his life. "I swear," he said.

The hoods of the eight newest members of the Ku Klux Klan were removed. They were given the honor of taking the first sips from a jug of 'shine. Man after man offered a handshake and his name.

Sam thanked Corky for vouching for him. "I don't mind tellin' you," Sam said, "Until I heard your voice, I was more than a mite scared."

"Yeah? You tell Bubba," Corky said. "We can't vouch somebody we sponsor, so Bubba and I traded." He turned and walked away.

Bubba handed Sam a jug. Sam raised it to his lips and tipped it until it was nearly vertical, but his tongue blocked the opening. Only a few drops of 'shine passed his lips, and they burned. He lowered the jug, mimed swallowing, and passed it on to the next man. He suspected that getting drunk was part of the initiation. As the night passed, the jugs seemed to reach his hands often. He played along. *I think I'll be a sleepy drunk*, he thought. *Better they think I can't hold my liquor than . . . .*

The thought died when he nodded his head, closed his eyes, and fell asleep.

Rough hands shaking his shoulders woke him. The fire had burned to embers. His back hurt where the stub of a branch had pressed into it. There was a glow in the eastern sky.

"Come on," Bubba said. "They'll be callin' for breakfast, soon, and you new guys gotta pull the cart back to camp."

§ § § § §

The routine of the day that followed failed to diminish the memories of the initiation. As he and Bubba watched a tree fall, Sam thought about the oath he'd taken and what it might lead to. They were cutting skinny trees, now—mostly pine, to be turned into log cabins. Bubba took out a whetstone and began sharpening the saw. Sam was puzzled for an instant: they'd sharpened the saw before starting, and it didn't need sharpening yet. Then he realized that Bubba wanted to talk. Sam stepped toward Bubba.

"What's up?" he asked.

"You're working mighty good for a fella who passed out drunk last night," Bubba said. His eyes were focused tightly on the saw.

116

"I ain't never seen you drunk," Sam said. His voice was level, matter-of-fact, and showed no sign of his nervousness. "And getting drunk didn't seem like a real good idea at the time."

Bubba hit the saw one more lick and pocketed the whetstone. He slapped Sam on the back. "I told Corky you was smart. Come on, trees won't cut themselves."

Influenza

Daddy brought Calvin and me into town. He dropped us off at Aunt Helen's and said he was going to the barbershop, even though it wasn't Saturday, and even though he didn't need a haircut. Calvin and I didn't mind. We knew Aunt Helen would tell us about Reverend Fletcher's sermon this past Sunday, but she didn't get too preachy and she always had cookies.

When she opened the door, I could tell she'd been crying. Her eyes were red, her voice was funny—like her nose was stopped up—and she kept dabbing at her eyes with a lace handkerchief. Calvin, who didn't notice, went straight to the kitchen.

Aunt Helen and I followed a little more slowly.

"Aunt Helen?" I said. "Something's wrong, isn't it."

I caught a little smile, then.

"You do pay attention to things, don't you?" she asked. I wasn't sure she wanted me to answer, so I didn't.

"After I feed Calvin," she said as we entered the kitchen.

After cookies, Aunt Helen asked if Calvin would like to play with the dog or sit in the kitchen with her and me. Calvin was out the back door before she finished asking.

118

"Little Clara Davis died last night. It was the influenza," she said. "This morning, Mr. Davis walked all the way here to tell me. In spite of his own sorrow, he walked all the way here from Colored Town to tell me."

She started crying. I sat at the table, miserable and wondering who Clara Davis was. It took Aunt Helen a few minutes to get over her crying. "It was just yesterday," she said. "I was walking to the post office when I saw Henry Davis."

§ § § § §

"Mornin', Mrs. Hunter." Henry Davis tipped his hat and shuffled onto the grass beyond the edge of the narrow sidewalk.

"Good morning, Henry," she said, and then stopped. "How is little Clara?"

"Not so good, ma'am," Henry said. "Thank you for askin'. She was mighty feverish last night. The ladies from the church? They's there prayin' all the time."

Helen pursed her lips. She didn't tell Henry what she was thinking—that if you believe God can heal the child, then you have to believe that God inflicted her. *It's been nearly twenty years since the Great Epidemic—the influenza that preyed on the young, and the soldiers in the Great War whose lungs had never recovered from the Hun's gas. Twenty years, that's one generation. Now, it's come back for little Clara.*

Instead, she smiled and said, "They must be a comfort to you and Christine."

"Tell the truth, ma'am, some of 'em are a mite too comfortin'. Miz Maybelle like to comfort my wife right into cryin'. Told her that Mr. Sam's temperature shot up like that just before he had a conniption fit an' died."

119

"Oh, I'm sure she wasn't being spiteful," Helen said. *Maybelle. She does for Mrs. Davidson. Chatters all the time. Opens her mouth a mite too often, and never thinks about what she's going to say.* "I'll send biscuits and a casserole around this afternoon. Please tell Christine she won't have to cook." I'll tell Hiram at the ice plant to deliver some ice, too.

The ice may have helped, but not enough, and the casserole was the first of many brought to feed the family and guests after little Clara's funeral.

§ § § § §

"Thank you, David, for listening," Aunt Helen said. "It helps to be able to tell someone."

"Why did God let the little girl die?" I asked.

"David, you know I don't know how to answer that." She looked out the window to where Calvin was playing with the dog, took a deep breath, looked at me, and then said, "The Bible's full of stories about God bringing plague and pestilence. Sometimes, it seems to me that if God is all-powerful, He is not being very good, and if He is good, then it seems to me He is not very powerful. One of the Greek philosophers first said that. I learned it long ago."

"Like Joey, you mean," I said. "Like Joey."

Aunt Helen didn't say anything for long enough for me to add, "Granny Meeks calls Joey a *blessing*; Grampa Yount said Joey was a *mission* and was sent to test us, I figured like the two angels that visited Lot before God destroyed Sodom and Gomorrah. Deacon Clement says we're saved by faith, and not works, and Joey is God's way of testing our faith."

"What do you think Joey is, David?"

120

Now it was my turn to be quiet and think. Then, "He's a trial, Aunt Helen. We're on trial before God to see if we can take care of Joey and love him. But it's not right! It's not right that we should have to do that! Why does God want to test our faith? Is it because we've done something bad?"

"No, David, I don't believe that. You're asking an old question: *why do bad things happen to good people.* I don't know the answer to that, either."

"That ain't . . . isn't the whole question," I said. "The rest of it's *why do good things happen to bad people?*"

"How do you mean, David?"

"Well, until he got sent to jail, Ebenezer Springer was a bad man, but he was rich. He killed his brother, and I know he beat Avery. He cheated his tenants and 'croppers. An' he got away with it for a long time."

"Maybe that's your answer, David. He got away with it for a long time, but he finally got caught."

"But that wasn't God," I said.

"I know what you mean, David. It was men, and the law of men, that finally caught up with him. But maybe it was God working through those men."

"Then God let him get away with it for a long time, and let him hurt people for a long time? Is that right? Is that the way it's supposed to be? And what about Avery? He's crippled, and I know it hurts him. And he gets beat by his daddy, now. Where's God in all that?"

"Quiet down, David," Aunt Helen said. I realized I'd been talking disrespectful to her, and I apologized.

"It's all right, David. Your questions are good ones. I guess I'm just not the right person to ask."

When Calvin came in looking for more cookies, Aunt Helen didn't have to tell him to wash his hands. That was an easy lesson that he'd learned long ago.

Women's Christian Temperance Union

"THE BATTLE IS NOT YOVRS BVT GOD'S."

Those were the words on a marble slab at the foot of a statue on the Ty Ty Town Square. The statue was an angel who modestly pressed her left arm against her breast. Her right arm held a pitcher as if offering it to a passerby. She was five feet tall and stood on a cast iron pillar that was another five feet.

§ § § § §

"Silver threads among the gold . . . ." Familiar words in four-part harmony drifted from the bandstand in the middle of the village green. Village green might be too fine a name for the grassy lawn of the square, but it was in the center of town and was the biggest open space in Ty Ty. People filled the square and the surrounding streets to celebrate the Fourth of July. Mama sniffed and wrinkled her nose at the smell of smoke. One of the men running for City Council had passed out a couple of boxes of cigars, and men who would never otherwise have smoked were standing around, thumbs hooked in belts or the suspenders of their bib overalls, puffin' and grinnin' at one another. Mama picked up one of the fans the funeral home had passed out and waved it briskly.

§ § § § §

Folks in Ty Ty were both serious and a little narrow-minded about religion. Mostly, that meant they didn't associate much with people except those who attended the same church as they did. Oh, they were polite enough to one another, but they didn't mix easily. Even at a Fourth of July picnic.

By tradition, the Berea Baptists staked out the corner closest to their church. The Methodists circled the bandstand. The Presbyterians set their blankets by the Confederate Memorial: a twenty-foot high granite soldier looking always to the north lest the Yankees try to sneak into town. The Episcopalians and Lutherans stared at one another from opposite sides of the shoofly. That left the northwest corner near the Women's Christian Temperance Union statue for us folks from the Gospel Truth Baptist Church. We were always separated by a wide space of grass from the others, who warned their children not to play with us—as if poverty was a catchin' disease. Being children, we didn't always obey. Besides, we knew each other 'cause we had been in school together since first grade.

Like the children, the men had fewer barriers to socializing. In the barbershop and the hardware store it didn't seem to matter much what church you went to. But it took a powerful force to bring the women together. Once upon a time, that force was the Women's Christian Temperance Union. On the Fourth of July, 1936, I learned how Ty Ty came to have a WCTU chapter.

§ § § § §

Mama had made Daddy bring one of the kitchen chairs to the picnic and invited Granny Meeks to eat with us. Mama and Daddy sat on a blanket with Joey between them. Calvin and I squatted in the grass. Calvin had a drumstick in one hand and an ear of corn in the other and couldn't seem to figure out which one to bite into first.

I looked up when the bell of the Berea Baptist Church struck twelve and then looked around the square. Most folks had sat down to eat, and I saw for the first time how separated everybody was. I looked closer and saw what it meant.

"Daddy? How come everybody's sittin' with the folks from their church?"

Daddy hemmed and hawed, but before he could come up with an answer, Granny laughed, and said, "It's human nature, Davy-boy. People are more comfortable associatin' with people who believe the same thing they do, who act the same way they do, and who dress the same way they do. The women folk, especially. They go to church together, to prayer meetin' together, to circle together. It takes a powerful force to get the women to cross the line between churches."

"How come we get the statue of the angel?" Calvin asked pointing with a drumstick. "And how come they don't spell right?" He was seven-going-on-eight, and wrapped up in his food in more ways than one—he had butter and chicken grease all over his face. However, he'd paid enough attention to understand what we were talking about.

Granny Meeks settled a little bit in the chair and told us the story of how Ty Ty got a WCTU statue.

"Mary and Adeline was twins. They'd been brought up in the Berea Baptist Church, but when they was eighteen, Mary married a Methodist. The family was scandalized. They was scandalized again two months later when Adeline married a Presbyterian. The family pretty much cast out the two women, an' they never quite got accepted by their husband's families, not even after they had children.

125

"I birthed all seven of their babies. Weren't nothin' . . . ." She seemed to remember where she was, and that Joey was lying on the blanket by Mama and didn't finish that sentence.

"Mary and Adeline went to church with their husbands. It was expected. They weren't turned out of the Baptist communion, but all the womenfolk pretty much shunned them. Mary and Adeline became a lot closer than just bein' twin sisters. They got to talkin' and realized besides marryin' men from different churches, they had married men who drank. They kept their eyes and ears open and listened to gossip and found some other women who were tired of puttin' up with husbands who drank and spent too much money on stump juice."

"What's stump juice?" Calvin asked from around a ham biscuit.

"Don't talk with your mouth full," Mama said, and looked kind of hard at Daddy.

"Stump juice is same thing as moonshine. You know about that, don't you? Some call it that 'cause they used to hide it in a hollow stump."

Calvin nodded and took another ham biscuit.

Granny Meeks took the biscuit Mama offered her and then kept talking. "Wayward husbands turned out to be a stronger bond between the women than any church doctrine, and their circle grew until it had women from most all the churches. They invited Miz Carson, even though she attended our church, 'cause her husband was the most notorious drunk in town. They asked me to join, too, even though I'd already been widowed."

Granny chewed a bit on her biscuit then tightened her lips for a minute. I figured it was something she had remembered that she didn't want to remember. Then I

126

understood: it was Miz Carson who'd discovered the body of the little girl in our church.

Granny started talking again. "I wasn't happy with some of what was going on. We heard about women who took axes to saloons and roadhouses. I never thought it would come to that, but some of the women got a little too excited and talked their husbands into puttin' on their Klan robes and going out on the Sylvester Road and burn down the roadhouse.

"Gettin' a bunch of drinkin' men to burn down the only saloon for miles from Ty Ty must have taken some powerful talkin'," she said. "I 'spect they used some pretty strong arguments."

"You mean like in *Lysistrada?*" I asked. Mrs. Purcell wouldn't let me check out the book, saying I wasn't old enough. Aunt Helen had gotten it for me but asked me not to let on that she had.

As soon as I said that, I knew I'd made a mistake. Mama knew exactly what I meant. I felt her frown even before I turned to look and knew I'd hear from her when we got home.

Granny Meeks must have figured something was going on between Mama and me and decided she shouldn't get into it. "It didn't matter much. Another roadhouse opened closer to Sylvester. All it meant was that people had farther to go when they drove home drunk."

"You mean, like Cletus Grant and Clora Mae?" I said. Again, I should have kept my mouth shut. This was another thing Mama didn't like me knowing about, but everybody knew that story. It happened Christmas Eve of 1933, only three weeks after prohibition had been repealed. And it happened right in front of the Gospel Truth Church. The oak tree still had a scar.

"That, Davey-boy, is something you shouldn't talk about. Some secrets are best kept," Granny said.

Mama figured this would be a good time to serve dessert and asked Granny Meeks to help her cut up the pie. While they were doing that, I thought back on what all I'd heard about the accident. Most of it I learned from other boys in the schoolyard.

§ § § § §

Edna watched the kitchen clock inch toward midnight on Christmas Eve. The diner was empty and she didn't expect anybody, but she didn't have anyplace else to be. The bell over the front door sounded.

"Hold on, I'm washin' my hands!" Edna called through the slot between the counter and the kitchen. A minute later, she pushed through the swinging door and gasped. "Sammy Holden! What on earth?"

The man who stood in the doorway was covered in red Georgia mud.

"Miz Edna, you gotta call the sheriff—and Doc Winter. Cletus Grant done run off the road. Him an' Clora Mae are hurt, real bad. I tried . . . ." Sammy's voice trailed off. He took a deep breath. "I couldn't get the door open!"

"Where are they?" Edna asked. She turned the crank on the phone four times and then picked up the earpiece.

"They run into the oak tree in front of the church."

Edna nodded and turned back to the phone.

"Matty? Call Doc Winter and try to find Deputy Donaldson. Cletus done run his car into a tree in front of the Gospel Truth Church. Him and Clora Mae—"

128

She stopped talking for a minute. "I know, I know, it's Christmas Eve." She looked at the clock. "No, it's Christmas morning. Just do it, Matty!"

Edna hung up the phone. Pulling a mason jar from under the counter, she poured two fingers of its clear contents into a coffee cup.

"Here." She pushed the cup toward Sammy.

Neither the mason jar nor the smell prepared Sammy. He tossed back the 'shine. He gasped. His face turned red and his ears purple. He caught his breath and exclaimed, "Edna! Where'd you—" He saw Edna's lips compress. "Uh, thanks, Edna."

"You feel up to goin' back an' meetin' the Doc?" Edna asked.

Doc Winter was there when Sammy arrived. Sammy told Doc he'd tried to get into the car, but couldn't.

"They never had a chance," Doc said. "You couldn't have done anything."

It didn't take long for the gossip to spread. Clora Mae was pregnant with Cletus's baby. They'd been at the roadhouse over toward Sylvester. Cletus was drunker than a skunk. They were eloping. It turned out that all the stories were true. Cletus had taken Clora Mae to the roadhouse for drinks and dancing. She'd told him she was pregnant and that the baby was his. Somewhere among too many drinks, Cletus had told Clora Mae he'd marry her and that they'd drive to South Carolina where it was a little easier to get married than in Georgia.

Eventually, the gossip died out, except for the part about Cletus being drunk. Sammy told folks that he'd smelled booze, and Deputy Donaldson's report said there was a broken bottle of whiskey in the wreck.

§ § § § §

"What about the angel?" Calvin asked. His face and hands were smeared with blueberries, and he was looking right hard at the last bites of my piece of pie. Granny told us to go for a walk and that she'd tell us more later. At first, Mama didn't want Calvin going off but I promised to keep hold of his hand.

The barbershop quartet—four men from the choir of the Berea Baptist Church—walked down the steps of the bandstand. The buzz of conversation picked up, and the peddlers who lined the square raised their voices. One in particular seemed to be attracting a lot of attention. His black, enclosed wagon sat across the corner from the hardware store. The mules that had pulled it into town were still in the traces. The wagon might once have been a hearse. The driver looked like an undertaker or a preacher—black suit and flat-brimmed hat, white shirt, black string tie, and a thin, unsmiling face.

Wonder what he's sellin, I thought. Then I saw the sign: patent medicine. He wasn't that Doctor Justin I'd seen at the flea market a couple of years ago. I didn't realize that I'd stopped, and was staring at the dark man and his dark wagon until Calvin jerked my hand.

"Davie, I want some cotton candy!"

I looked where he was pointing. A nickel for less than a penny's worth of spun sugar, my mind said. Then my heart spoke to me. *It's not the sugar, David, it's holdin' that big, fluffy mess in your hands. It's gettin' it all over your face and lickin' sticky lips and fingers long after it's gone. It's not sugar, it's fun.*

"All right," I said. "Come on. We'll both get one. I'll treat." We each had a dollar of our birthday money—the five dollars that Grampa Yount gave us each year.

I looked at the change the man gave me. "Hey, mister, you only gave me eighty cents. Ought to be ninety," I said.

"Go 'way, kid. Don't bother me," the vendor growled. He raised his voice and began his cant. "Fresh spun cotton candy! Biggest treat on the street! Only a nickel."

"And two for a dime means you owe me ten cents!" I said. Calvin jerked on my hand, but I shook him off.

"If the boy says you owe him a dime, you had better be paying it."

I turned to see Deacon Clement standing behind me. The deacon was dressed exactly like the man with the black wagon, and he was sweating profusely.

"Ain't none of your business, mister—" the vendor began.

Deacon Clement's voice seemed to gain strength as he spoke. "This boy's family are members of my congregation," he said. "And that makes it my business. This boy's not a liar or a thief. If he says you owe him a dime, you owe him a dime."

I snatched the dime the candy man spun into the air.

"Come on, David," Deacon Clement said, his voice shaking now. "Let's go find your folks."

§ § § §

131

I gave Calvin back to Mama, who spit on her kerchief and cleaned his face, despite his protests. Daddy stood by a pickup truck decorated with political signs. He was smoking a cigar, and Mama had run him away from where she'd spread our blanket.

The deacon leaned against the WCTU statue. I poured him some water from Mama's jug. His hands shook as he drank it. I wondered about that but was afraid to ask. Back then I was afraid of the deacon. He was the one who said what was right and wrong and who was going to Heaven and who was going to Hell. He was the one who had baptized me just last month on the Sunday after my twelfth birthday. He was younger than my daddy, but Daddy still said *Sir* to him.

I had just gotten up enough nerve to thank him for taking on the cotton-candy man, when the Municipal Band started playing. It was time for the political speeches.

"Sometime, maybe we can talk," the deacon said over the music and then turned to leave. I nodded, and went back to where Mama, Calvin, and Joey were on the blanket.

The politicians stood on the bandstand. They all faced the Berea Baptist Church crowd, so it was hard to hear them from where we sat. When they finished, Calvin pestered Granny about the angel, so she told us the rest of the story.

§ § § §

Mrs. Ruthie Jones Hudson, undisputed first lady of Ty Ty, cleaned her parlor, dining room, kitchen, and the downstairs bathroom like she did for Christmas, when the mayor held a weeklong open house for "the right people," meaning political supporters and members of the Berea Baptist Church. She knew the reason she'd been asked to host this meeting was only partly because she was the mayor's wife. It

132

was mostly because she had the biggest parlor in town, and when she opened the double doors leading to the dining room, she had room for at least fifty people. She frowned at the folding chairs that had come from the church social hall, but Mrs. McCorkle was sure they'd be needed. Then she smiled at her dining room table. Pushed against the back wall, it held two silver punch bowls—although she suspected the one she'd borrowed from Mrs. Baucomb was plate. Between the bowls she had arranged plates covered with cookies.

Mrs. McCorkle hadn't asked for, nor expected, the refreshments. "I am so sorry, Reverend Young," she whispered. "I thought we'd get started right away."

The Reverend James Read Jones knew the politics of religion in small southern towns. He saw the separate clusters the women made. "Oh, Mrs. McCorkle, that's quite all right. Breaking bread—or cookies—in Christian fellowship is a fine thing to do."

Mrs. McCorkle smiled, but it was a tight smile. She was more upset by the cookies than anything else. Everyone knew they were Mrs. Hudson's cookies. She always made the same ones for church suppers and festivals and didn't let anyone in on the recipe. Mrs. McCorkle was mad, too, because she had done all the organizing, and thought that Mrs. Hudson would get all the credit.

"Ladies? Ladies!" Mrs. Hudson's voice was barely loud enough to be heard over the whispers of conversation and gossip. "Will you all take a seat, please?" Movement and conversations subsided, and she continued. "We are all grateful to Mrs. McCorkle for putting all this together. And, she was entirely right about the number of chairs we'd need. Mrs. McCorkle, would you take the floor and introduce your guest?"

A rather flustered Joyce McCorkle stepped to the front of the parlor.

"Ladies, we are honored to have with us Temperance Preacher and former Candidate for Governor of North Carolina, the Reverend James Read Jones."

Mrs. McCorkle had planned to say more, but polite applause from the assembled ladies interrupted her and by the time she gathered her wits, Reverend Jones was standing beside her. She nodded to him, and then sat in the front row.

After listening to Reverend Jones, the ladies agreed to bring their husbands to the square that night, when Reverend Jones would preach from the bandstand.

The Reverend Jones' voice filled the square, and there were those who swore it echoed off the bank building more than a block away. "They call him *Leather-lungs Jones*," Mrs. McCorkle confided to Mrs. Hudson. "I read it in the newspaper."

Jones called for the community to set aside differences and to unite against a common enemy—Demon Rum. He acknowledged a tradition of making moonshine, declaring it a sin to convert corn into alcohol if that corn could be used to feed starving children.

"How does he 'spect us to get it to starvin' children?" George McCorkle asked his neighbor. "Railroad's chargin' more to ship corn than it sells for."

Mrs. McCorkle elbowed him. "Hush!" she hissed.

"I will not hush!" George retorted. "Hey preacher! Where you from you don't know it costs more to ship the corn than it'll bring at market?"

Many of the men in the square nodded. Calls of "yeah," and "that's right" gave the preacher pause, but only for a moment.

"Why, then, feed the corn to your swine, and ship *them* to market," Jones said.

"What pigs? The government done made us kill half of 'em!" someone yelled.

There were more shouts. Men tugged at their wives' arms and some turned to leave. Reverend Young pulled them back by the force of his voice and his personality. Something he said must have worked. A few of the men "took the pledge," and became teetotalers. A bunch of others took the pledge, too, but didn't stop either drinking or making 'shine. The women continued to meet for a few years, but after a while the WCTU just sort of disappeared.

§ § § § §

"An' the angel?" Calvin asked. "What about the angel?"

"It wasn't long after the preachin' that Mayor and Mrs. Hudson's little boy died from the polio. Only a day later, Mrs. Carson's husband died. He'd been shot up in the Great War and had never been well.

"The two grievin' women ran into one another at the funeral home. They decided to do somethin' together. It took liquor and then tragedy to break down the difference in religion and social status. If'n you look on the back of the statue, there's some little letters that nobody ever reads."

In Memory of
John Carson
and
Andy Hvdson, Jr.

Granny never said why we poor folks from the Gospel Truth Church got to sit by the statue. I figured it was just tradition. I asked Mrs. Purcell about the spelling, and she helped me find a book that said it was because in the old English alphabet, "U" and "V" were the same letter, and it was just tradition. I thought about the tradition of folks sitting only with other folks from their church and decided that tradition was just an excuse for doing stupid things.

Boarding House Fire

Mama was listening to her daddy's Sunday night preaching program. The front of the radio looked like one of the stain-glass windows of Grampa Yount's church, except it was wood. It had three knobs and a lit-up dial that showed station numbers. On a winter night the radio station in Athens came in right good. We couldn't get the station during the summer. I asked Uncle Neal about that 'cause he had been to college and ran the electric co-op. He said it was the way radio waves bounced off the air and to ask him again when I was older.

I wasn't paying much attention to what Grampa Yount was saying, because I was waiting for *Jack Armstrong, the All American Boy*, the program that came on after.

Grampa's voice stopped in the middle of a sentence and the room got dark. I looked up. Mama's reading lamp was out. Daddy came in from the kitchen.

"Fuse blew," he said. "Meant to get some extras at the hardware last Saturday." A match *skritched*, and he lit a candle.

"Little David? Get the kerosene lanterns—"

"Can't you put a penny behind the fuse?" I asked. I just knew I was going to miss *Jack Armstrong*.

"Where'd you learn that?" Daddy asked. He snapped each word out like he was cracking a whip.

"Jimmy Barringer said that's what his daddy did. He said there was sparks and flame shootin' out of the socket when his mama plugged in her iron."

"Jimmy Barringer's daddy is a fool," Daddy said. "Fuses are to protect you. You put a penny behind one, and you're sayin' that your life and your house are only worth a penny. Don't you never do that, you hear?"

"Here's a fuse," Mama said. "There's a whole bunch in my sewing drawer. I'll turn off my lamp so David can hear his program."

It wasn't long after that I remembered what Daddy said about the fuse and the penny.

§ § § § §

On Monday morning, George Wilson lit the first cigarette of the day, spooned sugar and powdered milk into his mug, and poured in coffee. The milk powder floated to the top and made a fluffy island. Even before he felt the side of the pot, George knew what he would find. The coffee was cold. The hot plate had blown another fuse. George sighed and dumped the mug into the sink. The day had hardly begun, and already it was going badly. He'd broken a shoelace. Lacking a spare, he had re-threaded what was left up to the second holes from the top. If he were careful, his pants leg would cover it. George made a mental note to stop by the hardware store for a fuse, shrugged on his overcoat, and stepped from his room at the Overton Railroad Hotel and Boarding House.

Twenty minutes later, George hung his overcoat from a hook on the door of his office at the Ty Ty Insurance Agency. At nine o'clock he lit a cigarette and began typing.

138

November 2, 1936

Mr. Harrison Weil
Rural Route 42
Ty Ty, Georgia

Dear Mr. Weil,

Thank you for your purchase of a life insurance policy from the Ty Ty Insurance Agency. Your policy has been placed with a carrier in New York; however, payments will be made to this Agency. A set of payment coupons is enclosed. Please mail payment to the letterhead address, or drop them in the mail slot in the office door.

Sincerely yours,
Mr. George Wilson, Agent

George rolled the paper out of the typewriter and separated the carbon paper and the second copy. He typed Mr. Weil's address on an envelope bearing the agency's return address and inserted the letter. He looked carefully at the policy before adding it to the envelope. It was an impressive document, with a fancy border and printing. The only thing missing was the address of the insurance carrier. George smiled, stuck on a three-cent stamp, and sealed the envelope. Then he inserted another sandwich of letterhead, carbon paper, and second sheet into the typewriter. By noon he had typed up ten identically worded letters.

The policies had not been placed. Neither the policy document nor the carrier was real. The payments would go into Mr. Wilson's account. If one of the policyholders died? He would deal with that when it happened. If he were still in Ty Ty.

George ate his lunch at Edna's Diner. Monday was egg-salad-sandwich day. George always ordered the special. It was a nickel cheaper. He spent the nickel he saved on a second cup of coffee, even though he knew it would make him jumpy all afternoon. Jumpy was good, though. He'd need the energy if he were to sell life insurance policies.

At 7:00 PM, George returned to the boarding house. Cursing his forgetfulness, he put a penny behind the blown fuse and warmed a can of soup on the hotplate.

Doc Winter testified at the inquest that George died of asphyxiation and didn't feel the flames that gutted the Overton Railroad Hotel and Boarding House. The melted wires of George's hot plate and the slug of copper that had once been a penny were buried in the rubble, and the cause of the fire was listed as *smoking in bed.*

§ § § § §

I was twelve years old when the railroad hotel burned. It happened on a Monday night. Soon as school was let out on Tuesday, all the boys ran to see what was left. It wasn't much. There had been four brick chimneys; two of them were still standing. The sidewalk and cement steps leading up to the porch were there. The rest of the building was nothing but burnt timber, piled up like chicken bones after a church supper.

They said only one person was killed. Still, somebody had died, which made it a little scary. The older boys teased the little ones about the ghost of Mr. Wilson, and said his body was lying somewhere under the charred wood just waiting for one of us to be alone in the dark. Buddy Horton said that wasn't true, and we believed him—partly because his father was a volunteer fireman and had been there, and partly because we didn't want to be afraid.

It didn't take long for folks to figure out that there was no such thing as the Farmers and Merchants Equitable Life Insurance Company of New York. Mrs. McCoy at the bank

140

said there was a bunch of money in Mr. Wilson's account but by the time the lawyers were through with it, there wasn't much left.

Barbershop

Around Ty Ty, about everybody had something to do with moonshine. If you weren't making it, you were selling it. If you weren't involved, at least you knew somebody who was. Most people turned to barter, especially after the social security started taking a penny out of every dollar folks earned. After piglets and chickens, I reckon moonshine was about the best thing to barter. About the only place you couldn't spend it was in the collection plate at church, and I wasn't entirely sure about the Presbyterians.

During prohibition, Daddy could get ten dollars a quart for his 'shine. After prohibition the price went down to about five dollars a quart. Daddy got more than most 'shiners because he never did a second run with sugar, and his 'shine was quality stuff. Even after the price went down, making 'shine was a good way to make money. Besides, it was a tradition.

Some of the 'shiners let people come to their stills, where they would fill jugs for them. Most, though, would carry their 'shine to a barn in a barrel and fill jugs, there. Daddy never let anybody know where his still was and Mama wouldn't let him bring the 'shine to the house or the barn. So, most every Saturday as long as the corn lasted in the fall, Daddy would bring a corrugated box with a dozen or so Mason jars—quarts and pints—filled with 'shine to the barbershop.

§ § § §

Saturday was cold, but it wasn't raining, so Calvin and I rode in the back of the truck. Up front, Mama held Joey. Joey was four-goin'-on-five, but still no bigger than a two-year-old. Mama said she thought he was stronger today. I knew she was fooling herself.

Daddy drove down the Ty Ty-Sledge Road slow enough that Calvin and I could talk.

"How come Daddy's got two boxes of stump juice for the barbershop?" Calvin asked.

"What do you know about stump juice?" I said.

"That's what Granny Meeks calls it. And Uncle Neal, too," Calvin said. "Uncle Neal said it was 'cause that's where he hid it from his mama when he was growin' up—in an old stump."

"Naw, people call it stump juice because that's where they hid it from the revenuers," I said. "An' you ain't supposed to be talking about stump juice and 'shine, anyway."

"I never said about Daddy!" Calvin said. "Honest, I never!"

Soon as we stopped at the barbershop, I jumped down and had one of the boxes under my arm by the time Daddy got out of the truck. He looked at me funny, and then picked up the other box.

"Come on," he said. "Ain't gonna make your mama any madder than she already is."

We went in the back door and Daddy set his box on a shelf. Daddy told me to set down my box and wait while he went in the shop. When he came back, he gave me a silver dollar. "Here. This is for you and Calvin. Don't tell your mama."

§ § § § §

After Uncle Frank's hardware store, Mr. Horton's barbershop was the busiest place in Ty Ty on a Saturday. Men and older boys waited their turn for a haircut. The men sat on cracked leather chairs with chrome armrests and talked crops and boll weevils. The boys stood in a corner or sometimes

outside the door when the weather was good. Most of the little boys got their hair cut by their mamas. I don't think any of them really put a bowl on the kids' hair and followed around with scissors, but the bowl cut was mighty common all the way through about sixth grade, when boys started getting real haircuts. Mama's sister, Aunt Lucille, had been to beauty school in Atlanta and she cut Calvin's and my hair when we were little. She had a beauty shop in her house, and we'd walk over there about once a month on a Monday evening. She didn't charge, but Mama always gave us a jar of honey or a basket of eggs or something for her.

Uncle Neal Goodson

Aunt Lucille was older than Mama. Her husband, Uncle Neal, was a veteran of The Great War. He'd been in the Signal Corps. They didn't have any kids. I asked Mama why once and she said it was because something had happened to him in the war. I asked her what and she said Daddy would tell me— when I was older. When I was older, I forgot about it and never did find out. Uncle Neal and Aunt Lucille both died while I

144

was overseas in World War II. After I got back from the war, Mama gave me a picture of Uncle Neal in his Army uniform. He had been a sergeant and looked mighty dashing. As many times as I'd been to their house, I'd never seen the picture. Mama said they'd found it in Aunt Lucille's Bible.

About the time I was twelve, Daddy started taking me to the barbershop instead of Aunt Lucille's. Calvin whined a little, until I asked Daddy to take him, too, even though Calvin wasn't but eight.

The barbershop smelled like cough syrup, Grammy Yount's bath soap, and men's sweat. The chairs were massive and swiveled all around. Above each chair was a ceiling fan with blades shaped like a ship's sails. On the back wall, next to the door to the storeroom, was a calendar with a half-naked woman on it.

Art Horton was Calvin's age. Most of the time he sat on a stool in the corner, kind of staring at nothing until Mr. Horton snapped his fingers. Then Art would grab a push broom and sweep the hair from around the chairs. I watched him when I couldn't find an old *Field and Stream* magazine to read. He was more like a dog than a boy. Mr. Horton would snap his fingers and nod in a certain way and Art would pick up all the magazines and put them on the rack. A different nod and he would take all the dirty towels into the back and bring out a stack of clean ones.

He was what they called *retarded*. Like my littlest brother, Joey, but not nearly as bad. Calvin told me that Art had been in his first grade class but hadn't come back after the first week of school.

After us boys got our haircuts, we'd usually hang out in the alley behind the barbershop. It meant going past the calendar and sneaking a look at the picture of a half-naked woman then walking through the storeroom. There was usually a game of mumblety-peg going on and marbles for the younger ones. Once C.W. brought a pair of dice and tried to teach us to play craps, but he got run off when Mr. Horton came out to use the necessary. The barbershop had indoor plumbing, but it was on septic. The drain field was mostly clay, so it backed up a lot. The outhouse got plenty of use.

I guess it happened the summer I turned thirteen. We'd gotten our haircuts, and Calvin and I were out back. Calvin was nine and the youngest kid there, and he hung onto me while I watched C.W. arm wrestling Ronnie Babb. Art came out and headed for the outhouse. I didn't pay any attention until Calvin jerked my arm and pointed.

Darrell Fletcher, Jr., the preacher's kid from the Berea Baptist Church, and Tommy, his buddy, had blocked the door to the outhouse and wouldn't let Art in. Art didn't say anything. He never did. He just mewed like a cat. He kept squeezin' his knees together. It was pretty obvious that he had to go right badly. I turned back to watch the arm wrestling, but Calvin pulled my arm, again.

"Davie, you gotta do somethin' !" he said. I must have looked pretty blank because he said, "What if it was Joey?"

Out of the mouth of babes and sucklings, I thought. Calvin's innocence had seen something I hadn't. I turned and walked toward Darrell and Tommy. Calvin tried to follow, but I pushed him back. I didn't know if I was trying to protect him or make sure he could get Daddy if things went wrong.

I got right close to Darrell and told him, "Hey, Darrell. Come on, let the kid in."

"Kiss my grits, David Sasq. Who do you think you are, tellin' me what to do?"

146

"Who do you think you are, Darrell Fletcher, pickin' on a dumb retard? Come on," I said. "Let him in."

"You gonna make me, David Sasq?"

I don't know if it was what Darrell was doing to Art or the way he said my name, like he was spitting out a cat hair that had gotten on his tongue. Anyway, I stuck out both arms and pushed him to one side of the outhouse, then pushed Tommy to the other. Before they got their balance, I opened the door and Art ran in.

"David, look out!" C.W. yelled.

I stepped back in time for Tommy's fist to graze my cheek. If C.W. hadn't warned me, Tommy would have hit me upside my head and I'd probably been knocked out. As it was, I got a real shiner that took more than a week to go away.

I don't know why C.W. got into the fight on my side, but he did. He grabbed Darrell's arm before he could hit me, spun him around, then planted a right cross on Darrell's nose. I heard Calvin behind me, yelling, "Daddy! They's fightin'!"

I managed to lay an uppercut on Tommy before a couple of men from the barber shop grabbed our arms and pulled us apart. I heard somebody retching like they had the stomach flu. It was Darrell. His nose was bleeding worse than a lung-shot deer, and he looked sicker than a dog. I thought C.W. had punched him in the stomach, but it was seeing his own blood that made him sick.

The guy who pulled me away from Tommy let me go, but there was somebody tugging on my belt. It was Calvin, and he was about to cry.

"Davie . . . Davie . . . you all right?" he said.

I knelt down and hugged him. "Sure, I'm all right."

Over Calvin's shoulder, I saw my daddy, standing in the door of the barbershop. C.W. was talking to Daddy, and pointing to Art, who had just come out of the necessary. Daddy smiled. I didn't know whether he was more proud of me for taking up for Art or for the uppercut I laid on Tommy. It was a fine uppercut, if I do say so myself.

Old Man Moss

I dug my bare toes into the freshly turned earth of the
bottomland next to the creek. First thing this morning, Daddy
and Old Man Moss, the colored man who had just bought the
farm across the creek, had hitched their two mules together and
plowed it. Tomorrow they'd do the same for the Moss bottom
on the other side of the creek. For the next two weeks or so,
they'd plow each other's land, turn and turn about. After that,
they'd not speak to one another until next year, when it was
again time to plow.

The bottom was the best land on the farm. It was
especially good this year. Nineteen thirty eight was the first
year in about five that the creek had overflowed onto the
bottom and dropped a load of silt. The soil was dark, nearly
black. We'd get 250 bushels of white corn from the bottom.
The white corn would be malted and then combined with
cracked yellow corn to make 50 gallons of moonshine. We all
would work the fields—corn, peanuts, beans, sorghum, and the
vegetables in the kitchen garden—from dawn to dusk from
now until harvest.

Why does anyone want to be a farmer, I wondered.

§ § § §

Every morning, including Sunday, Calvin and I began the day in the field of white corn. There was always something to do. If nothing else, it had to be weeded and hoed. Across the creek, Old Man Moss's two sons tended their daddy's corn. The four of us looked across the creek at one another but never spoke.

The spring flood that had dropped soil on the bottom had also scoured the creek and created a natural swimming hole where the creek curved back on itself. Sometimes on a hot afternoon, Calvin and I would sneak away from the dusty fields and skinny dip. Sometimes on a hot afternoon, the Moss boys would sneak away from the dusty fields of their farm and skinny dip in the same pool. It wasn't long before we ran into one another.

The two Moss boys had shucked off their bib overalls and were standing on the west bank ready to jump in the water when Calvin and I pushed through the brush on the east shore. Calvin and I looked at the Moss boys for a few seconds, and they looked back. Then the older boy jumped into the water, as if to establish his claim on the pool. The little one—whether following his older brother's lead or because he realized he was naked in front of us—followed.

Calvin looked at me. "What are we gonna do, Davie?"

I shrugged. "We ain't got much time before Daddy sees we ain't in the peanut field. Come on."

"I'm scared, Davie," Calvin whispered. "They's Coloreds, an' you know what people say."

I snorted. "People say a lot more than their prayers. Come on." I shucked off my bib overalls and jumped into the water. Calvin turned his back to the pond and took off his own overalls. He turned and jumped into the water without looking where he was going. He nearly hit the older Moss boy, who had swum to the east side of the pool. Calvin was startled, and swallowed a mouthful of water. He gasped, choked, and

150

coughed. The colored boy lifted Calvin's head from the water and held it until Calvin stopped gasping.

"Y'all all right?" he asked.

"Uh, yeah," Calvin managed.

"Thanks," I said. I'd seen what had happened and swum up. "I'm David. This here's my little brother, Calvin."

"I's Joshua," the older boy said. "This 'un's my little brother, Luke. Y'all is Mr. Sasq's boys, ain't 'cha?"

"Yeah, an' you two are Old Man Moss's boys, huh?"

I watched as Joshua's eyes looked from side to side. The boy's lips tightened and his cheeks twitched.

"I mean, you're Mr. Moss's boys," I said.

Joshua's face stopped twitching, and he smiled. "Yeah, we is."

"Where'd you live, before you came here?" I asked Joshua. We were sitting on a log while our little brothers splashed and played.

"Valdosta," Joshua said. "We was—"

Whatever else he might have said was interrupted by Daddy's voice.

"David Sasq, you put your clothes on right now and get over here! Calvin Sasq, you get out t' water. Get here!" His voice told us we'd better hurry.

Calvin tried to pull up his overalls but his wet legs got all tangled up and he would have fallen if I hadn't grabbed him.

We hurried to where Daddy was standing. My stomach churned. Daddy had cut a thin branch from one of the ti ti trees—that was not a good sign. "Come on!" He grabbed my arm and pulled me away from the creek. "I ain't gonna whip you in front of Coloreds."

When brush screened us from the eyes of the two Moss boys, Daddy stopped.

"Pull them overhauls down, boy," he told Calvin. Calvin already had tears in his eyes.

"Daddy, please don' whip Calvin. It was my fault we went swimming," I said.

I pulled one overall strap off my shoulder and reached for the other one. "Just whip me, please, Daddy?"

Calvin's overalls were a puddle at his feet. Daddy grabbed his arm. "I ain't whippin' you 'cause you went swimming. I knowed you done that every time you done it. You're getting whipped 'cause you was playing with Coloreds. An' that's a lesson you both need to learn."

The switch hit the back of Calvin's legs. The branch had burrs along it. A red stripe and a few drops of blood appeared. If Daddy had looked, he'd have seen blood coming from Calvin's lip where he had bitten it to keep from crying out. If Daddy had looked, he'd have seen tears falling from Calvin's eyes. If Daddy had looked, he'd have seen my hand reach out and grab the whip.

The burrs raked my hand. I grabbed harder and pulled the whip away from Daddy. He turned loose of Calvin's arm. "What in tarnation you doin' boy?" He swung his fist at me. At the last instant he opened his hand so that it was his palm that hit my cheek.

I spit out blood from where a tooth had torn my cheek. I held the whip out to Daddy. "You told me I was my brother's keeper, an' I asked you not to whip Calvin. Please, Daddy?" I turned and slid the second overall strap across my shoulder and down my arm.

152

Daddy stood motionless for a second, then for another. He drew back his arm. The switch left a red streak and a couple of drops of blood on the back of my legs. And then it made a second streak.

"Pull up your overhauls, boy, and look at me. You too, Calvin."

When we had obeyed, he continued. "*Raise not your hand in anger*, the Bible says. But, it also says *spare the rod and spoil the child*. I don't whip you boys 'cause you done wrong. I whip you so's you'll remember what you done wrong and won't do it, again.

"You boys is not to play with the Coloreds, you hear? You can go swimming. But, if they's there, you can go back later or stay on your side of the creek. I'll talk to Mr. Moss and he'll tell 'em the same thing."

The next time we ran into the Moss boys at the creek, they were on their side. Calvin and Luke exchanged brief smiles, but Joshua's eyes were tight with anger. He saw that I was looking at him, and turned away. My stomach curled up and pressed against my backbone. "Come on, Calvin." I took my little brother's hand. "We'll come back, later."

Daddy and I were tying up beans when I got the gumption to ask a question that had gnawed at my belly until I couldn't hold it any longer. "Daddy? Why can't we play with Mr. Moss's boys? You an' him, you plowed together, and I know Mama carried a casserole and medicine to them when Miz Moss was sick."

Daddy handed me the roll of twine and then knotted the string. "Son, what Mr. Moss an' I do is strictly business. Ground's too hard 'cept in the bottom to plow deep enough with one mule." He looked way over my head, like he was

153

thinking. "An' what your mother did? It was plain Christian charity. You don' play with them boys 'cause I told you not to. 'Honor your father an' mother,' you hear? You're not so old you don' have to listen t' me."

"No, Daddy, but I am old enough to want to know why." I tried to keep my voice quiet, but firm.

"I told you why. 'Cause I told you so."

"No, Daddy, I mean why you told me so," I said.

" 'Cause that's the way it is, boy. Whites and Coloreds don't associate 'cept for business." Daddy looked at me, then far away, again.

"You're growing up," he said. "I guess just telling you ain't gonna work for much longer. You listen and you listen good. An' you don't never talk about this to nobody, you hear?"

I nodded and Daddy continued. "A lot of folks around here—white folks—believe that Adam was white, just like God. Noah was white and so was his family. God cursed Noah's son Ham, 'cause he saw his father nekked. God turned Ham black. Ham was the first of the Coloreds. They is cursed by God, so we don't associate with 'em unless we have to, and we never make friends with 'em."

Daddy looked hard at me. "Son, I don't believe that, Deacon Clement don't preach it, and I don't want you to believe it. But they's too many people around here that do believe it. They's too powerful, and they's too dangerous. You do what I say, you hear?"

154

I nodded. "Yes, sir." Then I thought, *Whatever happened to love thy neighbor?*

§ § § § §

Calvin and I set a scarecrow in the middle of the white corn. Across the creek, Joshua and Luke had built one, too. The scarecrows weren't so much for crows as for redwing blackbirds. Both scarecrows wore an old pair of overalls that had been patched as many times as could be. Both had on two shirts. The cloth of one covered most of the holes in the other. Between them, they kept in most of the straw stuffing. The arms were left loose to flap in the breeze—what there was this time of year. From a sapling at the edge of the corn, I hung a couple of old forks that had lost too many tines, and a spoon whose bowl was worn through. They'd tinkle together, if there was a breeze.

After breakfast Calvin and I headed for the bottom. Mama held out an old kitchen towel that still had a little color in it. "Put this around the scarecrow's neck," she said.

I must have looked at her funny because she said, "Crows are smarter than you think. If the scarecrow don't change a little now and then, they'll figure out it ain't real. Things got to change—people too—or they get so set in their ways they'll never be able to change."

I thought about what Mama said over the rest of the summer. The only thing in my life that changed were the seasons, and they came and went regular-like—so that didn't count. Was I going to be a farmer, like Daddy? Why couldn't I be something else? a doctor like Doc Winter? a teacher like Miss Goodman? I even thought about being a preacher like Deacon Clement, but every time I thought about that, something inside me said, *no.*

The scarecrows weren't keeping the blackbirds out of the corn. Daddy told Calvin and me we'd have to chase off the birds ourselves. Each morning we'd gather small rocks from the stream. Then we'd patrol the field, running and yelling at the birds that got close enough and throwing rocks at the ones that didn't.

Across the creek the Moss boys were doing the same thing, except they had slingshots.

§ § § § §

"Come here, boy." Daddy sat on the stump where an oak tree had once shaded the west side of the house. Its replacement was a row of what Daddy called *trash trees,* locusts. "They'll grow fast an' won't last long," he'd grunted while digging holes for the saplings he'd fetched from the woods. "But they'll keep t' sun off in summer and block t' wind in winter." I remember nodding, and then going back to playing marbles with acorns. I'd been five years old. Now I was about to turn fourteen, and the trees were more than twenty feet tall.

"Sit, boy," Daddy said. I squatted on my haunches at his feet. "No, I mean sit." I rocked back and tucked my feet under my bottom. Daddy held out his hand. "Here, boy. I know your birthday ain't 'till next week but there's no reason you can't have this now."

I took the brand new Barlow knife from Daddy's hand. I barely heard what he said.

"I knowed you wanted your Grampa Sasq's knife, but I'm gonna hold on to it for a while. When I'm ready to give it you, you give that 'un to Calvin, you hear? An' don't be

156

cutting what you ain't supposed to cut, you hear? An' that includes you."

Daddy looked hard at me. I knew what he was thinking: *It'll sink in, in time.* The reason I knew what he was thinking was that he said that to me right often.

"First things first. You make you and Calvin slingshots to keep the crows off the bottom corn, you hear?"

Daddy and I spent the afternoon together making my slingshot. An old shoe tongue, cut right, made the best sling. The elastic came from a worn out inner tube. "The red ones is best," Daddy said. "You can use pebbles, but marbles are good, too." He grinned. " 'An I know you and Calvin win a lot of marbles at school."

The next day, I helped Calvin make a slingshot. The slingshots worked a lot better than throwing rocks. Still, Calvin and I spent hours in the cornfield. One afternoon the heat was so oppressive even the crows seemed to be asleep.

"Calvin," I said. "If you promise not to tell, I'm gonna go across the creek and talk to Joshua."

Calvin looked at me. I knew he was thinking hard about that. I'd helped him make his slingshot, even let him use my new Barlow knife. He'd appreciated that, so right now our relationship was good. It wasn't always. We were brothers. I loved him, and he loved me. But we weren't expected to get along all the time.

Calvin nodded. I handed Calvin my slingshot and the bag of marbles and walked toward the creek.

Joshua saw me and sat on the same log we'd sat on when Daddy had called Calvin and me away. I sat beside him. We looked at one another, waiting for the other to speak.

"Uh, you go to church?" I asked.

"Yeah," Joshua said. He seemed surprised by the question.

"What they teach you 'bout Ham?"

"Ham?" The boy was clearly puzzled.

"Yeah, like Shem, Ham, and Japeth—Noah's sons."

"Oh. That Ham. Nothin' much."

"My daddy says Ham was the first colored man."

"Naw, that ain't right. We was made, long with everybody else, at the Tower of Babel. An' that was after Ham and his brothers. The Coloreds went to Africa and was Kings and Queens of Egypt and built the pyramids."

Before I went to sleep that evening, I looked at the picture on the wall of my bedroom—the picture of a white Jesus surrounded by white children—and wondered about what Daddy had said about Ham and what Joshua had said about the Tower of Babel and whether "Suffer the little children to come unto me" meant only white children.

§ § § § §

About a week later I walked across the creek again. The legs of my overalls got wet to the knees, but they dried quickly in the July heat. I walked past the rows of the Moss's corn.

That's white corn, I realized. And nobody grows white corn except to make moonshine. Wonder where Old Man Moss will cook it? There's no running water on his farm except the creek. A thought pushed its way into my mind. *Well strike me for a rattlesnake!* I thought. *Daddy and Mr. Moss are going to make 'shine together.*

I followed the sound of hoes striking hard earth. The first person I saw was Old Man Moss. "Howdy, Mr. Moss," I said.

The man looked up. "Howdy, Young David. Your pa know you're here?"

I didn't take offense at him calling me *Young David*. Most people called me *Little David*, just like they called Daddy *Big David*. I figured Mr. Moss was being friendly-polite.

"No sir," I said. "I was hoping you'd let Joshua and me talk a while."

Mr. Moss looked at me for what seemed like a long time, and then hollered, "Joshua, your friend's here."

Joshua walked around the end of a row and stopped six feet from his father. "You boys go up t' house and get a dipper from the well," Mr. Moss said.

Joshua slung his hoe over his shoulder and walked away. I followed him. He hadn't said a word.

The field of yellow corn went all the way to the hardpan yard of the house. Joshua set his hoe against the stone wall of the well and let the bucket down. He brushed aside my offer to wind up the bucket and turned the winch himself. When the bucket came up, Joshua scooped out a dipperful, looked hard at me, and drank. He held the half-full gourd dipper out to me. I took the dipper and drank.

"Thanks."

"You'd drink from the same dipper as a colored boy?" Joshua spoke for the first time.

"Yeah," I said. "I knowed you was testing me, but I'd a' done it, anyhow." I looked at Joshua as hard as Joshua had

159

looked at me. "Your daddy called me your friend. Was he right?"

Joshua's shoulders slumped. "Come on and set under the tree," he said. When we were comfortable leaning against the trunk of an oak, he spoke.

"Ain't no white boy and no colored boy in Tift County bein' friends. Maybe not in the whole state of Georgia."

"Why not?" I asked.

"You really don' know?" Joshua looked at me, again.

I shook my head. "Why?"

" 'Cause if folks knowed we was friends, they'd shun you—and hurt me, maybe," Joshua's voice grew softer. "Maybe lynch me . . . an' Daddy."

I was slow to speak. When I did, my voice, too, was soft. "I saw two Coloreds who had been lynched by the Klan. They wouldn't do that to you, would they?"

Joshua nodded.

What about, *Thou shalt not kill?* I wondered.

§ § § §

"Thinkin', that's all," Joshua said.

I had waded across the creek to where Joshua was lying on a rock, eyes closed. I asked him what he was doing.

"Thinkin' 'bout what?" I said.

" 'Bout movin' to Atlanta," Joshua said.

"How come?"

160

"Don't wanna be a farmer. 'Specially don't wanna be a share-cropper, and Daddy's afraid he's gonna lose the farm."

I waited, and Joshua kept talking. "He had to borrow from the bank for seed money and guano, and couldn't make the payments. The bank's gonna foreclose us off the farm if we can't come up with five hundred dollars. Where's a colored man gonna get five hundred dollars?"

I knew folks were losing their farms to the bank. But I didn't know anybody it had happened to. "Don't know," I said. "Don't know if there's that much money in the whole world."

"Daddy? Is Mr. Moss gonna' lose his farm?" I asked. Big David and I had been shuckin' white corn since daybreak. My hands were raw, but knowing how important the white corn was, I didn't mind so much.

"Why do you think that?" Daddy said.

I looked at my daddy. "You know why. You know I been talking to Joshua. You know, and you ain't said nothing, so I know it's all right," I said.

Daddy took a deep breath. "You know there ain't much you do that I don't know about. You're right. I know you and Joshua been talking."

He looked me squarely in the eye. "Boy, they's some things I tell you that you have to do. They's some things I tell you that you don't have to do. Part of growing up is learning the difference. You can talk to Joshua all you want, but don't let anybody know, you hear? That's not something you can disobey."

I nodded. "Yes, sir."

"We've got forty-five days to get Mr. Moss enough money to pay off the bank. It's gonna take a lot of work. We have to get this corn and the yellow corn ready. You know 'bout that, too, don't you?"

I nodded. "I know it's for making 'shine. I just don't know where you make it—you and Mr. Moss, too."

"You figured that out for yourself, or did somebody tell you?"

My stomach dropped to my toes. I hadn't meant to let on that I knew. "I figured it out, Daddy," I said. "It was the white corn in the Moss bottom, and there's no creek on his land to cool the still."

"Hmph," Daddy said. "That's something else you don't talk about, your hear?" He paused. "Does Calvin know?"

I was pretty sure Calvin didn't know about the still or where Daddy was making 'shine. "No, sir. I'm pretty sure Calvin doesn't know."

"You keep it that way, you hear?"

"Yes, sir."

It wasn't a week later that Mr. Moss broke his leg when he fell climbing a tree to a beehive. Calvin and Daddy and I helped Mrs. Moss and the boys as much as we could. Together, we got in the Moss corn. Daddy and I, and Joshua, tended the still in the cave up the creek, and somehow managed to make enough 'shine to pay off the note on the Moss farm.

It was a lean winter but we made it through. I think that knowing that we had done a good turn for somebody else was the reason we did.

"Do unto others." Maybe there's something to that.

Blockadin' and Raidin'

About once a month, somebody got arrested for blockadin'. That's what the old folks called making moonshine—blockadin'. It's an old word, that came over from England where people had been making liquor and smuggling it past the navy for centuries. Some of the folks around here would get arrested for bootlegging. That's selling moonshine, not making it. I was thirteen when I figured out my Daddy was a blockader. I was dumber than road-kill, or I'd of figured it out sooner.

§ § § §

I was sitting in the shade, sweating from the heat and itching from the hairs down my neck. Daddy had dropped Calvin and me at the barbershop first thing and told us to walk to the square as soon as we were finished. He'd walked in with us, and looked to see how many folks were waiting. "No hangin' around, you hear? You be back to the square by 11:00, you hear? Your mama will have need."

He handed his box to the barber, Mr. Horton. The box held Mason jars filled with moonshine. Mr. Horton hefted the box, and then raised his eyebrows.

"Only six, today," Daddy said.

Mr. Horton nodded. "That will do. Thank you."

Daddy just nodded.

Mama didn't have anything for us to do when we got to the square. Daddy said that we could play with our friends but not to leave the square and to come back for lunch by a quarter to twelve. Calvin whined about wanting to go to East Creek and hunt for crawdaddies, but I talked him out of it by saying I'd play marbles with him, for keepsies. Calvin was better than I was at marbles and figured he'd do pretty well. It was about then I figured that something was going on.

About 11:30, Daddy started pulling out his watch and looking at it, and then squinting at the clock in the steeple of the Berea Baptist Church. I looked around, but couldn't see anything and couldn't figure out what was going on. Then, just before noon, I heard sirens, and watched four sheriff's cars come up the Tifton Road heading west, toward Sylvester.

I jumped up, and Calvin was just a second behind me. Before we could take a step, Daddy snapped at us. "Sit down, boys." He looked at his watch, again, and nodded, and then asked Mama to start unpacking lunch.

Mama looked at Daddy. "The barbershop?"

Daddy nodded.

"Mr. Horton?"

"He'll be all right."

"What about Mr. Horton?" I asked.

"Not now, David," Daddy said. "It's lunch time."

164

We didn't stop at the barbershop on the way home like we usually did. After supper, and Mama had put Joey and Calvin to bed, Daddy took me on the front porch, and sat me in the swing next to him. There was a breeze. It was coming down the creek from the north, and was cool. Daddy lit his pipe and then started talking.

"Little David, you're old enough to know certain things and old enough to know not to talk about them to anybody. Not nobody, you hear?"

I nodded. "Yes, sir."

Daddy puffed his pipe a couple of times. "You know that Mr. Horton at the barbershop, he sells our 'shine. Mine and Mr. Moss's and a handful of other folks. He gets a little cut from each bottle. It ain't much, but he knows that we'll take care of him. One of the men is a friend of the Sheriff's, and he finds out when there's going to be a raid on the barbershop. That's why we only took in six bottles today, and why you got your haircut early.

"Uncle Neal has already been to the jail in Tifton. He paid Mr. Horton's fine, and got him home in time for supper. On Monday, he'll buy back Mr. Horton's car from the sheriff. The judge will get a cut—that's the Superior Court Judge in Tifton. The sheriff will get most of the money. Everybody will be happy for a couple of years, and the barbershop will be open on Tuesday.

I was scared to ask, but I had to know. "Daddy? If it's again' the law, why do you do it?"

Daddy must have heard my voice shake 'cause he put his arm around my shoulder. "Hit's all right to ask, David." He knocked out his pipe in the flowerpot. I almost giggled thinking of Mama giving him what-for when she saw it.

"There's lots of reason, son. We've been making 'shine here since before there was a US of A. President George Washington made rye whiskey, but he was rich an' he could afford the taxes on it. One of the first things Washington did when they made him president was to send out the army to make poor people pay taxes on 'shine. We don' think that's right.

"It's good for barter. It's makin' money that the government can't take, and it's tradition."

Daddy had told me that there were some things he told me I had to obey and others I didn't. Now, he was telling me that there were some laws that didn't have to be obeyed. I think that's when I really started wondering about what's right and what's wrong, and how was I supposed to know the difference.

The Worth of a Man

Mama had given me a basket of eggs to take to the produce stand to sell on consignment. She could probably sell them for more at the Saturday market, but I knew she was trying to help Sam and Mrs. Brown. Seemed as if I had always spent a bunch of time delivering things. I'd take a casserole to one house and tote a basket of eggs from there to somebody else's house. Pick up a bag of quilting squares there, deliver them to somebody, and carry a jar of preserves home. At school, I'd learned about the triangular trade. Ships carried trinkets and guns from England to Africa where they traded for slaves. The slaves were carried to the West Indies or the American Colonies where they were traded for rum or tobacco. The rum and tobacco went to England. When I was littler, I pretended I was a merchant ship carrying cargo from port to port, fighting off pirates and privateers.

§ § § § §

Sam and I had been friends for a couple of years, since he worked at the CCC Camp across the county line, and Daddy sold beef to them. Mrs. Brown was Everett Springer's widow until she married Sam. The first time I met Sam, I had a book with me and he asked me what it was. I told him, and from then on, he wanted me to tell him about what I was reading. He always had a question for me or something to say about the books. Seems like he'd read most every book in creation.

When I got to the store, Sam was busy inside helping a customer and asked if I'd feed the piglets. Folks did a lot of barter in those days, paying in pigs and chickens, so Sam and Mrs. Brown kept a pen for pigs and a chicken coop.

When I came back inside, Sam held out a nickel. "Here, David. Thank you."

"What's this for?" I asked.

"For feeding the piglets," Sam said.

"Heck, Sam, that was just a favor, and you've done me plenty of them," I said.

Sam smiled. "Yes, we've traded favors and I hope you and I, and your family and mine, will always do that. But this was business, and in business *the workman is worthy of his hire*, don't you know?"

Sam surprised me when he said that. It was from the Bible, and Sam hadn't struck me as a particularly religious man. Mrs. Brown was a member of the Gospel Truth Church, and Sam would come with her to weddings, funerals, and church suppers, but he didn't attend services. It was quite a few years before I found out why.

§ § § §

I set the table that evening and then sat in the dining room flipping the nickel into the air with one hand, catching it with the other. Calvin came in and asked me, "What you doin', Davie? What you got?"

"A nickel," I said.

168

"Where'd you get it?" Calvin asked. He knew I'd spent my allowance because I'd asked to borrow a dime from him.

"Mr. Brown gave it to me."

"Naw!"

"Yep. Mr. Brown."

"What's the story, there, David?" Daddy asked. He'd come in while I was talking.

I jerked forward, slamming the front legs of the chair onto the floor. "He paid me to feed the piglets they keep out back." I said. "I told him he didn't have to pay, but he said it was a fair bargain."

"Um, hm." That was all Daddy said.

The next morning was Saturday, and while I was helping Daddy change the oil in the truck, he asked me if I wanted to work for Mr. Brown.

"Don't you need me?" I asked. I think I was a little put off that maybe Daddy didn't need me to help on the farm.

"Not all the time, David. I was thinking maybe Fridays after school and Saturday you could work for Mr. Brown. The rest of the time, you got your chores to do."

"Do you think Mr. Brown would want me to work for him?"

"The only way to find out is to ask," Daddy said. "Hand me that wrench. Now, why don't you get yourself cleaned up and put on shoes and a shirt, and go ask Mr. Brown if he'd hire you? You'd have to be home in time to clean up for supper, so you'd have to stop work at 6:00."

"What do you think he'd pay me?" I'd worked the sorghum pressing for a dollar a day, but that was hard work, toting buckets of juice and pouring them into the evaporating pan over a hot fire.

"How much do you think?" Daddy asked.

"A dollar a day? A dollar for Friday afternoon and Saturday?"

"Hmm. A dollar a day is pretty good wages for a grown man," Daddy said. "Why don't you ask a dollar and see what he says. Let him talk you down a bit, if that's what it takes."

"How much down?" I asked.

"That depends, David, on how much you think you're worth. Now go get cleaned up." Daddy stuck his head back under the hood of the truck, and I knew I wasn't going to get any better answer.

Mr. Brown didn't blink when I asked for a dollar. He did say the same thing Daddy had said—that it was a pretty good wage for a grown man. Then, "You're fourteen, right? You're going to be a man, soon enough. I'll pay you a dollar, but no dawdling, no loitering, no fooling around. Agreed?"

I agreed and we shook hands on it. Then he handed me a bucket of lime and pointed to the outhouse. When I finished that, he told me to clean the floor of the chicken coop and put what I found in the compost pile—and then turn over the compost pile. At the end of the day, Sam handed me a silver dollar. It had been a lot harder to earn that dollar than at the sorghum boilin' but somehow I felt a lot better about it.

I figured out later what Sam had done. He'd given me the nastiest, dirtiest jobs there were to see if I'd do them. Not only do them, but do them well and without complaining.

170

Once I started working for Mr. Brown, I figured Daddy would stop my allowance, but he didn't. I still had chores, and when I found out that Calvin was doing some of my Saturday chores, I took over clearing the table after supper, which had been his job. I didn't find out until months later that Daddy had talked to Mr. Brown about me working for him before Daddy had sent me off to ask him for a job.

§ § § § §

"States rights? No. That war was fought so his grandfather could continue to own slaves." Mr. Brown looked up and saw me standing at the counter.

"David, I'd be grateful if you didn't repeat what I said."

"No, sir. I won't," I said. Then—talking without thinking—I asked, "What did you mean by it? They all say the war was fought over the states' right to determine their own destiny."

"Yes, their destiny to keep slaves and to sell their cotton to England and France."

I froze. Mrs. Brown had said that. I hadn't seen her sitting in a corner shelling beans.

Mr. Brown looked at me and said, "David, I'd be grateful if—"

"If I didn't tell. Yes, sir. But you got to tell me what all that means." I thought for a second and then added quickly, "That's not a condition of not telling. It's an asking."

That was the day I started learning Mr. Brown's history of the world. He'd been to school until he was twenty-two when he left home to join the CCC. Shoot, he had more schooling than anyone in Ty Ty, except maybe for Doc Winter.

171

"They teach you dates, they teach you names, they teach you facts. But, they don't teach you what to do with them. They don't teach you to think!" Mr. Brown said. He had asked me what I'd learned in school that day, and I said we'd learned about the Great War—what some people were starting to call World War I. They were also calling what was going on in Europe the beginning of a second world war. He asked me why the United States had entered the first war, and I told him "the Zimmerman telegram." I thought I was pretty smart.

"They told you that? They told you that the United States of America entered the war because of a telegram? And that's all? And you accepted that?"

I couldn't answer, and that's when his voice raised and complained that I hadn't been taught to think. When he calmed down, I asked him what had caused the war.

He blinked, thought for a minute, and then said, "Same thing that causes all wars, David. Greed. The real reason the war started wasn't the assassination of a minor member of the nobility and his wife. The reason the United States got into the war wasn't some telegram with an idiotic proposal that Mexico ally with Germany and attack the United States. The war was fought over who would get control of the raw materials of Africa and the Middle East. And the real reason the United States entered the war was because it looked like we'd be left out of the divvying up if we didn't get into the fighting."

"But, Mr. Brown, that's what the teacher said. It's what the textbook says." I lifted the book and was about to open it, when Sam held up his hand.

"I'm sure that's true, David. You don't have to show me. You don't have to prove to me anything you say. As long as you think before you speak."

He stopped talking and looked like he was thinking, so I kept quiet. "David," he said, "there's something I'd like you

172

to think on. It was written a great many years ago. The fellow who wrote it—his name was Peter Abelard—he messed up his life more than anybody I ever heard of. But what he said was maybe the real beginning of science and clear thinking. First, he said to question everything because questioning leads to truth. Then, make sure you know how to distinguish rational proof from propaganda or persuasion. Part of that is to use words precisely, and demand that others do so, too. Finally, he said to be wary of error, even in the most sacred texts."

Sam chuckled. "When Abelard talked about *sacred texts*, he was thinking of the Bible and the writings of the fathers of the Catholic Church. He couldn't have predicted your school history book. But if he had known about it, I think he'd have included it."

The next Saturday, Sam asked me, like he always did, what I was reading. I told him I'd finished *The Sword in the Stone,* a story about King Arthur. It was a brand new book that my Aunt Helen had given me for my birthday.

Sam nodded then handed me a slip of paper. "Here's a book I want you to read, so we can talk about it."

On the slip Sam had written, *Democracy in America* by Alexis de Tocqueville. It was the first time Sam had asked me to read a particular book, so I figured it was important.

There wasn't a copy of *Democracy in America* in the Ty Ty library. Mrs. Purcell at the library looked at me funny when I asked, but she said she'd get me a copy from the university library at Athens. After I read what de Tocqueville had to say about slavery—that he figured it was un-Christian, and he wondered how slavery could have existed in a country based on individual freedom—I understood why the Ty Ty library didn't have a copy.

§ § § § §

Morning fog billowed from the creek, climbed the shallow banks, and covered the corn. I stood in the field. I could not see more than a few feet in front of myself. The fog was only a few inches higher than my head. Directly above, a half moon shown. *That's two hundred and fifty thousand miles away*, I thought and marveled at that. *I can see a quarter of a million miles into the sky, but I can't see past two rows in front of my face.* Most of the stars were washed out by the moonlight and coming dawn, but a few were visible. *Starlight that began its journey millions of years ago*, I thought. *I can see that, too.* I lay down in a furrow, stared up at the sky, and felt the cool of the earth through the denim of my overalls and against the bare skin of my arms, and I thought.

I'm connected to the earth. I kicked my bare heels against the dirt and pounded it with my fists, and grinned to think how silly I must look. *But I'm connected to the sky, too. I just don't know how.* I stretched my right arm upward. Then my left. Both legs. My head. I strained and wished, but remained firmly in the dirt. I let out the breath I'd been holding and flopped back onto the ground.

"Ow!" I'd hit my head on a rock. Angry—at the rock, I reckoned—I grabbed it and flung it into the corn, startling a crow that had come for breakfast.

I lay back more carefully this time. *Wishin' and wantin' ain't gonna make anything happen any more than believin'. An' I ain't gonna find answers in a corn field.* The sound of Mama swinging the bell on the back porch brought me back to the world. "Oh, oh," I muttered. "I ain't fed the chickens, yet."

The next Friday, I told Sam the story of fog and moon and stars.

"You are connected to the sky," he said. Then he chuckled, and then added, "At least to the sun. Plants turn sunlight into chemical energy that we and other animals eat. Without the sun, there would be no energy and no life."

§ § § § §

It was years before I thought about this, again. I'd flown to Wichita for a tradeshow sponsored by a big military airplane company, and woke the next morning to find that the Wichita airport had been closed by a blizzard. I was stuck in a motel. I faxed my story to my editor, then had little to do but watch television. I was flipping through channels when a familiar voice caught my attention. I paused long enough to hear the phrase, "We are made of star stuff," and was hooked.

When the episode of *Cosmos* was over, I lay back on the hard motel mattress and stared upward at the flocked ceiling. *Shucks*, I thought. *I knew that all along.*

§ § § § §

I learned a lot about people that year. Mr. Brown said I had to wear shoes, and a shirt under my bib overalls. He made me wash my hands and face and slick back my hair, too, before letting me work inside the store.

"Clothes do not make the man," he said. "And you shouldn't judge a book by its cover. But people do. They see what you are wearing and they think that is you. If you smile and say 'Yes, sir,' and 'Yes, ma'am,' not 'yassir' and 'yessum,' people will look at you differently."

Mama and Daddy were happy I had a job, even though I made only a dollar a week. I never told them about the stuff Mr. Brown taught me. I probably should have. Mama would have understood. I didn't know until later that Daddy would have, too.

Party Line

Two longs and a short was our first telephone number. We were on a party line with fifteen other families. Everyone had had a different ring, and that was ours. In the summer of 1938, they ran another line, and we shared with only six other folks. Of course, two of them were the biggest gossips in Tift County. Most any time you picked up the phone, one of them would be on talking to somebody. If there wasn't anybody else to talk to, they'd talk to each other.

They usually knew when somebody else was on the line listening, but I figured out a way to listen without them knowing. The phone wires came in the house through a hole in my bedroom wall, and then went through a hole in the floor to the kitchen. Uncle Frank had seen me admiring a crystal radio in the hardware store, and gave it to me for my fourteenth birthday. I scraped a place on the phone wires, took the earphones off the crystal radio, and clipped them to the wires. I could hear everything and didn't have to worry about anybody hearing me. I thought I was going to have to whoop Calvin to keep him from telling on me, but he said he wouldn't tell, so I let him listen some.

I guess we knew we were doing something wrong, but we really didn't think it was bad or anything. We shouldn't have been surprised that it nearly got us in trouble.

§ § § § §

Calvin wasn't supposed to listen unless I was there, but he'd been home sick for two days, so he'd unclipped the earphones from the crystal set and clipped them to the phone wires. He was sitting on the edge of the bed listening when I got home.

His eyes were open wide. He was shaking his head and whispering, "No, no, no!" He was scared and it took a minute before I figured it wasn't me he was scared of. "Davie," he said, "they gonna kill Mr. Moss!"

We were about the only white folks who called him Mr. Moss. Most folks called him Old Man Moss, 'cause his hair was white from the time he was a boy. I knew, and I think Calvin suspected, that Mr. Moss and our daddy made moonshine together. Mr. Moss made enough money by hard work and selling 'shine that he wasn't in debt to anybody and owned his farm free and clear. A colored man owning a farm didn't set well with some folks.

"What do you mean, *kill Mr. Moss*? You still got a fever?" I asked. Granny Meeks said people with fever sometimes saw and heard things that weren't real, like the little girl she'd nursed during the influenza epidemic who said she saw angels just before she died. I put my hand on Calvin's forehead. It wasn't hot.

"Mr. McCorkle was talking," Calvin said. Calvin and I had come to recognize the voices of the people on the line. "He was talking to somebody called Mr. Lee. The Lee feller told Mr. McCorkle to get the Klan to take care of that uppity ni—" Calvin stuttered. Daddy had told us never to use that word. "—to take care of Mr. Moss once and for all."

That got me scared. Mr. McCorkle was a Hydra—one of the nine deputies to the Grand Dragon of the local Ku Klux Klan, and Mr. Lee was Mr. Arpie Lee. He was on the town council, and was about the richest man in western Tift County now that Ebenezer Springer was in prison.

178

"*Once and for all.* Is that exactly what he said? *Once and for all?*" I asked Calvin.

"Uh huh. An' then Mr. McCorkle said he'd get the boys together and get some rope and they'd string him up and that there was an oak tree down the road that'd work fine."

Calvin was babbling, now, but I knew what was about to happen. The Klan would take care of Mr. Moss and his family. Probably horse whip Joshua and Luke. I was glad Calvin wasn't old enough to know what they'd do to Mrs. Moss.

"When?" I asked.

Calvin was glassy-eyed and breathing hard. "You're gonna tell Daddy, ain't you?"

I nodded. "Got to. When? Did they say when?"

"Tonight," Calvin whispered. He pulled the sheet up to his chin. "Daddy's gonna whip me, ain't he?"

"Don't think so. Here, drink your water and lie back down." As soon as Calvin was settled, I hurried to the barn where Daddy was working. It was already nearly five o'clock.

Daddy didn't say anything about listening to people on the telephone, and he didn't get as excited as I thought he would. He didn't waste any time, though. "They'll get together at the Volunteer Fire Department—get likkered up. Probably won't get up the courage to go out to the Moss place until after dark. That don't give us much time. The sun will be down in half-an-hour."

He put down his tools and walked toward the house, talking as he went. I could hardly keep up with his long legs. "David, run over to Mr. Moss's house. Tell him what Calvin heard. Tell him you told me. Tell him I asked him to bring his family here. Right now, you hear?"

I nodded and lit out across the field. I was halfway to the bottom when I smelled smoke.

They hadn't waited until dark. I could smell a lot more smoke when I crossed the Moss bottom. When I got to where I could see the house, it wasn't there. I got a little closer and saw that the house was burned down with nothing left but the chimney. I stood there, breathing heavily and staring, when the chimney fell. Then there was nothing.

Where are they? Did they kill them all? I was afraid of the answer. Maybe just Mr. Moss. They wouldn't have killed Mrs. Moss and the boys.

I knew where Mrs. Moss and the boys would go, if they could. I turned and ran back to the creek, then upstream, splashing through the water.

About a mile up the creek, hidden by bushes, was a cave where Daddy had set up his still. The smoke from the fire went through cracks in the rock. Daddy never did learn where it came out, but when it did, it couldn't be seen. There was an underground stream that gave him cold water for the still's condenser. It was a sweet setup, for sure.

"Don't come any closer!" I couldn't tell where the voice was coming from. "I got a gun!" It was Joshua. I felt like I'd been punched in the gut, but it was a good feeling.

"Joshua! It's me, David! Is your daddy there? Your mama? Luke?"

Joshua stepped around the boulder that helped hide the entrance of the cave. He didn't have a gun, but I didn't figure he would.

"They took Daddy. He made us run. He made us run! I wanted to help him, but he made us run!"

As soon as it was dark, I led Mrs. Moss and the boys across the fields to our house. Mama drew the curtains and fed them supper by the light of a single lamp. It was nearly midnight before Daddy got home. Mama was sitting with Mrs. Moss. Calvin and Luke were asleep, curled up like a couple of puppies. Joshua was sitting in a corner, staring at me. It wasn't a hateful stare or a sad stare, more like the empty eyes of a pole-axed steer before his brain realized he was dead.

I could barely see Daddy's face in the lamplight, but Mrs. Moss must have seen something. She let out a wail that ran up and down my spine. Luke woke up knowing something was wrong and started crying, too. Joshua closed his eyes. Daddy didn't need to say it, but he did. "I'm sorry. Mr. Moss is dead."

He hardly took a breath before he started talking again. "Mama, pack some food. Stuff that'll keep. And a couple of jugs of water.

"David, you and Calvin—you're of a size as Joshua and Luke—get a couple pair of your best overalls, shirts, and socks. Wrap them up in those two Army blankets in the chest. Tie everything up good. Bring it all to the barn.

"Mrs. Moss, we're gonna get you and the boys away from here. I'll carry you to some people I know."

Mrs. Moss nodded. Luke was crying. Joshua had opened his eyes and was looking at me, again. "Come on, Joshua, help me," I said.

It was sunup when Daddy got back. I ran outside to meet him. "Where'd you take them, Daddy? Where are they?"

Daddy's eyes narrowed like he was thinking, not like he was mad. It had taken me a lot of years to learn the difference.

"David, did you ever hear about the Underground Railroad?"

"The folks who helped slaves escape to the Free States?" I asked. Before he could answer, I nodded and said, "The Quakers—a lot of the conductors and station agents were Quakers. You took Mrs. Moss and the boys to that Quaker family in Sylvester, didn't you?"

Daddy nodded.

"Where are the Quakers going to take them?"

"I don't know, and I don't want to know," Daddy said. "And don't you ever say anything about this, you hear? And you talk to Calvin. Tell him never to say anything. He'll listen to you."

§ § § § §

Two months later, I got a letter from Joshua. It was postmarked in Charlotte, North Carolina. They weren't there, though. Joshua wrote that one of their new Friends has Friends in Charlotte, and they will mail the letter from there. I figured the way he wrote *Friends* with a capital letter, he meant Quakers.

The next time I heard anything about Joshua was when I was overseas in World War II. Mama wrote that Mrs. Moss and the two boys had moved back and were living with Mrs. Moss' sister in Colored Town, and that Mrs. Moss and Joshua were working in the cotton mill out toward Sylvester.

Mrs. Moss died in 1947, two years after I got out of the Marine Corps. I was in school in Athens and took the train home for the funeral. It would be the first colored funeral I'd ever gone to, but it wasn't the first time I'd been to the AME Zion Church.

182

§ § § § §

I had been thirteen when Avery and I snuck through the woods, waded across the creek, and hid in the brush until dark and a drum inside the church started beating. Then we'd crept close enough that we could see through the windows without being lit up ourselves by the kerosene lanterns inside.

"They's glory-shoutin' and jumpin' around and carryin' on like . . . like I ain't never seen!" Avery's whisper was breathless in his excitement. "Do you see the one in the white dress? Her ba-zooms are gonna jump right out—"

"They's all in white dresses," I said. "But I know the one you mean. Them are the most righteous ba-zooms I ever seen."

"Seen a lot of 'em, have ya?" Avery's brother's voice cut through the darkness. Avery and I jumped. "And where'd you hear 'em called that, anyway?"

"Lonnie, don' you sneak up on a feller like that!" Avery said. "An ba-zooms is what Junior Lind calls 'em. Anyhow, what are you doin' out here?"

"Tryin' to figure why my little bro ain't done his chores and ain't in his room," Lonnie said. "I saw you leavin' an' followed you. An you shouldn't be listenin' to Junior Lind. His mama's raisin' him to be a right sissy boy." A match flared. Lonnie touched it to a cigarette. He smoked the store-bought kind since he'd gotten a job at the Post Office in Tifton.

"I done my chores!" Avery protested. "An I ain't sleepy. 'Sides, me an David are goin' after coons in a little bit. Wanna come?"

"How you gonna tree a coon?" Lonnie asked.

183

"I brought Blue," I said, and then pointed to the dog lying behind Lonnie. "He's not really a blue tick, but he's a mighty righteous hound. Daddy gave him to me for my birthday. If he'd been a snake, he'd a bit you."

"Is that Pa's shotgun?" Lonnie wasn't gonna turn loose of us. "Did he say you could use it?"

"He's asleep," Avery said. Lonnie and I knew Avery meant his daddy was passed out, drunk.

"Just so you get it back before he wakes up," Lonnie said.

§ § § § §

I took the train from Athens to Ty Ty. The train's whistle at the crossing in Colored Town woke me from that memory in time to get my coat and hat from the overhead before we reached the station. I stepped onto the platform and looked through the window of the stationmaster's office. Jed wasn't there; the fellow at the telegraph was someone I didn't know. He saw me looking and waved. I waved back. Maybe Jed would be there when I got back from the funeral.

I walked the mile or so from the railroad depot to the church, glad that the temperature was cool, and there was no rain. At first, there wasn't anyone walking along the street. I passed the place where the Hooverville had been and remembered going to the flea market with Avery. I wondered if I'd have time to try to find Avery before my train left that afternoon. As I got closer to the church, I saw other people. They were all colored and they were dressed up. They were walking in the same direction as I was. I felt kind of funny 'cause I was the only white person there.

The church was just as I remembered it: plain, whitewashed building in the middle of a hardpan yard. The

184

trees and brush where Avery and I had hidden had been cut down, and there were houses there now. The clothes and hats the women wore were much more colorful than what the women wore at the Gospel Truth Church. It was if they were trying to make up for the plainness of the building.

Mrs. Moss was laid out up front in a coffin that looked like oak. *They hanged Mr. Moss from an oak* tree, I remembered.

Joshua and Luke sat in the front pew. I watched from the back of the church for a couple of minutes. It looked like the thing to do was to walk down the aisle, stare at Mrs. Moss for a minute, and then go talk to Joshua and Luke. If you were a woman, you could cry and wail a little. I figured I could do that. Not the crying and wailing part.

I guess I did it right, although I'm pretty sure the whispers I heard when I walked down the aisle were about me. Joshua and Luke were surprised. I mumbled something, and Joshua said, "Not afraid of the Klan?"

"Please stand up," I said.

Joshua looked at me really hard, but stood. I hugged him and slapped his back a couple of times. The whispers got louder. "You're my friend, our daddys were friends," I said, "and I don't care who knows it."

I didn't have time to go looking for Avery, and Jed wasn't at the station when I got there. I exchanged a couple of letters with Joshua after that, but we didn't have anything in common any more and kind of drifted apart.

Coming of Age

I was pretty dumb when I was a teenager, and it took me a long time before I figured out that Calvin copied about everything I did. I caught him imitating me and thought he was mocking me. He got hurt when I called him on it. I finally realized he did it because he admired me. After that I was very careful what I said and did when he was around. I did manage to get him in trouble when I said a bad word, and he repeated it in front of Daddy. Daddy strapped him—not hard—and then turned him over to Mama, who washed out his mouth with soap. When I found out Calvin hadn't told where he'd heard the word, I told Daddy it was from me. Daddy was so surprised that I confessed he didn't strap me. The next Saturday, he gave me thirty cents to take Calvin for ice cream.

That happened last month. Today was my fifteenth birthday and we were in Athens, staying with Grampa Yount and Grammy. Grampa had sent train tickets. He didn't send one for Daddy 'cause he knew Daddy wouldn't come. They got along right politely, but Daddy always had a reason he couldn't visit, usually something to do with the farm.

After supper, we left Joey with the colored woman who did for Grammy and walked to the church. Grampa Yount preached a powerful sermon, even for the Wednesday night prayer meeting. His voice rang through the sanctuary. He stopped every once in a while to let it echo a couple of times before he started talking again.

186

About halfway into the sermon I pretty much quit paying attention to what he was saying. I counted all the lights in the chandeliers and all the panes in the side windows. I tried to count the panes in the stain glass window over the altar, but there was too many and they weren't regular or organized. The heat made me sleepy. I had nodded off a couple of times, but Calvin had poked me before Mama noticed. The second time he did, I touched a finger to the side of my nose. That was our private signal that we shared a secret. Calvin would figure out it meant that I owed him a favor and would pay it back.

Grampa was preaching from *Ecclesiastes* about how we should glory in our youth but that young people got tempted by Satan and led from the narrow path, and how we needed to be watched and guided. I thought about what I'd heard on the radio that afternoon about Lou Gehrig having some disease that was going to make him weaker and weaker until he just died, and wondered where was the glory in that.

It was one of those questions I should have asked Grampa when I could have, but I didn't want to upset him. Mama was his youngest child, and I was his first grandson even though I had a different name from him. Grampa always gave me good presents at Christmas and birthdays and I sure didn't want to spoil that. After he was dead and I couldn't ask him any questions, I wished I'd been a little more curious and a little less greedy.

Grammy had made a birthday cake and set it out when we got back from the prayer meeting. After we ate cake, Grampa pulled out a long box done up in colored paper and ribbon.

"Your daddy and I talked about this, David, and he said you were old enough and mature enough—and careful enough." Grampa handed me the box. Mama's lips were tight, and she didn't look happy, so I figured she knew what was in the box. At that instant, I knew, too. It was a gun, probably a shotgun. I was right. It was the prettiest double-barrel, 12-

gauge shotgun ever made. The blued barrels drank up the light but the walnut stock glowed.

I stood up and walked to where Grampa was sitting and held out my hand. "Thank you, sir. I'll not disappoint you." It was the right thing to do. A year before I'd have hugged him, but I figured he'd given me a man's gift and that it deserved a man's thank you, even though I was just fifteen.

"Can I shoot it?" Calvin asked. It didn't take Mama's gasp to tell me how to answer that.

"Yes, when Daddy says you can," I answered. Calvin's grin was big enough to tell me I'd repaid the favor I owed him for keeping me awake in church.

§ § § § §

People living around Ty Ty had been poaching and hunting out of season ever since people had been living around Ty Ty. Daddy was more strict, though. "They don't make hunting seasons just 'cause they can," he told me. "They make 'em to keep people from killing too many and from killing pregnant females an' such. Besides, you kill an animal out of season, and it'll give you worms."

I didn't know if I believed that last part, but I sure was excited when Daddy took me to Uncle Frank's hardware store to buy shells. He made a big thing out of it, telling everybody how his boy got a shotgun, and he was taking me dove hunting. Some of the men asked him if he was going to take me snipe hunting. They winked and elbowed each other, but I knew what they were talking about.

Calvin wanted to go with us, but Daddy said not this time. I said, "Next time, though, huh, Daddy?" Daddy looked at me right funny but nodded his head. Calvin waited until

188

Daddy wasn't looking and touched his finger beside his nose. Now, he owed me a favor.

Daddy kept telling me what to do and what not to do. I'd been reading the hunting magazines at the barbershop for years and knew it all, but I listened anyway. I knew about buck fever, too and was glad Daddy started me out on dove. I didn't have any trouble pulling the trigger on them.

When deer season rolled around I got my first buck with just one shot. Calvin went with us and was as proud as he could be carrying the extra shells. I thought he was going to be sick when Daddy field dressed the deer. Heck, I thought I was going to be sick, too, but we both did just fine.

Paid God

Mr. Brown had sent me to deliver some tomatoes to Edna's. When I got to her kitchen, I could hear the radio that Edna kept playing in the front. I couldn't make out the words, but I recognized their cadence. It was a hellfire and brimstone preacher, the kind of preacher who paid the radio station to put on his services and then made money off the radio audience. It was what the radio people called "paid God." My grandfather was that kind of preacher. The best preaching I ever heard him do was the time he did the revival at our church just after my fifteenth birthday.

§ § § § §

A figure rose from the shimmer of the mirage where the road dipped into a hollow between two hills. Deacon Clement stood by the road and watched Granny Meeks approaching. She stopped when she reached the top of the hill.

"Mornin', Deacon," she said. She sucked on her corncob pipe, frowned, and knocked the dottle onto the ground.

"Good morning, Sister Meeks," the deacon said. "Will you have a drink of water?"

The bucket dropped a long way before splashing into the water at the bottom of the well. Rain had been scarce of late, and some folks' wells were dry. More and more folks were

190

hauling water from the creek. More and more were watching the corn and peanuts and sorghum cane dry up. The kitchen gardens shriveled even though they were carefully watered with rinse water from dishwashing, bathing, and clothes washing.

"Church was built forty-nine years ago," Granny said. "Dug the well then, too. Dug it deep, they did. There were a drought then. Seven times seven years ago. Reckon it's a sign, Preacher?"

"A sign? How do you mean?"

"A sign the people hereabouts have fallen into evil ways. A sign that God has turned his face from us," the old woman replied.

It doesn't work that way! Deacon Clement thought. That's old covenant—the Old Testament God of retribution. But it's what's been preached around here for so long. He sighed. I can't contradict Granny Meeks. She'd not listen. If she listened, she'd not understand, and she'd likely tell people I was preaching heresy.

"Oh, I surely hope not, Sister Meeks. And so long as there are upright people like yourself hereabouts, I'm sure we'll be fine." While he was not brave, Deacon Clement was sincere.

Granny Meeks paused in stuffing her pipe with rabbit tobacco and looked hard at the deacon. He wasn't sure what the look meant.

"What we need, Preacher," she said, "is a revival and a singin' and a prayin' for rain."

The deacon shucked and shuffled but before he knew it, and quite against his will, he'd agreed to hold a revival the week following the Fourth of July. *At least, it will take their minds off the drought,* he thought. *And the revival suppers . . . won't get much in the collection plate, but there's no better*

191

fried chicken and pie than gets brought to revival suppers. Now, where am I going to get a revival preacher?

§ § § § §

Deacon Clement sat in the waiting room of the train station. He was hoping for a reply to one of his telegrams. He'd sent seven to preachers in nearby towns asking them to preach a revival. Three had said no. Three had said yes, but they'd asked for more expense money than he could come up with. He had only four days before the revival was to start. His hopes were pinned on the seventh preacher. He looked up as he heard the clatter of the telegraph machine behind the ticket window.

Jed Harmon pulled the strip of yellow paper from the machine. "Sorry, Deacon, not for you. It's railroad business." Deacon Clement's shoulders slumped. The heat of the late afternoon was only slightly abated by the slow movement of the ceiling fans. Flies buzzed lethargically around his head. Deacon Clement fell asleep.

"Brother Clement? Brother Clement?" A familiar voice woke him. "Brother Clement, it's nearly dark. Are you waiting for someone? For if you are, that was the last passenger train."

Deacon Clement woke and realized that the voice addressing him belonged to Mrs. Sasq's father—Reverend Yount from Athens. Deacon Clement stuttered, "Reverend Yount, I fell asleep." He tried valiantly to rub the fatigue from his eyes.

Reverend Yount frowned. "You're troubled, son. Why are you here?" He chuckled. "Only my daughter knew I was coming to visit, so you're not here to greet me." He frowned

192

again when he realized that the deacon hadn't reacted to his little joke. "What's wrong?"

"Reverend Yount, what's wrong is that I've promised a revival, but I can't find a revival preacher. The only ones I know can't come, or won't because I can't pay enough. I don't know what to do."

The Reverend Yount's eyes seemed to lose focus. *This may be a chance to pick up some pocket change*, he thought. "When's this revival supposed to start?"

"Tomorrow night, Tuesday," the deacon said.

"And last how long?"

"Four nights," the deacon said.

"Hmm," Yount said. "Tell you what. We'll split the collection plate, and I'll preach your revival."

Word that the Reverend Yount would be preaching the revival spread quickly through Tift County and beyond. Two of the preachers who'd turned down Deacon Clement's invitation drove in to ask if they might be included. Deacon Clement dithered. He'd have to ask Reverend Yount, he told them, but Reverend Yount wasn't available. He'd taken his grandson Calvin fishing somewhere in Worth County, but no one knew exactly where.

The preachers weren't the only thing Deacon Clement had to worry about. Two fellows from the radio station in Athens showed up with a thing they called a wire recorder, and a microphone that had to be screwed down to the pulpit. When they found out that the church didn't have electricity, they drove Deacon Clement to the Electric Co-op where he talked Uncle Neal into sending some men to put in some poles and run a line from the road. Nothing was said about who would pay for it, but Deacon Clement had a bad feeling.

The poles had been set, and a wire run to a fuse box nailed to the side of the church. From the fuse box, another wire ran through a hole they'd cut in the wall behind the pulpit. The fuse box and wire had required a trip to the hardware store. Nothing was said about who would pay for it, but Deacon Clement had a bad feeling.

§ § § § §

I heard the dynamite they used to make a hole for the first pole and got to the church in time to see them blast the hole for the second. The ones after that went in easier. After the electricity got hooked up, the two fellows from the radio station started running around the church hollering, "Testing: one, two, three, four," and then listening to their voices on the recorder.

Mr. Spencer, the president of the men's group, came in the church to where Deacon Clement and I were standing watching the two men. He pointed out the door to the electric poles that marched up from the road. "Deacon Clement?" he asked. "What in thunderation is goin' on?"

At this point, one of the fellows from the radio station let out a particularly loud, "Testing: one, two, three, four." Mr. Spencer took Deacon Clement's arm and pulled him outside.

"Reverend Yount's gonna preach our revival," Deacon Clement said. "Those men are from the Athens radio station and they've got something that will take down his voice so they can play it on the radio, like a Victrola, but with wire."

"And who's payin' for it? The co-op charges ten dollars to set a pole—more in rocky ground like this."

Deacon Clement confessed that he didn't know.

194

"By golly, you leave this to me," Mr. Spencer said before he stomped up the steps of the church yelling, "Hey, you radio fellers, come here a minute."

Mr. Spencer was shaking his head when he came out of the church. He took the dipper Deacon Clement offered and drank a slug of well water. Then he pulled out a block of tobacco and opened his pocketknife.

"Want a chaw, Preacher?" he offered. "No? Well, I need a bit of soothin' after hearing what they had to say. Free God and paid God. They call it paid God and free God." He put a plug of tobacco in his cheek.

"Seems" he said, "that folks get to vote once a year on whether a radio station gets to keep its license. It ain't a real vote, but if enough people don't like a station, they can lose their license. The station in Athens these boys are from—an' they say most stations in the state—puts on church programs to show people the station's servin' the community. They don't charge for 'em. And these fellows call it 'free God.'

"Then they's churches and preachers who pay the station to put on their programs. The radio guys call that 'paid God.' And those fellows said that Reverend Yount's preaching is about the best paid God they got. They put on his Sunday services—both of 'em—and his Wednesday night service, and he pays 'em real good. Anyway, I told 'em that they'd be paying for the electric poles and the other stuff, and they said they would, just send 'em the bill. They said Reverend Yount was paying a lot more than what a couple of 'lectric poles cost."

§ § § § §

The preaching was set to start at 7:00 PM, after the day had cooled a bit, but folks started arriving in late afternoon.

Food covered the picnic tables. Folks sat in the shade of the oak trees or the two tents the funeral home had erected. The funeral home had also put out fans—a thin piece of cardboard stapled to a tongue depressor. The cardboard had a picture of Jesus on one side and the name and address of the funeral home on the other.

Don't know why they need to put on their address, I thought. There aren't but two funeral homes in town—one for white folks and one for the Coloreds. It isn't likely anyone will get them confused.

I hadn't wanted to come, but Mama insisted. "It wouldn't be right if you didn't come and hear your grandfather preach. Besides, I'm not fixing supper except what I'm taking to the church."

Her second argument was the stronger, and I spent the afternoon figuring how I might slip away—after supper, of course—without being missed.

Fans waved and tongues flapped. The story of the electric poles and the fuse box bought at the hardware store passed from mouth to mouth. I grabbed the windlass at the well and hauled up buckets of water to fill pitchers and Mason jars. Calvin clung to me. I would have run him off except I figured I'd need someone to bring me supper. Working the windlass was the best plan I'd come up with for avoiding the preaching.

Toward dusk, boys started congregating near the picnic tables. They'd have to wait until Deacon Clement offered the blessing and wait again until the old women tottered up to serve themselves, but the boys would be close to first in line. I pushed Calvin to join them. "You get two plates, you hear, and don't let anyone tell you nevermind, either."

The talking stopped but the fans beat even more furiously as Deacon Clement and Grandpa Yount stepped onto the top step of the church. For a moment, the only sound was the whisper of fans. Then the door to the outhouse behind the

196

church slammed, drawing a giggle from some of the boys and stern looks from their parents. Deacon Clement had asked Reverend Yount if he wanted to offer the blessing, but Reverend Yount had turned him down, like he'd turned down Deacon Clement's offer of the first speaking spot on the evening's schedule. *Boy doesn't understand what warmin' up an audience means,* Yount chuckled to himself. *Doesn't know how to project his voice, either.* Deacon Clement's blessing didn't reach the ears of those farthest from the church, but they didn't expect it to. The surge of people toward the picnic tables was signal enough.

Miss Mary Clampert, the organist, was traditionally the first in line at the picnic tables. No one begrudged her, because the singing that began the service couldn't start until she was ready to play. Nor was it long before she walked into the church followed by a dozen folks. Minutes later, the traditional first revival hymn fled through the windows into the evening air. *Shall we gather at the river . . .*

Reverend Yount had given Deacon Clement the scripture for his warm up sermon. *Job said, "Naked came I out of my mother's womb, and naked shall I return thither: the Lord gave, and the Lord hath taken away; blessed be the name of the Lord."* Yount had also given the deacon a theme—Job's comforters—no matter how bad off you are, there's someone worse off; things may be bad, but they could be worse. It was a dark theme that would cause the audience to welcome Reverend Yount's uplifting message.

When Deacon Clement went to the pulpit, the fellow from the radio station looked at Reverend Yount and raised his eyebrows. Reverent Yount frowned and shook his head. *No sense recording this,* he thought. Five minutes later, he regretted his decision. *The boy's good,* he thought. *I'll give him that.*

My plan to get away hadn't worked. When the preaching started, I was sandwiched between Mama and Calvin on the first pew, right in front of the pulpit. My brief fascination with the turning reels of the wire recorder wasn't enough to keep my mind away from Grampa's sermon. The message was simple: Job didn't doubt the Lord; we must not doubt the Lord. There were words about loaves and fishes, about cups running over, about milk and honey, and about manna from heaven. Grampa praised Miss Goodman's huckleberry pie, and Mrs. Brown's Hoppin' John, and made all the ladies proud of their contribution to the picnic. *Done his homework*, I realized. *But I know for a fact that he didn't get any huckleberry pie. Calvin said Mr. Spencer's boys got the whole thing until Calvin threatened to tell, and got us a piece.* I caught Calvin's eye, and touched my finger beside my nose in our private signal. Calvin must have caught on about the huckleberry pie, 'cause he grinned.

I couldn't help but notice that the radio guys from Athens turned on the recorder for Deacon Clement's sermon the next three nights. He kept preaching from the Book of Job. The deacon preached the bad things and Grampa preached the good things. The collection plate was passed after the good things.

Grampa Yount took the train back to Athens Saturday morning. I sat in the station with him while he waited and asked him about the huckleberry pie. He was surprised and, I think, amused. He wasn't upset and may have been proud that I'd caught his lie. I didn't understand that and asked him why he'd told those stories.

"David," he said. "God is the God of Truth—"

I could see the capital letters in what he said.

"—and sometimes the Truth needs a little help. The congregation of your church are simple people. They see things

198

in simple ways. Talking about that woman's huckleberry pie and the other person's Hoppin' John were ways to make them listen to me so that I could give them a greater truth.

"I see that you do not understand. You will, as you get older." The train whistle sounded at the crossing. We had only a few minutes. Before I could ask another question, Grampa stood up, hugged Mama, and offered his hand to me. I shook it, but all the time I was thinking, *'That woman?' You don't even remember her name since Tuesday? It was Miss Goodman's huckleberry pie and Mrs. Brown's Hoppin' John. And what do you mean by 'greater truth'? Are you the only one who knows what's true?*

Mama sent me straight from the train station to the church to help with the cleanup. Daddy and I and a couple of other folks picked up trash from all over and took it to the ravine. Daddy was surprised that I volunteered to put lime in the outhouse. After that, I watched the radio guys unscrew the microphone from the pulpit. Mr. Spencer was there to supervise. He wasn't happy about the damage they'd done to the pulpit and the wall but agreed that he'd find someone to fix it.

When we finished, Deacon Clement made a point to thank me for taking care of the outhouse. I figured it would be a good time to ask him a question, so I asked about Grampa and the huckleberry pie.

The deacon didn't say anything right away, and when he did, he didn't answer my question but asked one of his own.

"David, I confess to being a little uneasy about what Mr. Spencer said about *paid God*. After I heard that, I went home and read the part about Jesus driving the moneychangers out of the Temple. Do you remember that story?"

"Yes, sir. But what about what Grampa said about truth?"

"Who knows the truth?" Deacon Clement said. "Do you remember when God told Jonah to tell the people of Nineveh that God would destroy the city in forty days? God knew that the people would repent and that He would not destroy the city. God never intended to destroy Nineveh, but He told Job to tell the people that. Was God lying to Jonah, or was he using Jonah to lead those people to a greater truth? Maybe that's what your grampa meant."

Ave veritatum, I thought. *Hail truth.* I was taking Latin that year from Miss Stewart, and that was one of the first things in Latin I learned. Was that just as empty of meaning as was the "Hail, Caesar," Brutus said before stabbing him?

§ § § § §

On the Monday after the revival, a thunderstorm boiled across the county line from the west. The creek overflowed, but the water went down before the corn in the bottom was hurt.

It was the first real rain we'd had all summer, and the storm seemed to sit over the western half of Tift County for nearly a week, giving us a gentle, soaking rain. Granny Meeks was happy, telling anybody who would listen that God was answering the prayers lifted at the revival meeting. It just gave me something else to think about: why would God send a drought and then send rain just because we prayed?

200

Sinkhole

Bobby Gordon and I were standing behind the bob-wire fence the Works Progress Administration fellows had put up around a sinkhole where Barney Bonds's house used to be. We could still see some of the roof near the bottom of the hole. Two bulldozers and a stream of trucks from the WPA had half-filled the hole. Mr. Bonds, Mr. Barringer, and Bobby's daddy were on the other side of the hole, leaning on the fence and talking, but we couldn't hear them over the bulldozer.

Bobby had a big mouth, though. All it took to get him started was to say something about his dad, and Bobby would start telling stuff that his dad would have whipped him for saying. Of course, I guess Mr. Gordon had a big mouth, too, or Bobby wouldn't have known the things he told me.

§ § § § §

"Ought to of bulldozed your garage while they was at it." Danny Barringer gestured toward a rusty, tin building about ten feet from the edge of the sinkhole, and then spat. A greasy gob of tobacco juice fell beside Nate Gordon's feet.

Nate sidestepped a little and glared at Danny. "Your mama ought to of drowned you when you was born." His words were without heat. The July day held enough of that. Nate pulled out a bandana to wipe the sweat that dribbled down his neck and under the collar of his blue work shirt. Another in the stream of WPA trucks dumped a load of dirt and gravel near the sinkhole. The bulldozer driver moved toward it.

"They'll be finished 'fore dark," Nate said.

"An' then what?" Barney Bonds asked. "Don't do me no good. Can't build on a sinkhole, even if I had the money. Can't live in the garage. It's chock full of you-know-what. It'd kill a man."

"They ought to bulldoze the garage," Danny repeated. He knew what was in the garage, and he was afraid the sheriff would find out about it. At that moment, the edge of the sinkhole closest to the garage slumped. The bulldozer driver gunned his engine and backed up in time to keep from being pulled in. The men watched as the sinkhole widened. The walls of the garage creaked. Nails popped out as the building leaned toward the bulldozer. The driver dove for the ground.

As if trying to resist its fate, the garage leaned slowly over the pit. Two windows looked down into the hole and blinked as their glass shattered. The garage with its load of DDT stolen from the WPA fell into the pit. The concrete slab on which the garage had been built slid down the side of the hole. It caught, and stood upright.

That night I dreamed about the sinkhole and the standing-up slab of concrete. I dreamed the hole was a grave and somebody was being pulled in, and a hand was coming down to write a name on the concrete that was now a gravestone. I woke up just before the hand started writing. I was shivering even though it was July.

For the rest of the night, I sat on the front porch with nothing but the darkness for company. Even Blue abandoned me and slept in the cool spot he'd dug out under the porch.

202

The next day was Friday. I was walking home from working for Mr. Brown, and sweating in the heat. I'd just passed the church and reached the crossroads at the Old Sylvester Road when Granny Meeks called to me.

"Afternoon, Mrs. Meeks. You don't want to be getting too close to me," I said.

"You got something catchin?"

"No, ma'am. Mr. Brown and I've been turning the compost pile. I 'spect Mama won't let me in the house until I wash up."

"Well, then, don't dawdle 'cause she won't be serving supper until then, either."

"Mama asked you to supper?" I asked.

"And what's so wrong about that?"

"Why, nothing, Granny. It's about time you got some meat on your skinny bones."

"That's Mrs. Meeks to you, Davey-boy, and we can't all be great oxes."

"You mean like Mr. Barringer?" I asked.

"I was thinking more of you, boy. You've growed a lot this summer."

"I'm sixteen, Granny, and working a man's job."

Granny *harumphed* and fell in beside me. I had to slow down a bit.

"Granny? What do you know about dreams?"

"Dreams? Why you askin' that?"

"Granny, I'm scared. Every night, I dream about the sinkhole that swallowed Mr. Barnes's house and garage. In the dream, I know it's a grave, and there's a hand coming down from heaven to write on the gravestone, and I'm afraid of the name it's going to write."

By now, we were almost home. "After supper, Davey-boy. After supper, we'll talk."

"You help Granny Meeks up the steps," Mama said. Her voice was sharp. She was standing on the porch holding Joey. He was struggling and flailing, and it looked like he was going to have one of his fits. I offered my arm to Granny Meeks like Mama had showed me how to do.

"Thank you, Davey-boy," she said. "You're turnin' into quite a gentleman, ain't you."

Calvin had come to the door. He made a face at me but was careful not to let Mama or Granny Meeks see. I showed him my teeth, and he grinned at me. I'd get him, later.

"There's lots a things goin' on out there," Granny said, and waved her hand at the gathering darkness. We were sitting on the porch after supper.

Granny's way of talking changed, and I knew she was telling me one of the stories that she told so often she likely believed them.

"There's powerful things that run around in the dark while you're asleep—things that would make your flesh creep. The noise they make is the silence of the night. They are the shadows that fly with the wind. Some are dressed in moonshine, carded and spun finer than silk. They ride white, winged horses. They are dreams. Some are dressed in darkness, and the horses they ride are night mares. If you're fast, if you're clever, you can catch a dream and it's yours, forever."

"Granny, I don't want to catch this one!"

204

"Seems like you already have, Davey-boy."

"How can I let it go?"

Granny didn't answer my question, but asked, "What name is the hand going to write?"

My answer caught in my throat. I had to swallow and take a couple of breaths before I could answer. "*Joey*," I said. "And then, *David*. And I'm afraid, afraid I'm going to Hell."

"Davey-boy, the Gates of Heaven and Hell are a lot closer to one another than people know. And there ain't no signs at either one. There's only the road you take in life that's gonna lead you."

What she said was frightening; what she said next was more frightening. "Davey-boy, I 'spect you're right about Joey. He looks mighty poorly. But you don't say a word to your mama."

"No, ma'am."

§ § § §

It took the WPA four more days to fill the sinkhole. By then, Barney had left Ty Ty on a westbound freight train. A couple of years later the county tried to sell the land for back taxes, but nobody bid on it, so they gave it to the city. The city at least kept the grass mowed, and for a while it was a good place for a pickup game of baseball.

Nobody thought any more about it, not even in 1965, when what they called a "cancer cluster" broke out in Colored Town. The government scientists tested the well water and then covered up the wells just like they'd covered up the sinkhole.

Funeral Casseroles—Part II

Granny and I were right. My dream was a foretelling. On September 5, 1940, Joey didn't wake up. I had dreamed that night, dreamed that Joey's grave was a hole waiting to suck him down to Hell. Mama's crying woke me up. Daddy came in the room.

"Joey's gone away."

That's all he said; we knew what he meant. Calvin and I cried. I stopped first and went to do the milking. Things had to go on.

Daddy wrote out a telegram for Grampa Yount in Athens and Daddy's sister, Aunt Mary, in Valdosta. The funeral would be Saturday. He gave me the writing and a handful of dollars. "Don't know what a telegram costs, now-a-days," he said.

Grampa Yount wasn't at the funeral. I don't think Mama noticed. Everybody else that counted was there. Aunt Lucile and Uncle Neal, Aunt Mildred and Uncle Frank, Aunt Mary and Uncle Beau from Valdosta, and Aunt Helen and Uncle Robert. Just about everybody in the church was there, too. Didn't any of them really know Joey, but I guess they all knew Mama and Daddy, so it was for them that they came.

Mama hurried us away after speaking to people, and Daddy drove us home. Nobody said anything, and the only sound was Mama's crying.

§ § § § §

When she reached her bedroom, Martha poured water from a pitcher into the basin and splashed some on her face. She had sent David and Calvin to their room to change out of their good clothes. Their voices came through the thin wall and echoed down the short hallway.

"It ain't true, you know." That was David.

"What ain't true?" Calvin asked.

"It ain't true what Deacon Clement said, about Joey being with Jesus," David said.

Martha's hand, which had been reaching for a towel, froze. A drop of water fell from her chin onto the unfinished pine of the dresser.

"What do you mean, Joey ain't with Jesus?" Calvin asked.

"Because," David said. "Deacon Clement's always preached that you have to accept Jesus and repent of your sins 'fore you can be saved. Well, Joey was too dumb to know his own name, and he sure didn't know anything about Jesus. He didn't know what sin was. If he didn't know about Jesus and sin, he couldn't accept Jesus and repent, and he couldn't be saved. So, Joey's burning in Hell, right now."

David's words pierced his mother's heart. *Oh, Lord, please don't let him believe that!* She splashed more water on her face.

"David Sasq, don't you say such a thing!" Calvin said. "Joey's not in Hell! He's in the arms 'a Jesus."

"You're so dumb," David said. "You think Jesus got nothing better to do than hold dead kids?"

Her husband hollering up the stairs drowned out whatever else Martha might have heard. "Martha! Your pa's here."

Calvin finished changing out of his funeral clothes, which were also his Sunday-go-to-meetin' clothes, and which had been David's, and would have been Joey's, except that Joey was dead. David had stomped out of the room. Calvin looked at the picture of Jesus on the wall and gave in to the tears that he'd last shed when his daddy had told them that Joey was dead.

Minutes later, Calvin sat on a straight-backed chair in a corner of the kitchen. His lap held a paper plate heaped with macaroni and cheese and a drumstick. Aunt Lucille had brought two chickens and fried them up while everyone else was at the funeral.

"Calvin? Where's David?" Martha asked. "He's had time t' change."

"Don't know, ma. He changed his clothes an' took off."

"You just go find him," Martha said. "Grampa wants t' see him."

"Aw, Ma," Calvin whined. "I'm eating."

Martha looked at the dinner table. It was covered with bowls and plates of food. "Calvin, there's plenty a' food. I'll save you chocolate cake. Now go on, git." She took the boy's plate.

208

Fall wildflowers have more pollen than the spring ones, Deacon Clement thought as he swept up the petals that had fallen from Joey's coffin. They left a trail of yellow that lodged in the grain of the rough, dry wood. The deacon sighed and leaned on his broom. Through a plain glass window that provided little protection from the cold in winter and even less relief from the heat in summer, he stared at the mound of red earth that covered Joey. *No sparrow shall fall,* he thought. Then he whispered it. "No sparrow shall fall but that God sees it."

"No, but it still falls, doesn't it?" Startled, Deacon Clement turned to see David Sasq standing only a few feet away. He'd not heard the barefoot boy enter the church.

"There was this sparrow," David continued. "Actually it was a wren, that built its nest up under the eaves. Joey could see it from his crib. He watched the little ones hatch out. He watched them bein' fed. He saw the one with a crooked wing. When the others flew, that one just fell. Joey couldn't see it, but he heard it when the cat got it. God must have seen it too, huh?"

Deacon Clement opened his mouth to speak, but David kept talking. "Joey cried for the rest of the day and most of tomorrow. Why did God make Joey cry? Why did God make the sparrow die?"

Deacon Clement leaned the broom against the wall and clasped his hands behind his back. "God works in mysterious ways—"

"Deacon, that's no answer, an' you know it," David said.

Deacon Clement squeezed his hands together. Something in the boy's voice bothered him. "David, you need to be getting home," the man said. "Folks will be coming to visit."

"That's no answer, either," David said. He seemed to stare at something miles past where Deacon Clement was standing.

"Think on it, Deacon," David said. "You and Jesus, you think on it." He turned, and walked away.

When Deacon Clement turned to retrieve the broom, he realized where David had been looking. From the velvet painting above the communion table, Jesus stared at him.

Deacon Clement shook his head and then lowered his eyes—not in prayer, but in shame. He didn't have the courage to tell David that he didn't understand it any better than the boy did. He knew that wasn't what David wanted to hear, but it would have been better than what the deacon had told him.

People filled the bottom floor of the Sasq home. The aunts played hostess while Martha sat with her father. Reverend Yount took his daughter's hand. "Now, Martha, don't cry. Joey's with his Lord, now."

Martha stifled a sob. The words didn't seem to help coming from her father any more than they had coming from Deacon Clement. *Speaking of the deacon*, she thought as he appeared in the doorway.

Deacon Clement tugged his coat sleeves over the frayed cuffs of his second-best white shirt. Like Calvin, he anticipated a full belly. What he didn't anticipate was finding Joey's grandfather sitting on the sofa. Wishing he'd worn his best white shirt, Deacon Clement went to greet the Reverend.

Martha watched Deacon Clement tug at his coat sleeves and then speak softly to several people before reaching her.

"Reverend Yount, I didn't know you were here, sir."

"I'm sorry I missed the funeral, Deacon. Everyone has said that it was a comfort. My train was on time, but the telegram was late, and there was no one to meet me at the station."

Martha didn't know quite how it happened, but the deacon managed to take her place on the couch, and began talking with her father. David and Calvin appeared at the front door. Calvin went straight to the kitchen to claim his place and his plate. Martha watched David move toward the stairs before Lucille demanded her attention. The two sisters put leftover food in Mason jars or wrapped it in wax paper. It would have to be eaten soon. The old refrigerator didn't hold the cold like it used to.

David and his grandfather sat on the porch swing. Inside the house, Calvin slept uneasily. His dreams were dark and his tummy grumbled from unaccustomed fullness. David's father slept, too, but Martha lay awake, listening to the voices of her father and her son drifting in the stillness.

"What did you and the deacon talk about so serious-like?" David asked.

"Mostly about you," the man answered.

"I kinda' figured, the way you kept looking at me. What did he say?"

"He said you had asked why God made Joey cry."

David was silent for a while and then told his grandfather what he had told Calvin about Joey not knowing sin or Jesus. Now, it was the man's turn to sit silently. When he spoke, his voice was soft.

"David, there are only two things in the Bible that are really important. The first is that God cursed mankind because Adam and Eve sinned. They were our parents, and we inherit their sin. The second is that God still loves us, and a couple of thousand years ago, He sent Jesus, His Son, to die to redeem that sin. Most of the rest of the Bible is telling us things about that, or useful things for living the right way. I know that you've been taught that every word in the Bible is true. But you know that isn't so, don't you?"

"Yes, sir," David said. "I looked up the sparrow thing. Matthew says two sparrows for a farthing. Luke says five sparrows for two farthings. And neither of them says exactly what the deacon said."

The man nodded. "The Bible was accurate once, but it's been translated and printed so many times, and not always by men of God, that some mistakes have crept in. That's why you have to read it prayerfully, so God will help you find what's true and what isn't."

Then Grampa surprised David. He said, "People don't come to church for truth; they come for comfort."

David shivered and thought, It wasn't but a few months ago he told me how important the truth was. Now he's tellin' me something different. What am I supposed to believe?

§ § § § §

I was brought up in the Gospel Truth Church and was taught to believe some things as being true. Things like, *For God so loved the world, Love thy neighbor, Do unto others,* and *Suffer the little children* were drilled into me from the git-go. The only picture in my bedroom was Jesus, surrounded by little children. Beside it was a framed copy of the Ten Commandments. Now, Grampa Yount had told me maybe it wasn't all that certain.

After Grampa Yount went to bed, I brought my Bible down to the kitchen and read by the light of a candle. I knelt on the linoleum floor and prayed. And I thought. *If a preacher can make you believe you're born sinful and have to be saved, and then make you believe that he's the only one that knows how to save you, then you have to listen to him and do what he says. That's what's true. The rest of it isn't. And Joey isn't in Heaven or Hell. Joey is just dead.*

Granny Meeks came early the next morning and found me doing my chores.

"Granny, you were right about my dream. I should have told Mama!" I challenged her.

Granny answered with a poem. I knew where it came from—the stories and verses of Joel Chandler Harris, the *Uncle Remus* book.

> *Little children die, and you think they are gone,*
> *And you weep and wail, with black mournin' on;*
> *Family and friends, they're taken, too,*
> *And it seems like the Reaper won't never get through;*
> *Both big and little, both young and old,*
> *They all got to answer to the Call of the Roll;*
> *They answer, and go. Do you 'spect that's all?*
> *Is the oak tree sorry when the acorns fall?*

"Bless you, Davey-boy," she said. "I know what I know a lot better than I did fifty years ago." Granny Meeks said. "And I 'spect you'll understand. I told you that Joey was a blessin' to you. I hope it won't take you fifty years to figure that out."

Charles Robert Darwin

Let justice be done though the heavens fall.
—Traditional

"This is not what we believe! This man believes that human beings came from apes and were not made by Almighty God in His image." Mr. Ronnie Babb's voice was louder than proper in a library and earned a stern look from Mrs. Purcell. She raised her finger to her lips and was about to *shush* Mr. Babb, but he had turned toward the shelves where the spines of the books bore a cross: the symbol for safe, Christian books.

A young man who sat at a nearby table looked up from his newspaper. He saw the man put the book on a table then grab the hand of a boy and pull him away. The boy turned his head, and saw the young man looking at him. The young man caught the boy's eye and raised an eyebrow in question. The boy shrugged, grimaced and followed his father. The exchange took but an instant. When the man and boy were out of sight, the young man retrieved the book and stared at the title: *The Origin of Species by Means of Natural Selection, or the Preservation of Favoured Races in the Struggle for Life* by Charles Robert Darwin. The young man put the book back on the table and then returned to his newspaper to read of the London blitz and about a scientific discovery on radioactivity by a fellow from Cambridge.

214

Across the street at the Ty Ty Consolidated School, Miss Lillian Goodman was preparing her classroom for the beginning of the school year. She stood behind her desk and smiled. Her classroom was bigger than the entire one-room school where she'd started teaching right after the turn of the century. Down the hall were what they called "restrooms" with indoor plumbing. In 1902, they didn't have those, either. There was a separate restroom for teachers next to the teachers' lounge. *A teachers' lounge—imagine that—a room just to sit down in. Those boys from the Works Progress Administration did a fine job building this place.*

The school building was faced with marble from the quarry in Jasper. It was already beginning to darken. The coal-fired power plant in Albany was too far away for anyone to make the connection, and the world hadn't yet heard of acid rain. There was another school across town for the Coloreds. It was brick and had outhouses instead of indoor plumbing.

The WPA had brought more to Ty Ty than the school. They had also built a city hall and a post office. Afterwards, many of the WPA men who had learned carpentry, bricklaying and other building trades had stayed on to build the cotton mills and warehouses that sprang up west of town. With reliable and cheap electricity coming over the new high-tension lines, mills didn't have to rely on waterpower as they had in New England. Besides, the people in the south were willing to work for a lot less money and the mill owners had the KKK to take care of the union organizers and other Communists. Boys and men from the CCC camp had been among the first hired to work in the mills. Many had sent for their families, and the builders were kept busy putting up tin-roofed, wood frame houses. These were rented to the mill workers, with the rent coming out of their pay before they even saw it. Everyone with a spare bedroom took in a boarder or two, and those who didn't have a spare bedroom doubled up the kids to make one.

The following Monday, Miss Goodman sat at her desk, hands folded and spectacles balanced primly on her nose. The children squirmed. It was the first day of school, and the weather was unconscionably warm. Miss Goodman cleared her throat. "During this school year, you will each select nine books from the library. You will read one book each month. On the last Friday of each month, you will turn in a one-page essay—" She paused to allow the groans to subside. "You will turn in a one-page essay. You will tell what the book was about, what you learned from it, and why you think someone else should read the book. You will read your essay aloud to the class."

There were more groans. She spotted one raised hand.

"Yes, Jonathan?" she asked.

"Any book, Miz Goodman?"

"Any book in the library. Except, of course, the picture books in the children's section."

§ § § § §

Jonathan Babb stood confidently in front of the class. "The book I read was *The Origin of Species* by Mr. Charles Darwin. This book is about how over time, random mu . . . mutation creates new species, and how new species survive by natural selection, or die, depending on whether they're suited to the place where they live. He says it's like a farmer will breed his cows to the best bull to improve the herd, or like Mr. Barringer put his best bitch with Mr. Horton's blue tick and got them champion coon hounds.

"Anyway, I learned that the world is a lot older than it says in the Bible, and that it's more complicated and beautiful than I had ever thought. I figured out that the story of creation in Genesis is a, uh, *allegory*—I had to look that word up. I

216

think that everybody should read this book because it explains a lot of things I wondered about."

§ § § § §

The following Monday, the School Board moved the venue for its meeting to the new City Hall—the WPA-constructed, neo-classical monstrosity that dwarfed even the Berea Baptist Church across the town square. Save for the stairwells, the entire second floor of the building was a meeting room. Across one end, an elevated platform held a long oak table and chairs for the members of the city council and the mayor. On Wednesdays, all but one chair was removed, and Judge Robert McCoy conducted municipal court. The chamber, which could hold perhaps three hundred spectators, had only fifty chairs. The Town of Ty Ty could not afford to furnish this gift from the taxpayers of America.

The windows were open to the soft air of an Indian summer evening. The sky held a glow from the setting sun, but the bright lights in the council chamber pushed it away. The mayor glanced up at the twenty-two frosted glass globes. Each held four, one-hundred-watt light bulbs. He did the arithmetic in his head every time he walked into the chamber: *8,800 watts. Almost nine kilowatts per hour. And the bulbs burn out right regular-like.* Neither he nor the WPA architect who had selected the fixtures understood that the heat of the bulbs, captured in the glass globes, caused the bulbs' early failure and one day would start a fire that would gut the building and kill seven people.

The School Board had only four members; however, five of the chairs behind the bench were occupied. The Chairman of the Board rose and gaveled the room to silence. The people who had thought themselves lucky to get seats were already squirming. The wooden chairs were uncomfortable and promised to become more so. People stood two- and three-deep around the walls.

There were only a few children in the room. David Sasq was there. Sam Brown had told him to go and listen carefully to what people said. "Say nothing, yourself. Nothing!" Mr. Brown had commanded.

Jonathan Babb sat in the front row between two men. One of the men was his father. The other was Reverend Darrell Fletcher, pastor of the Berea Baptist Church. Also on the front row, separated from the others by empty seats on both sides of them, were two women—Miss Goodman, of course, and Mrs. Purcell, the librarian. Although the School Board did not have jurisdiction over the public library, they had enough political clout to get the mayor to bring her before the board. Preachers from the other churches sat in the second row. David saw Deacon Clement standing across the room from him.

The chairman cleared his throat. "This special meeting of the Ty Ty School Board will come to order." People strained to hear. "Uh, due to the . . . gravity of the situation, we've, uh, asked Judge McCoy to preside." He handed the gavel to the judge, and sat. The chairman was not happy, but he was a politician who had learned to conceal his true feelings. The mayor and Reverend Fletcher had made it clear that he must agree to this if he expected to be re-elected.

"Thank you, Mr. Chairman." The judge's voice filled the chamber. He was accustomed to speaking here, and he was ambitious. He was going to make sure people heard him and understood who was in charge tonight. "Reverend Fletcher, would you invoke the blessing of Almighty God upon this assembly?"

Reverend Fletcher offered an invocation. He did not sit down after the "amen," however, but kept talking.

"Last Friday, my daughter came home from school and told me that they were teaching that the Bible is full of lies, and

218

that children were reading books that they had no business reading, including this piece of trash by some uppity Englishman named Charles Robert Darwin." His lips curled and his voice became a snarl when he said the author's name. He might have been saying *Satan*.

He waved the copy of *Origin of Species*. "I have since removed this book from the library."

Judge McCoy was reluctant to silence the preacher, but the babble that arose from the audience gave him the justification he needed. He rapped his gavel, silencing the room. "Thank you, Reverend Fletcher. We are here to address charges that Miss Goodman is guilty of teaching the subject of *evolution . . .*" He stretched out the four syllables of that word, and managed to convey a sneer as he did. " . . . and that Mrs. Purcell has made *unsuitable books* available to children."

A young man leaned against a pillar near the front corner of the room. He could not see the faces of the School Board, but he wasn't interested in them. He wanted to see the faces of the mayor and Reverend Fletcher—whom he recognized as the real powers in the town. He wondered silently at the judge's words: *Charges? Guilty? Does he not know the difference between the School Board and his petit court? And the School Board has no jurisdiction over the library!* The young man turned his attention back to the proceedings.

"Reverend Fletcher, perhaps you should continue. Would you be kind enough to take the witness stand? Bailiff, would you swear in Reverend Fletcher?"

The *witness stand* was a vainglorious name for a small table and chair in front of the platform on which the School Board sat. The young man fumed, silently. *Witness? Swear in? The School Board doesn't have that kind of authority!* He watched as Reverend Fletcher was sworn to tell the truth.

219

Judge McCoy stood and looked toward the assembled people. "Reverend Fletcher, please tell us in your own words what happened last Friday afternoon."

"Thank you, Your Honor." The preacher turned toward his real audience—the townspeople who filled the room. "Last Friday, I was in my study working on my sermon for the following Sunday. The subject was to be *obedience to the will of God*. My daughter, Rebekah, came in. She was in tears. 'Daddy,' she said. 'Daddy, they said in school that the Bible was a lie and that God didn't create us!'

"She threw herself into my arms and cried her eyes out. I comforted her and sent her off to her mother. Then I started making telephone calls. It seems that there's a banned book in the library and Miss Goodman let one of her students not only read it but also report on it to the entire class. Thirty innocent children were exposed to an attack on their faith!" Reverend Fletcher spoke even more loudly than had the judge.

"When I learned that the boy who had done this was a member of my congregation—not a communicant, you understand—I summoned him and his father to a meeting with the Deaconate. The boy has recanted." Reverend Fletcher smiled at the boy seated in the front row. "But the damage had already been done, and the fault is not entirely the boy's. There are two women, entrusted with the minds of our children, who have betrayed that trust."

You smug, sanctimonious son-of-a-bitch, the young man thought. He scanned the faces of the audience. *And these people are eating it up.*

"Naturally," Fletcher continued, "I changed my sermon, and preached from Genesis."

Preached from Genesis. Stirred the pot is more likely. No wonder so many people came, tonight. The young man scribbled a few notes on his steno pad.

Reverend Fletcher waved the book, again. Before he could speak, Mr. Babb shouted, "That book ought t' be burned—"

The young man spoke. "Mr. Babb, the National Socialists are burning books in Germany and the Fascists are burning books in Italy. Are you suggesting that we should follow their example?" He knew that his argument was a straw man, an exaggeration, but he figured Mr. Babb wouldn't know that.

He was right. "Well, no," Babb stuttered. "But it shouldn't be in the hands of children. My son disobeyed me—"

"No sir," Jonathan interrupted. "You didn't tell me not to read it. You said it was something we—I guess meaning you and Mama—didn't believe. You said Mr. Darwin said mankind came from apes, and that's not what the book says—" The boy seemed to realize what he was saying and stopped, abruptly.

The young man stepped forward. His voice filled the room but without the harshness of the judge or the singsong whine of the preacher. "The book also says this, 'There is a grandeur in this view of life . . . from so simple a beginning endless forms most beautiful and most wonderful have been, and are being, evolved.' The book doesn't challenge God. It glorifies Him."

The judge rapped his gavel. "Who in tarnation are you, and why are you talkin' in our meetin'?"

"I am Charlie Lowder and I'm speaking because someone has to stand up to superstition, ignorance, and bigotry."

"Did you encourage this boy to read that book?"

"I did not have that opportunity, Judge. He took it from the shelf himself, before his father wrested it from his hands."

"Huh? You saw that?" Mr. Babb blurted.

"Yes, sir, I saw it. And I looked at the book after you'd placed it on the table."

"I seen him talkin' to the boy!" a woman called from the back of the room. "I was in the library, and seen 'em."

"Is that true?" the judge asked. He was looking at Charlie.

"What? That she saw us? I can't answer that," Charlie said.

"Don't get smart with me or I'll slap you with contempt," the judge replied.

"Judge, this isn't your court, it's a meeting of the school board, which doesn't have the power to cite for contempt, and of which you are not even a member." Charlie folded his arms.

"I have been empowered by the school board to conduct this meeting," the judge asserted. "Now, answer the question, or—"

"You don't have the power to threaten someone, Judge."

"Boy, I have the moral authority . . . ." He sputtered to a stop when Charlie walked toward the bench.

"Judge, I respect your office, and the authority of that office which the people of this community have conferred on you. I respect the right of the school board to set the curriculum for the schools in this community. But I will not suffer the fate of Socrates."

Miss Goodman and Mrs. Purcell exchanged glances.

Charlie continued. "Yes, a few days ago I spoke to this young man in the library. I didn't know his name then. But I recognized him as the boy whose father I had seen wrest Mr. Darwin's book from his hands. The boy saw me reading a book on geology and asked me about it. I explained how index fossils were used to determine the relative age of sedimentary rock and how science had shown that the earth was as much as three billion years old. This answered his question about the theory of evolution—how evolution by natural selection, which would take billions of years to occur, could have happened."

"So, you admit that all this is just a theory?" the judge asked.

"The word 'theory' has a meaning that I believe you are ignoring, Judge. A theory is a comprehensive explanation of facts and observations that is accepted by science until and unless it is disproved. The Theory of Evolution explains everything we know about biology and is completely consistent with the sciences of paleontology and geology. Evolution does not need the intervention of a divine creator—except perhaps at the exact instant of creation."

"You admit to teaching blasphemy to a child, and to suborning his faith!" Reverend Fletcher challenged.

"There's no blasphemy in what I said. If your faith cannot stand up to the evidence of your senses, if your faith keeps you from seeing what lies all around you, if your faith closes your mind instead of opening your heart, if your faith is so fragile it rests on jots and tittles, then perhaps it is deserving of challenge and question."

"You're not from around here, are ya' boy?" The mayor finally figured how he could safely inject himself.

"Yes," Charlie said, "in a way, I am. Seven years ago, I broke your son's arm in two places when he tried to bully me. You called me Charlie Winter, then."

"You're Charlie Winter?"

"I'm Charlie Lowder, but that is the name Doc Winter lent me when I came here. When I first came to Ty Ty, I found some very fine people including Mrs. Hudson and Doc Winter. I found some pretty intolerant people, too. I hoped when I came back that I'd find more of the former, but it seems as if the town has been taken over by the bigots." Charlie turned and walked from the room.

No one noticed when David Sasq slipped down the stairs and ran after Charlie.

"Mr. Winter—I mean, Mr. Lowder?" David's voice was soft as the night. Charlie paused and looked back.

"Mr. Lowder? Please? May I talk to you?"

Charlie folded closed the steno pad and tucked his pen into a shirt pocket. "About what?"

"About what you said. About . . . about what's real . . . and true."

"Who are you?"

"David Sasq. Of Sasq Farm."

"Little David? You were just a kid. Don't you remember? Doc Winter and I used to visit. Doc got stump juice from your Dad. Used it to make tinctures."

"Yeah, I knew who you were. Wasn't sure you'd remember me, though. Can I ask you what you were talking about?"

Charlie and David sat on the porch of the Sasq house until nearly dawn. David's father came out to find David asleep on the swing and Charlie about to fall from the rocker.

§ § § § §

224

The next Sunday in Edna's Diner the radio was tuned to the Tifton station. A tenor voice backed up by a steel guitar slid smoothly from note to note. The words weren't important: love unfaithful or unrequited, good times or hard, Christian faith or sins of the flesh. Edna had decided a long time ago that she had heard every story that could be told. "Nothin' new under the sun," she muttered as she filled the salt and pepper shakers, getting ready for the Sunday lunch crowd. "Nothin' new under the sun."

The community was being torn apart by an argument over evolution, and folks had turned to their churches for an answer. The Gospel Truth Church was always full. This Sunday was no exception. For his sermon, Deacon Clement had taken Ecclesiastes 1:9, *The thing that hath been is that which shall be; and that which is done is that which shall be done: and there is no new thing under the sun.* He preached that this meant that God was all knowing and that nothing His children did could surprise Him. The deacon asked the congregation to look beyond the argument over evolution and the age of the world and to look for the wonder of the world as revealed to them by their senses. He encouraged them to open their hearts and minds to the notion that what was different wasn't necessarily evil, and that evolution wasn't heresy but another way of looking at things and trying to understand them. He told them that new knowledge shouldn't be of concern to people who had raised their children in the faith, and that if faith was strong, knowledge wouldn't challenge it.

"Questioning leads to knowledge, and in the end, knowledge can only affirm what is true," he said. "In the end, knowledge can only affirm your faith and the faith of your children."

The Berea Baptist Church was always full. This Sunday was no exception. The choir led the congregation in but a

225

single hymn: "All Things Bright and Beautiful." Deacons collected tithes and offerings before Reverend Fletcher began his sermon. He knew that's what the congregation wanted, what they came for, what they were waiting on.

"When Moses came down from Mount Sinai, he saw the Children of Israel worshiping an idol. An evil had risen among them, an evil that took the shape of a golden calf and crept into their hearts and minds and souls.

"An evil has crept into our Community of Believers, an evil that seeks to corrupt the hearts and minds and souls of our children. This evil slinks through garbage and filth. It slithers like the snake slithered up to Eve and tempted her. Adam and Eve were cursed for eating of the Tree of Knowledge. This new serpent pretends to offer new knowledge, knowledge that contradicts the Word of God. Questioning the Word of God is blasphemy!" Reverend Fletcher held up his Bible shaking it at the congregation as if he could sprinkle its words upon them.

"Open your Bibles to Ecclesiastes 1:9. *There is no new thing under the sun.* God made each animal and plant *in its kind*, and there is no new thing under the sun. No matter what this serpent says, there is no new thing under the sun. There is no such thing as evolution.

"This serpent pretends to offer knowledge, but what he offers is a pack of lies! He claims that his science has the answers. He claims that his science and not the Bible tells us the age of the earth. He claims that his science, and not the words of Genesis tells us of the glory of Creation."

Reverend Fletcher paused to catch his breath before shouting, "But for the Godly, it is enough to believe that the First Cause of the Universe and of all created things is the Lord! We believe in the authority of the Scripture, since greater is that authority than all the powers of the human mind!

"At first afraid to show his face, he tempted a child—a child of this Community of Believers—to do his work. He

226

tempted the child not with an apple, but with a book. Through his agent, a schoolteacher who is entrusted—entrusted! with the minds of our children, the blasphemy of that book was sown into their minds. The child has recanted. The schoolteacher, who was this Satan's tool, remains unrepentant—"

"Reverend Fletcher, that is a hateful thing to say!" Mrs. Ruth Simmons stood in her pew. "Miss Goodman is no more an agent of Satan than you are. And there isn't anything for her to repent."

"Woman! Know your place! I suffer not a woman to teach but to be silent. For Adam was first formed, then Eve. And Adam was not deceived, but the woman being deceived was the transgressor!" The preacher commanded.

Mrs. Simmons stood in silence for a moment and then sidestepped along the pew to the center aisle. She faced the pulpit. "I know my place, Darrell Fletcher, and it isn't where you preach hatred. *Faith, hope, charity, these three; but the greatest of these is charity.*" She turned, clasped her hands on her purse that she held like a shield in front of herself and marched toward the rear of the church.

Two pews behind where Mrs. Simmons had sat, Jonathan Babb shifted his weight again, trying to find a way to sit that didn't hurt. His father had used a harness-leather belt to beat the boy's bare bottom.

Before Mrs. Simmons could reach the back of the church, the preacher seized control, yanking the flock's attention back to the pulpit: "Let us pray," he thundered. The sheep bowed their heads. "Lord God," Reverend Fletcher began, "when You founded Your Church on the Rock that was Peter, You told him that whatsoever he bound on earth would be bound in heaven, that whatsoever he blessed on earth would be blessed in heaven, and that whatsoever he condemned on earth would be condemned to eternal damnation. As his successor through the laying on of hands and the Gift of the

Holy Spirit, I invoke that promise. Lord God, in your name, I curse Charlie Lowder and cast him into eternal perdition. I require of all Believers that they shun him, that they, too, cast him out of their lives. He came here years ago as a liar, an agent of that Prince of Lies. He came as a boy pretending to be someone he was not. He returned as a liar, revealing this time his true nature."

Mrs. Simmons closed the door of the church. The preacher's words rang in her ears. She strode briskly down the steps and continued walking.

She did not hear Reverend Fletcher pray for Miss Goodman and Mrs. Purcell and ask that God would show them the truth and bring them back to the fold. She did not hear his thanks to God for showing Jonathan Babb the light and for Jonathan's confession and recanting. Reverend Fletcher did not mention the beating which had taken place in his study in front of the entire Deaconate.

She did not hear Reverend Fletcher conclude his prayer, "In Jesus' Name, Amen."

A group of young men met after church at the Volunteer Fire Station. "You remember when he broke your arm?" one asked.

"You think I'd forget that, you stupid jackass?" Milky snorted. "He's gonna be trouble."

"He always was a trouble maker."

"Get the boys together," Milky said. "We'll show him."

"Don't we need to ask Reverend Fletcher?"

"He appointed me Chief Terror of the Klavaliers. We're supposed to do things like this. I don't need nobody's

228

permission, especially after what he said in church today," Milky replied.

Mrs. Simmons's warning reached Charlie in time. When the men in hooded white robes burned the house that had been Doc Winter's, Charlie was gone. With skills he learned as a youth and never had forgotten, he hopped a freight train to Albany.

Charlie spent the rest of his life moving from town to town, working as a schoolteacher during the winter and for the American Civil Liberties Union in the summer. He didn't teach biology, geology, or paleontology, but somehow, whether he was teaching arithmetic or English literature, he managed to work in the principles of Peter Abelard.

Charlie seldom held a teaching job for more than a year. For reasons that were never explained, school boards simply declined to renew his contract. He never saw the fruits of his labor, the seeds he had planted.

The welts on Jonathan's bottom faded, but the scars on his brain never did. When he was eighteen, he was charged with manslaughter for beating to death the girl he was living with. He spent the next few years in and out of jail and died after a brawl in an Atlanta bar. He was twenty-seven years old.

§ § § § §

Word got around that the Klan tried to kill Charlie by burning down the house thinking he was in it. Miss Goodman had been around forever, and taught just about everybody in Ty Ty, including everybody on the School Board, and there wasn't a person who hadn't, as a kid, gone to the library to hear Mrs. Purcell read poems from Mr. Stevenson's *A Child's Garden of Verses*. Neither the School Board nor Reverend Fletcher could find support for censuring Miss Goodman or Mrs. Purcell, but the copy of Mr. Darwin's book that Reverend Fletcher took from the library was never returned.

Deacon Clement's Visit

Calvin stuck his head under the spout while I pumped the handle. Then we switched places, and I let the cool water rush over my head. I stood up and rubbed my hands across my hair, pushing the water until it ran down my back.

"Come on, Calvin," I said. "We got to—"

"Who's that?" Calvin interrupted, and pointed toward the road. A dark figure stepped from the shadow of an oak and moved toward us.

I started to shrug like I didn't know. Then, the figure raised its hand and waved a wide, flat-brimmed hat. He fanned his face a couple of times and then put the hat on his head.

I snorted. "Who else? It's Deacon Clement. Come on. We got chickens to tend."

The bell hanging from the back porch summoned us to supper. After another rinse under the pump, we pounded up the steps. Mama was waiting for us.

"You boys put on shirts and shoes. Deacon Clement's staying for supper."

Daddy was waiting in the upstairs hall, grinning. "She made me change my shirt," he said, adding unnecessarily, "Don't dawdle; supper's ready."

Calvin saw only the positive side of the Deacon's visit: supper included both fried chicken and ham. I knew, however, that after supper I would be told to take the Deacon to the parlor while Mama and Calvin cleaned up. Daddy would find something to keep himself away, and the Deacon and I would be left alone. I was right.

"Little David? Please take the Deacon into the parlor while Calvin helps me fix dessert," Mama said. "Big David? Would you grind some coffee?"

"How have you been, David? It's been a spell." Deacon Clement began the conversation.

"Exactly fourteen days, Deacon," I replied. "It was the Thursday after Joey's funeral. We had pork chops and pecan pie. Calvin ate two pieces of pie and was up all night with a stomachache. You asked me if I thought about Joey, and I told you I thought about him every mornin' when I woke up and every night 'fore I went to sleep. I still do." Joey's memory lived inside me like a tapeworm eating its way through my gut, but I didn't say that.

The Deacon's eyes, which had been fixed on me, dropped to his feet. I saw a bead of sweat on the man's upper lip, but that may have been the heat. It was unseasonably warm for October.

"David, you know your mama asked me here to talk to you. And you know she'll leave us alone for at least half an hour." The Deacon hesitated. "What would you like to talk about?"

I didn't hesitate. "Last Sunday, after Charlie Lowder went to that meeting in the City Hall, Reverend Fletcher and you preached your sermons from the same verse. It's in Ecclesiastes. *There is no new thing under the sun.* But you said different things about it. How can you do that?"

232

Deacon Clement's eyes widened. He paused before he spoke. "The Sunday after Joey's funeral, your mama told me you wouldn't be coming to preaching for a while. Did she tell you about my sermon? And how did you know about Reverend Fletcher's?"

I grinned. "I asked. I ask every Sunday what you preached about. Calvin tells me, and he's pretty good at the tellin'. And Aunt Helen always finds some reason to tell me what Reverend Fletcher has to say."

I sat back in the chair and looked at the deacon. "Usually, it ain't . . . isn't all that interesting, but this time, it is."

"David, that's a serious question. You asked me a serious question after Joey's funeral, and I couldn't answer it. I have been thinking on it, like you said I should. I still don't have the answer. But I'm still thinking on it."

He looked at the floor for a minute. When he looked up, he laughed. It was the first time I remember him laughing. "I heard what Reverend Fletcher preached, and I heard what happened, after."

I knew he meant about the Klan going after Charlie, and Charlie disappearing before they could get him.

"David, I don't know if I'm smart enough or if I know enough to give you a good answer about the difference in the sermons, but I'll try. Your grandfather went to a real Bible college, one of the best in the South. I'm sure he had some fine teachers, and he's been very successful at that big church and with his radio program. The Bible School I went to wasn't even a real school. It was four young men who boarded in the home of a retired preacher and his wife. Our classes were held in his parlor. We had only one book—the King James Bible. We didn't learn Greek or Aramaic, like your grandfather did.

"I'll never forget the first lesson that Reverend Rosemon—that was his name—Reverend Rosemon taught us.

He had us open our Bibles to Matthew 5:2 and read the words just before the Sermon on the Mount: . . . *and he opened his mouth and taught them.* Then Reverend Rosemon told us that our calling was not to preach, but to teach. He told us that if we were going to teach, we'd have to learn ourselves, that we would have to make a commitment to learn for as long as we lived.

"He also told us that we should always question what we saw and heard and read, because only when we question something do we truly learn it. He surprised us when he said that we should be cautious about errors, even in the Bible. And he told us that we should be careful of the words we used, because words carry a lot more than meaning. They can carry a lot of emotion, too."

"Wait a minute!" I said. "That's what Charlie Lowder told me!"

"When did you talk to him?"

"After the meeting about Mr. Darwin's book. I followed him out, and he came here. We talked all night on the porch. He told me about Mr. Abelard, who had written that we should always question and doubt before we could learn, that we should always use words the right way, and that we should be on the lookout for people trying to fool us. He said it a little better than that, though."

I hesitated, and then said, "Mr. Brown's told me the same thing."

Just then, Mama brought coffee for the deacon and plates of pie for us both.

"You all getting along?" She asked. She looked at the deacon when she spoke and seemed surprised when I answered.

"Yes, ma'am. We're having a pretty good talk."

234

Mama raised her eyebrows, then shooed Daddy, who had started to come into the parlor, back to the kitchen with her.

After he took a bite of pie, Deacon Clement kept talking.

"Thank you, David, for saying that to your mother. But I've not answered your question."

I'd almost forgotten that.

"I believe that the Bible was written by holy men, inspired by God. I believe that the men who created the King James Version were inspired, too. But I'm not entirely sure that their translation was accurate. I think they sometimes sacrificed accuracy for some of the beautiful language they created. And I'm sure that God meant for us to read the Bible prayerfully and to listen to His voice—or our hearts and minds—to know what the Bible really means. I don't believe that there are any hateful messages in the Bible, and what Reverend Fletcher was preaching was pure hate.

"I'd be obliged if you'd not tell anyone I said that," he added.

Deacon Clement had finished his pie. He picked up his coffee cup and took a long sip. I think he did it to give himself—and me—time to think.

"No, sir. I promise," I said.

"David? What you said about words being important. Is that why you borrowed that book on rhetoric from Miss Goodman?"

"How do you know that?"

"Because, David, just as you ask Calvin about my sermons, I ask people about you. Last week, Miss Goodman told me about the book. She said you wanted to be a writer. Is that right?"

"I've not told anyone but her," I said. "Yes. Ever since I read *The Sword in the Stone* and *The Hobbit*, I've wanted to write something like that."

I think Mama was surprised when I walked down the lane with Deacon Clement. She probably couldn't see me shake his hand before he turned and headed down the road.

It was that night when Deacon Clement and I came to an understanding. I had surprised him when I said I'd asked about his sermons. He had surprised me when he said he'd talked to Miss Goodman about me. He had shared some important things with me—including his opinion of Reverend Fletcher. I had shared something important with him—my ambition to write. We had agreed on questioning and doubting. And we'd been civil to one another. We knew that we were going to disagree on a lot of things, important things like whether God was real or not and whether Joey was in heaven or hell, or was just dead. But maybe, just maybe, now we could at least talk about them.

Jesus Saves

"Folks say Brother Clement's got ambition," Sister Samantha said.

"Folks say more than their prayers," Sister Elizabeth answered, and the Wednesday morning quilting circle of the Gospel Truth Church officially started. The six women ranged in age from merely old to ancient. The circle, itself, was much older; it had survived the Civil War, although the sanctuary and fellowship house had been burned by Yankee soldiers. The sanctuary had been rebuilt, but fellowship took place around an outdoor barbecue pit or in the churchyard. The quilters met in the home of Sister Samantha who had the only parlor big enough for a quilting frame.

Sister Samantha was not only the hostess and leader of the quilting circle, but also Ty Ty's biggest busybody, with her nose in everybody's business. The last time someone had taken her to task for gossiping, she'd asserted, "It's because I care about people." *Maybe so,* thought Sister Amanda who had been there to hear it. *But it's always somebody else who makes the casseroles and visits the sick.*

"Well," Sister Samantha said, bringing attention back to Brother Clement and herself. "Ever since that Sasq boy's funeral, he's been preaching like Jesus was coming, tomorrow."

"No one knows the hour or the day," Sister Laura said.

237

"Amen," Sister Ruth added.

"Now, ain't you two all pious this morning," Sister Samantha said. She smirked. "The last person who'd know when Jesus was coming would be Brother Clement."

"Did something happen at the funeral?" Sister Rebecca asked. She was the youngest member of the circle. She and Martha Yount, the dead boy's mother, had never gotten along, not since Martha had married Big David Sasq out from under Rebecca. Rebecca had settled for Alvin Jackson who had joined the Army and then been killed in the Philippines. As the widow of a fallen soldier and the recipient of a government pension, she was set, both socially and financially. But, she still didn't like Martha Yount Sasq.

"Not at the funeral, likely after," Sister Samantha said. "Heard tell Brother Clement and the Reverend Yount had quite a long talk." The women's lips tightened. Rebecca may not have liked Martha, but none of the women liked her father. He'd been the first boy from the Ty Ty high school to go off to college. Now, he preached in the big Baptist church in Athens, and had his own radio show. It could be picked up on a winter evening after the Tifton station had signed off the air. There wasn't a person in Ty Ty who hadn't listened to it at least once.

"You don't think Brother Clement wants to go to college," Sister Ruth said.

"Brother Clement ain't got the choler for it," Sister Samantha said. "He's never finished anything he's started."

"What do you mean by that?" Sister Ruth asked.

"You all know he was spoonin' with Edna Sims for more than five years and never once asked her to marry him," Sister Samantha said. "She went and eloped with that railroad feller. Mighty peculiar, I say."

"Well, I guess—" Sister Ruth began.

238

"And he's got no gumption," Sister Samantha interrupted. "He wouldn't even stand up to that awful Carson Ord when he came into the church drunk."

"Well, but—" Sister Ruth tried to speak, again.

"An' speakin' of drunk, you know Brother Clement takes the train to Sylvester and back most every Friday, don't you? An what do you suppose is in Sylvester but a liquor store." Sister Wicker's face and voice were smug.

"Why Samantha, what a thing to say," Sister Ruth said. That's plain un-Christian! His mother lives in Sylvester!"

Sister Samantha's face turned red. "Ruth, don't you talk to me like that in my own dining . . ." Her face turned redder, and then pale. She slumped in her seat. Her head fell forward and banged softly on the quilt frame. Jesus had come for Sister Samantha.

Oh dear, Sister Ruth thought, *where will we meet, now?*

Encounter with Granny Meeks

Sam Brown had put in a gasoline tank and a pump, and Springer Produce was now Springer Gas and Produce. I was walking home from working there and had just reached the Old Sylvester Road when I saw Granny Meeks coming toward me. The sun was behind her, and she wasn't more than a silhouette; but I recognized her because she always carried a carpetbag and wore a poke bonnet. She saw me before I could get away.

"Davey-boy, you're runnin' afore your horse. Don' be so fast to turn away," she called.

I walked to where I could stand in the shade of a poplar tree while I waited for her.

"Howdy, Granny." I didn't say it very loudly, and I guess she thought I was being sullen or something because she snapped at me.

"I'm Mrs. Meeks to you, Davey-boy, and look at who you're talking to. I know your mama raised you better 'n that."

Granny Meeks walked to where I was standing and leaned against the tree.

"Heard you and the Deacon had quite a talk," she said.

"What did he tell you?" I felt betrayed that he would have told someone what we'd said.

"He didn't say anything, Davey-boy. It was your mother, and all she said was that you and the deacon had a long visit."

"Oh. That's all right then. We talked."

"What's bothering you, Davey-boy?" Granny asked. "And don't say *nothin'*—I know you better than that."

So I told her. I told her about the sparrow, and about Joey not knowing Jesus, and what I'd figured out about heaven and hell and being dead.

"I still don't know why God made Joey the way he was, and then killed him. And I don't know where Joey is—if he's anywhere."

"I know, Davey-boy." Granny Meeks sighed. "For the rest of your life—on this earth, anyhow—you're gonna wonder why God made that particular sparrow fall. You ain't gonna find the answer in those books, though." She gestured at the stack of books. I had tied them together with an old belt. Its tongue stuck out like the serpent in Eden.

I looked down at the books, although I knew what they were: Kant, Rousseau, and Nietzsche. Mr. Brown had lent them to me.

Granny Meeks continued. "You ain't gonna find it in what Mr. Brown tells you either."

I looked hard at Granny Meeks, my eyebrows drawn together, my jaw clenched. "What do you know about that?"

"Don't worry, Davey-boy. Ain't nobody in Ty Ty as watchful as me. 'Cept maybe Mrs. Fletcher, and she ain't half as watchful as she'd like to be. I heard you and Mr. Brown talkin,' and I heard him tell you that man was the measure of all things. If he is, it's 'cause God made him. No, Davey-boy, until you let God back into your life, you ain't never gonna find what you're looking for."

I opened my mouth. I wanted to tell Granny Meeks that it was all wrong, that the Bible didn't make sense in a lot of places. I wanted to say that we shouldn't thank God for doing good things if we didn't blame him for doing bad things. But I didn't. "Thank you, Mrs. Meeks for the talkin'. I got chores, now. I'll tell Mama I saw you."

I grabbed the belt that held my books, and stood up.

"Mind that you do, Davey-boy."

Bible Bee

Monday was Bible Bee at the school. It was like a spelling bee, except it was Bible verses. When Mrs. Bullard, the Bible Teacher, got to our classroom the class was split in half. Our homeroom teacher, Miss Goodman, picked sides so the Baptists weren't all on the same team. We lined up on both sides of the room. Going down the line, one side after the other, each kid had to recite a Bible verse. If you didn't know one, or if Miss Bullard said you'd said it wrong, you had to sit down. The last kid standing got a prize, usually a pamphlet with more Bible verses.

Girls are smarter than boys in most things, and you'd think they'd be smarter in this too. You'd have been wrong. There were three boys who knew more verses than anybody. I reckon that between them they'd about memorized the whole Bible. Henry went to my folks' church, the Gospel Truth Church. He wore glasses that got thicker every year, and he read a lot. His favorite verse was the one about Jesus healing a blind man. We probably should have figured it out, but we didn't. Henry went blind before he was eighteen, and went off to the Georgia Academy for the Blind in Macon. I heard later that he was teaching Braille to blind kids.

Another boy was Peter. I guess it was in the fourth grade we boys figured out what else his name meant. We gave him a hard time for a while but stopped when we were a couple of years older, and Peter was the first one to kiss a girl. Peter's daddy was the preacher at the Berea Baptist Church. It was the biggest church in town and the one the mayor and all the city council went to. My daddy told me nobody could get elected to anything, even dogcatcher, unless Peter's daddy said it was all right. I thought that was funny, 'cause we didn't even have a dogcatcher.

The last boy was C.W., and he was the most unlikely of the three. His family was always in trouble. His daddy was in and out of jail—usually the county work farm but once the state prison in Valdosta. His older brother had been sent twice to reform school in Waycross, and the judge was just waiting until he turned eighteen so he could send him into the Army. And it seemed rheumatic fever ran in the family. Both his sisters had been sent to live with relatives in the mountains for six or eight months. We all knew it wasn't rheumatic fever. More like "romantic fever," if you asked me.

C.W. was a Bible-quoting machine. There was this little sneer in his voice that seemed to bother Miss Bullard, but when she looked sharply at him, he smiled, and she forgot whatever she'd been thinking. C.W. was a bright-yellow blond, and about the only boy in the class without crooked teeth. I guess he had a right good smile.

I'd about had it with the smirks Henry, Peter, and C.W. gave each other when the rest of us got told to sit down. I tried to figure out how I was going to put them short, but I knew I'd never remember enough verses. One day, I figured it out. I spent the next two weeks studying and memorizing. Mama thought I was finally getting over my little brother Joey bein' dead. I wasn't.

On Monday when my turn came I was ready. *"Let him kiss me with the kisses of his mouth, for thy love is better than wine.* Song of Solomon, 1:2." I didn't look at Miss Bullard, but I knew her eyes had narrowed. I think there were a couple of giggles from beside me. Across the room, Betsy Young blushed. I stuck that in the back of my head for thinking about later.

244

My turn came again. *"I am black, but comely, O ye daughters of Jerusalem, like the tents of Kedar, like the curtains of Solomon."* This time, I looked at Miss Bullard. She knew what I was doing, but she didn't know why.

His left hand is under my head, and his right hand doth embrace me, was followed by *Thy lips are like a thread of scarlet, and thy speech is comely; thy temples are like a piece of pomegranate within thy locks.*

"Sit down, David." Miss Bullard's voice cut across the room.

"The verse wasn't wrong, Miss Bullard. Would you like to hear it again?" I asked.

"Sit down!" she said.

"Thy lips are like a thread of scarlet, and thy speech is comely; thy temples are like a piece of pomegranate within thy locks," I said. "I know the next one, too. And the one after that. Do you know that one?" I asked. "Thy two breasts—"

"David Sasq! Be silent!" she demanded. "The Bible Bee is over. You are all dismissed for recess."

I started toward the door.

"Except you, David Sasq," Miss Bullard said.

Kids learn early that when an adult calls you by both your names, you're in trouble. The noise of the rest of the class trooping out to recess had brought Miss Goodman back into the room. The two women had a whisper at the front of the room. I pretended I wasn't interested and watched out the window as the rest of the class reached the playground.

Miss Goodman looked at me. "David, what on earth were you thinking?" She crossed her arms on her bosom.

There were two answers to that question. I took the safer one. "I was trying to beat Henry and Peter and C.W.," I said. "I memorized a whole bunch of verses. Those were the easiest."

"You would turn the Bible Bee into . . . into some kind of contest?" Miss Bullard said.

"It is, ain't it? And one of them three always wins. And Samantha is always the first one out because she only knows one verse, and that's 'Jesus wept,' and somebody always gets it before she does. And she cries. Every week. Don't you know that? 'Suffer the little children' don't mean to make 'em suffer. Now, if you don't mind, I'm going to recess." Before they said anything, I was out the door.

We never had another Bible Bee. Some folks said it was because Sammy Kindle's dad—he was the town atheist—had complained. But I knew better.

Airplane

The drone of a thousand angry bees woke me. Calvin was already awake and sitting up in his bed. "What's that?" he asked.

"Airplane," I said. I jumped from my bed and grabbed a pair of overalls. "Come on—hurry—maybe we can see it." I ran from the room with Calvin close on my heels.

The soft patter of the boys' bare feet did not wake their mother. Big David had heard the plane, and smiled as his imagination followed the eager boys down the stairs and into the yard.

"Look! There he is," I pointed to the south. The plane, a double-winged contraption, was about to disappear below the tree line.

"He's turnin' around." Calvin said. "He's comin' straight toward us!" He grabbed my hand and tugged at it like he was trying to pull me away. "He's gonna hit the barn!"

"Naw, he ain't," I said. Then I gasped as the plane flew inches above the barn's weathercock and dropped out of sight.

Calvin had let go of my hand and clapped his hands over his ears. When he uncovered his ears, there was nothing to hear. "He's landed in the pasture," I said. "Come on."

We beat Daddy to the pasture only by seconds. "I saw him from the window," Daddy said. He was dressed like we were, except that where we were bare-chested, he wore a blue work shirt; where we were barefoot, he wore brogans.

The plane sat at the far end of the pasture. It was a two-seater, with open cockpits fore and aft. The fabric that covered it, once a bright red, had faded to a dull, brick color. The pilot was standing on the lower wing, fiddling with something on top of the engine. He turned as we approached, and Daddy called out a *hello*.

"Hello, yourself, sir. This must be your pasture. I'm mighty glad it was here. I don't think there's three drops of fuel left. The engine quit before I rolled to a stop. Must have run into a headwind. I don't suppose you have a couple of gallons of gasoline?"

"As a matter of fact, I do," Big David said. "But the hose ain't gonna reach. What say we hitch that contraption to the back of the truck and tow it? You can see the tank—" He pointed toward the barn.

The pilot nodded, but before he could say anything, Big David added, "After breakfast, though. Calvin, you run ahead and tell your mama we have company for breakfast. Little David? Hurry on and do the milking. Both of you, scoot!"

Martha frowned when Calvin blurted the news. Like as not, Big David had a reason, though. She scooped another cup of flour from the bin and started a second batch of biscuits. "Calvin? Break a dozen eggs into that bowl. Be careful! No shells. An' wash your hands, first."

By the time the pilot had visited the necessary and washed his hands and face at the well, assisted by David's pumping, breakfast was ready. Martha served scrambled eggs, biscuits with butter and honey, thick slices of ham, and a pitcher of sweet milk, still warm from the cow.

248

§ § § § §

Mama kept the pilot's plate filled while making sure Daddy and Calvin and I didn't go wanting. The pilot ate with manners and didn't talk with his mouth full. When Mama offered him a fifth biscuit, he declined. "No thank you, ma'am. If I eat another bite, I'd be too heavy to get the plane to get off the ground. Those were mighty fine biscuits, though."

It had taken most of the meal to learn his story. He had taken off from Ellijay at three o'clock in the morning, planning to get to Valdosta by seven o'clock. "I figured on hitting Highway 41 about dawn, and following it south. I picked up a headwind somewhere. It slowed me down and the plane ran out of fuel. I was mighty happy to see your pasture, I'll tell you!"

"Why you goin' to Valdosta?" Calvin asked. Mama opened her mouth to scold him for being nosy, but the pilot answered too quickly.

"Going to be a big fair there starting Monday. I figure to make money by giving people rides. It's what I was doing in Ellijay."

Big David had seen his boys' excitement and watched their eyes light up when the pilot mentioned giving people rides.

"David, Calvin, you help your mama with the dishes, and then you can come out to help with the gasoline. Don't argue—!"

Breakfast dishes had never been cleared, washed, and dried so quickly. Daddy had just hitched the plane to his truck when we got back to the bottom of the pasture. Calvin and I walked alongside the plane as Daddy pulled it toward the gasoline tank near the barn. The hose was barely long enough to reach the filler cap on top of the engine, but it did reach.

"You boys ready for a ride?" the pilot asked. Calvin and I must have looked like fools, standing there with our mouths open.

Daddy chuckled. "Captain Arnold and I made a deal—gas for the plane and a ride for you two. You do what he tells you, you hear? An' don't touch anything!"

The fabric may have been faded. The leather seat may have been cracked and leaking stuffing. The instruments in the front cockpit where we sat, strapped firmly to the seat by a worn leather belt, may not have worked. But in our minds, it was the most wonderful airplane in the world.

§ § § § §

Something about that plane resonated with Calvin. After that day, he ran to look every time he heard an engine. He saved up his allowance and bought himself a ride when a barnstormer came to the Tift County Fair. And, when he was seventeen, he joined the Army Air Corps. After the war, he joined the Strategic Air Command and was stationed in Great Falls, Montana. He fell in love with a girl and with the wide-open spaces of the west, and stayed on as her husband and a rancher. We exchanged Christmas cards, and I always sent a few dollars to my nephew and nieces on their birthdays. I was in Iraq, embedded with a Marine Ranger squad when Calvin died. I didn't find about it until long after the funeral. By that time, I was off to Afghanistan on another assignment, so all I could do was send a card.

Ushabti

It had rained the past two Decoration Days and Will Shackleford, the Sexton, had died. The cemetery was a real mess. Instead of flowers, we brought rakes, shovels, buckets, and brushes. Instead of Sunday clothes, the Children of the Confederacy wore work clothes. I tried not to snicker at the dark blue color and stiff creases in the bib overalls some of the Berea Baptist Church kids wore, fresh from Sears-Roebuck, and unlike anything they'd ever worn before. My overalls, and Calvin's, were faded, worn, and a whole lot more comfortable.

Avery was there. He was nineteen, now, and had just been hired as Sexton. It was hard on him, being crippled, but it also meant they didn't have to pay him a full wage.

I scrubbed the stone. The moss fell away easily to reveal the inscription:

Sgt. Matthew Gutson
Feb'y 19, 1828—July 12, 1863

Deacon Clement's boots appeared beside me. Without looking up, I asked, "Why is this one so clean?"

"It was put there only last year," the deacon replied. "He's not here, you know."

I snorted. "I know he's not here. Like Joey isn't in our cemetery." I didn't elaborate. Deacon Clement knew what I meant. *Joey isn't in heaven, either. Or in hell. He's just dead.*

"Sgt. Gutson's body isn't here, is what I meant," the deacon said. "He died at Gettysburg and is buried there. The stone is a cenotaph. Do you know what that is?"

I rocked back on my heels and looked up at the deacon. "Cenotaph. c-e-n-o-t-a-f—"

"C-e-n-o-t-a-p-h," the deacon interrupted. "It's Greek."

I spelled the word the right way. "Greek, huh?" Scenes from *The Iliad* flashed through my mind. "It's a memorial to someone who died but his body isn't here. Sgt. Gutson didn't come home with his shield or on it."

"You are right, David. Sgt. Gutson died of wounds received in the Battle of Gettysburg. He and several other Confederate soldiers were taken to a church that had been converted into a hospital. When they died, they were buried in the church cemetery."

The deacon chuckled. "Some of the members of the church weren't happy about Johnny Rebel bodies in their cemetery. A few of the men got together one night and dug them up, buried them somewhere else and never told where."

I stood and dusted off my hands. "Always . . ." I paused. "Always somebody making trouble. How come you know so much about it?"

"Sgt. Gutson left a wife and daughter. His daughter is my grandmother. His wife is buried here." He pointed to a nearby stone, still covered with moss.

252

I looked at the forsythia hedge and remembered what Aunt Helen had told me. "Do you know there's a slave cemetery behind the hedge?"

"Yes, David. I do."

"The Coloreds aren't allowed to use the white water fountain in the park. They have to go behind the fire department and use the tap back there. They can't use the restrooms in the train depot or any of the stores. They aren't allowed in the barbershop. If people don't want to be close to the Coloreds, why would they bury them so close?"

Deacon Clement looked right hard at me for a long time. "I've never thought of that, David. It's a good question." He hummed a little bit of *Just As I Am*, and looked at the forsythia.

"David, I've got a notion, but I don't know if it's right."

"That's all right, Deacon. I remember what we talked about questioning and doubting. I'll take what you say with a grain of salt. Shoot."

The deacon smiled. It was a genuine smile, I thought. "Do you know what a *ushabti* is?" he asked.

"I didn't even know that was a word!"

"It's not. Not English, that is. It's Egyptian, or how we think Egyptian was spoken. It means *answerer*. When the Egyptians buried their Pharaohs, they'd bury small clay figurines with them. These figurines were to become servants in the next life. When the gods wanted the Pharaoh to do something, he could call on his ushabti, who would answer, *I am here*.

"Most of the slaves who were buried here were house servants, the Mammies, the trusted men. I think maybe they were buried here to be servants, *ushabti* in the next life."

"What about in Matthew, when Jesus says in heaven people will not be given in marriage? Will they be given in slavery?" I thought it was a pretty good question, and the Deacon had a good answer.

"I think the part about marriage was supposed to mean that all bonds created on Earth would be dissolved, including slavery. These people," he swept his hands to mean all the folks buried on the white side of the forsythia, "these people didn't understand that."

The Daughters laid on more than punch and cookies this year. They had a regular picnic set up in the square. Before they let us to the tables, they made us wash up at the pump in the corner of the square. The boys took turns working the pump. Until it was Avery's turn. Avery had pumped for Darrel Fletcher, the preacher's kid, and then took his place at the spillway for the next boy to pump for him. "Not so fast," Darrell said. "You keep pumpin' for my friends."

There were only three boys left in line: boys who were Darrell's toadies. Avery shrugged, and pumped while they washed. As the boys turned to walk away, Avery asked, "Who will pump for me?"

"Nobody, crip!" Darrell said.

"I'll pump for you," I said. Neither Darrell nor Avery had seen Deacon Clement and me walk up.

"Yeah, *like and like,*" Darrell said. "Who let you in, anyway?" Without waiting for an answer, he turned and ran to the picnic tables.

"A whip for the horse, a bridle for the donkey, and a rod for the fool's back," Deacon Clement muttered. I jerked my head around and stared at the deacon. Deacon Clement winked.

Buggy Jugs and Other Mistaken Identities

I was walking home from the produce stand when I heard the chug-and-rattle of a car coming up behind me, then slowing down. "Come on, Davey-boy. Get in. I'll carry you home." I didn't have to turn around to know it was Granny Meeks. She was the only one who called me *Davey-boy*.

"Yes'm. Thank you," I called and walked across the road to where she'd pulled up. I started to undo the bailing wire that held the door closed, but Granny stopped me.

"Climb in, Davey-boy. You can skinny through the window, can't you?" She laughed. I wiggled in and bumped my feet against something on the floor.

"Why, Granny Meeks, you got a buggy jug down there. Wouldn't be 'shine in it, would there?" The clay jug between my feet was a low, wide version of the brown-and-white jugs the old folks used instead of Mason jars to hold moonshine. If Granny Meeks had been driving a buckboard or buggy the squatty jug couldn't have been seen above the sides of the wagon. It didn't matter in the Model T, though. She could have had a whole stack of jugs setting on the floor and nobody would have seen them.

"You got a quick mouth on you, Davey-boy," she said over the crashing of gears. "You got a mind to go with it?"

"Got straight A's in school last year," I said.

"That ain't what I mean, and you know it. What's Mr. Sam Brown been teaching you?"

"Huh?"

"Huh!" she echoed. "Mouth ain't so smart now, is it? I seen those newspapers he gets in the mail—*Socialist Workers' Weekly* and *National Socialist*—and I know you spend a lot more time there talking than workin'. What is he teachin'—"

"Mr. Brown isn't a socialist!" I said. "He told me a bunch of his relations have left Russia to escape from the communists, and what he says about the Reds is about how inhuman they are . . . about how inhuman people can be. As if I didn't know that, already."

"Now what are you down on, David?"

I looked hard at her. She hadn't ever called me *David*, before. "I'm thinking of what they did to Mr. Moss."

"That was three years ago. Why you thinkin' on it?"

"Got a letter from Joshua yesterday."

"He was the older boy, right?"

"Yes'm. He and I were about the same age."

"Was you friends?" she asked.

"We were working on it," I said. "He didn't want it much, mostly because he was afraid if somebody heard about it, they'd hurt him. Maybe his father, too." I couldn't say what was in my head—what had been in my head ever since Mr. Moss was murdered. *Did somebody find out that Joshua and I were friends? Is that why the Klan killed their daddy?*

Then like I'd had a dose of ipecac, I spewed it out. "Granny Meeks? Did I kill Mr. Moss? Did they find out that Joshua and I were friends?"

256

Granny Meeks didn't say anything right away. Then she said, *"By their works ye shall know them."* That was from the Bible, but it wasn't quite right. I knew better than to contradict Granny Meeks, though.

It was still light enough I could see her face. Her lips got tight for a minute. She clipped each word when she said, "What them rednecks did to Mr. Moss was more than inhuman, it was pure evil. But you didn't have nothing to do with it."

I wasn't sure if I believed her so it took me a minute to answer. "How do you know?"

"In the first place, Davey-boy it's more likely that they'd of killed Mr. Moss for blockading with your daddy. Oh yes, I know about that, but as far as I know, I'm the only one besides you and your daddy. That wasn't the reason they killed him, either."

It was comforting for her to call me *Davy-boy.* It made things seem more normal.

"No, they killed Mr. Moss because he didn't step aside on the sidewalk when Mrs. McCorkle passed. Mr. McCorkle tried to make something of it at the time, but Mr. Moss wouldn't speak. He just kept walking."

"No shi—" I stopped myself in time. At least I thought I had.

"There's that smart mouth . . ."

"I'm sorry, Granny. But really?"

"Yes, Davey-boy. Really."

Right then the radiator boiled over and a plume of steam shot up from the front of Granny's car. She pulled over and shut down the motor.

"We'll set till she cools a mite," Granny said. "Then you can pour some of the water from that buggy jug into the radiator." She grinned at that, knowing I thought she had 'shine and she'd caught me out. I had to smile back, and kind of ducked my head like I was embarrassed. She knew I was foolin', but she was a good sport about it.

"Granny? Darrell Fletcher said that the Sasqs were cursed—"

"That Fletcher boy? Far as I'm concerned, he's got nothin' to say and keeps on sayin' it. An' I know you don't believe in bein' cursed," Granny said.

"No, not for a minute. But I want to know why Darrell believes it."

"What did that boy say? All of it."

"He said Grampa Yount had sinned, and was cursed and we was cursed unto the seventh generation. He said his mama had told him."

"That story's been around for a lot of years," Granny said. "I guess you're old enough to hear it."

She pulled out her corncob pipe and stuffed it with rabbit tobacco.

"Your mama's daddy was a right handsome young man, and his family had money. There was plenty a' girls who was heartbroken when he took up with your grandma. There was talk of him spoonin' with a bunch of different girls. I think most of that was made up out of wishes and moonlight comin' in their bedroom windows on a spring evenin'. There was talk of him getting some girl in trouble. You know what that means, don't you, Davy-boy?"

"Yes'm. Like Samantha." Samantha only knew one Bible verse and didn't know enough about the birds and the bees. She'd wound up pregnant.

258

I hoped that the gloaming hid my blush. "Who's the daddy of her baby?" I really didn't expect an answer, so Granny surprised me.

She looked at me, and squinted. "People will know soon enough, I reckon," she said. "But you don't be saying, yet. Some secrets are best kept."

I nodded. I guess that was good enough. "Your friend, Bobby Gordon. As soon as Samantha's on her feet, her daddy's taking them to South Carolina to get married."

Granny lit her pipe and puffed it for a minute, before getting back to why the Sasqs were cursed. " 'Spect most of those stories were made up. But it only took a couple of people to believe 'em strong enough to start rumors. It never surprises me what Christian people can believe that ain't in the Bible, and how they can forget the Great Commandment."

"Huh?"

"Davey-boy, I thought you was smarter than that. The Great Commandment is, *Love thy God and love thy neighbor.* Them gossips, including Mrs. Fletcher, forget that, sometimes."

Granny chuckled. "Once she starts gossiping she don't know how to hush. All this happened more than 30 years ago, before your grampa went off to that Bible College in North Carolina but some of the women, they still talk about it."

§ § § § §

Mrs. Fletcher, Mrs. Hudson, and Mrs. McCorkle sat in the shoofly early on a summer evening. Their husbands were across the street at a meeting in the Volunteer Fire Department. That the meeting was of the Klan and not of the VFD was an open secret.

"Pretty night." Mrs. Fletcher sat on the front edge of the bench. Both her feet were on the floor. As proper for the preacher's wife, her dress was closed to her throat and hung below the top of her high-button shoes. Her hands lay folded in her lap.

"Hot, though," Mrs. McCorkle said. She wore a light cotton dress that revealed a little too much *décolletage* to Mrs. Fletcher's way of thinking although she'd never say that word aloud, much less say "bosom."

"At least the no-see-ums aren't bitin' up here," Mrs. Hudson said. The shoofly was just high enough off the ground to discourage biting insects.

An acrid smell caught Mrs. McCorkle's attention. The men's meeting was over. "George McCorkle, you take that see-gar over to the far corner!" Without waiting to see if her husband had heard her, she leaned against the trunk of the tree and waved her funeral home fan a couple of times.

"Getting a lot of these," she said. Seeing the puzzled looks on the others' faces, she added, "Funeral home fans. This is the fourth one this year, and it ain't even June, yet. Mildred Goodson, right after the new year. You know her husband Frank was gassed in the Great War, don't you?" she added.

"Is that why he and Mildred never had children?" Mrs. Hudson asked.

"Oh! I never thought of that. Don't know. And then William Russell and that lovely wife of his. She didn't last two weeks after he died. And only last week, Nana Hopkins. She looked right pretty for an 86-year-old. And that doesn't even count the little Sasq boy," added Mrs. McCorkle, concluding the list. "What was wrong with him, anyway?"

"He doesn't count," Mrs. Fletcher said. "He died last year. And I heard he was witched at birth. Never did grow to more than a baby. Oh! Maybe that's why the Goodsons didn't have children—they was witched, too!"

"Constance Fletcher, I don't see how a Christian woman can believe in witching," Mrs. McCorkle exclaimed.

"There are witches in the Bible." Mrs. Fletcher crossed her arms over her bosom.

"One," Mrs. McCorkle said. "The Witch of Endor."

"Call it what you want," Mrs. Fletcher said. "It was God's punishment on Lucille and Mildred and Martha Yount."

"What did they do to deserve that kind of punishment? How can you say—"

"Not them, their father. The sins of the fathers, you know, are visited upon the children unto the seventh generation," Mrs. Fletcher declared.

"That's a plum evil notion," Mrs. McCorkle said.

"It's in the Bible!" Mrs. Fletcher said.

The hard silence was broken only by a low laugh from the women's husbands, sitting on the base of the Confederate Memorial, enveloped in the cigar smoke that protected them from the insects. Mrs. Hudson tapped the funeral home fan on her palm. "What did Martha's father do, anyway?" The tension between Mrs. McCorkle and Mrs. Fletcher was broken.

"You have to understand," Mrs. Fletcher began. "I learned the truth of this from my mother, and she was known to be a truthful person."

Granny chuckled, and then said, "Mrs. Fletcher's mother was known to be the biggest gossip in town, and Mrs. Fletcher was getting to be just like her." Then she continued the story

"You all remember what Vernon Yount was like as a young man?" Mrs. Fletcher asked.

"Mighty handsome," Mrs. McCorkle said.

"I'm sure I never noticed," Mrs. Hudson said.

"Why you story-teller!" Mrs. McCorkle said. "You had your sights on him just like the rest of us!"

"He had money, too. His daddy owned the feed store," Mrs. Fletcher said. "Had a lot of brawn from totin' around those bags of feed. And he'd work in the summertime without his shirt on." She put the funeral home fan over her mouth as if to deny having said those words.

Mrs. Hudson snorted. It was a soft snort, but a snort nevertheless. "Never had call to go to the feed store. Wouldn't have been seemly."

"Saw him when you walked by, I suspect," Mrs. Fletcher said. The other women's nods were nearly lost in the gathering darkness.

"About the only place we girls could get close to him was in Sunday School or at a church social. There was many a Presbyterian and Methodist mama who had to put her foot down to keep her daughter from becoming a Baptist." This brought a chuckle from Mrs. McCorkle and a smile to Mrs. Hudson.

"We Baptist girls would dress as prettily as we could."

"And pinch our cheeks scandalously to bring up color," Mrs. McCorkle interrupted. Mrs. Fletcher thought of denying that she'd ever done such a thing.

"Vernon Yount was as clever as he was handsome, and he knew what was going on. He'd slick down his hair and put

262

on a new celluloid collar, and dress himself up right fine. For a long time, he pretended to be friendly to all of us—"

"Constance Fletcher, we know all this. Get to the point!"

"You hold your horses, Joyce McCorkle," Mrs. Fletcher bit off the words. Then, her voice softened.

"It turned out that he was making eyes at Marilyn Lafferty. Don't know how they arranged it. Some say she was sick, and left the church supper early. Anyway, she disappeared right after the supper, and so did he. Three months later, she and her family left Ty Ty and never came back."

Mrs. Fletcher lowered her voice. "Those who knew said she was pregnant with Vernon Yount's baby. And that's the curse that was visited on Martha and Lucille and Mildred Yount."

The three husbands had finished their cigars and walked to the shoofly. Each of them had heard the end of Mrs. Fletcher's story. Only one felt his heart race. He knew it was Vernon Yount who had left early because he was sick, and that Marilyn Lafferty had gone behind the hardware store with him that night.

"Andrew Hudson? Where in tarnation are you?" His wife's voice interrupted his thoughts. "I'm ready to go home."

§ § § § §

Granny squinted at the thermostat on the radiator cap. "It's cool enough, but you be careful takin' the cap off."

I climbed through the window and took the jug she handed me. I slung it over my shoulder, and mimed drinking from it. She laughed.

263

I looked up in the Bible the part about sins of the fathers being visited on the children. Mrs. Fletcher was right except for the number of generations. If the story were true, if Grampa Yount had really sinned, then Mama was cursed. So was Joey—and Calvin and me, and our kids and maybe their kids. And that just wasn't right!

I wanted to hate God, but I realized: if I were going to hate him, I'd have to believe in him, and I wasn't sure I believed in him any more.

Truth or Consequences

After years of drought a wet spring and summer were welcome, although some farmers complained that the fields had been too wet to plow. They managed somehow and now were hoping that the rain would let up before their bumper crops of corn, beans, peanuts, and sorghum cane rotted in the fields. Besides the farmers, the folks who benefitted most from the rain were the boys. Swimming holes that had been pretty much dried up for a couple of years were full, and we had scrambled to replace the rope swings that had been neglected for so long. Of course, most of us had chores and not much time for swimming. However, by unspoken agreement, during the summertime we were excused from Wednesday night prayer meeting. Most of us managed to spend Wednesday afternoon and evening at a swimming hole.

Not everybody did—or could. If you'd misbehaved since Sunday, your folks might think you needed another dose of preaching. Every once in a while, one of the churches would have a covered dish supper on a Wednesday. All the boys who went to that church—and anyone else who could wrangle an invite—would go to that before anything else in the world.

We figured that was why C.W. didn't show up that Wednesday. Now, don't get me wrong: C.W. didn't go to any church. In fact, my mama said his family had been thrown out of about every church in these parts. But C.W. did have a way about him. He could get himself invited about anywhere—

unless a girl's folks found out about it, in which case he was likely to be uninvited real quick.

Like I said, nobody made anything about C.W. not being there, and I didn't think anything of it until he showed up at my folks' house before sunrise the next morning. At least that's what I figured when I went outside and found him asleep on the back steps with dew on his hair and eyelids.

"C.W.? What in tarnation?" I nudged him awake with my toe. He woke up right fast. I'd never seen anybody look so scared. Then he must have figured out where he was, 'cause he calmed down. A little.

"David, you gotta tell 'em I was with you last night," he said. "You just gotta!"

"But you wasn't," I said. "And what do you mean, I gotta?"

"David, please! My brother and me, we broke into your uncle's hardware store last night. He stole a rifle." C.W.'s voice shook. "Somebody seen us. He got caught, but I got away. He won't tell on me, but . . . ."

He took a deep breath. "David, I don't want to go to jail! I'm scared. Oh, God, I'm scared! If you tell 'em I was with you. Please?"

"We ain't friends," I said.

"That's why they'll believe you," he said.

I thought for a minute.

"Wait here." I went inside and got my shotgun. I got back outside and whistled for Blue.

"Come on," I said. "We been coon huntin' all night. Didn't find any. That's all we say to anybody, you hear? Come

266

on, we gotta get into the woods 'fore my folks and Calvin wakes up."

§ § § § §

Daddy gestured me to follow him onto the porch after supper, then to set in the swing beside him. After seventeen years, I thought I'd pretty well figured out his moods, but this was a different one.

"David, you know you're not supposed to go out huntin' without tellin' me," he said.

He said that slow and quiet, then sat in the swing. He was waiting for something, and I knew what it was.

"I wasn't hunting," I said. "I didn't leave until dawn." I blurted out the whole story. When I finished, I was trying mighty hard not to cry, and almost doing it. Still, some tears trickled down my face and I hiccoughed a couple of times.

All Daddy said was, "Um, hum."

We sat there. It started getting dark. Calvin came outside after helping with the dinner dishes, but Daddy waved him back inside. I was glad it was dark enough that Calvin couldn't see my face. I was too old to be crying.

"What are you going to do about it?" Daddy asked.

Now I was crying like I hadn't cried since Joey died. Daddy grabbed me and pulled me to his chest and let me cry for a little.

"That's enough crying, now," he said. "You start feeling sorry for yourself, and cry enough, you start liking the feeling of feeling sorry for yourself."

Daddy hugged me and then turned me loose. "You are feeling sorry for yourself, aren't you?"

I wiped my eyes and sniffled a couple of times. "Yes, sir. But, I'm not feeling sorry 'cause I did wrong. I'm feeling sorry 'cause I don't know what to do! I can't tell on C.W.!"

I hoped Daddy would come up with the answer, but he didn't. He made me think it through. We talked about truth. "Something isn't true 'cause we want it to be true," he said. "Something's either true or not. If it's not true, it's a lie."

"Is it always wrong to lie?" I asked. "What about Mama telling Miz Clampert she played good at the service when she always misses a bunch of notes? An' what about in the Bible, when it says God sent a *lying spirit* to lure a king onto the battlefield where God knew he'd be killed?"

Daddy didn't answer for a few minutes, and I thought I'd made him angry. But he chuckled.

"You know I can't answer the first question, and I'm not even going to try to answer the second one. You talk to Deacon Clement about that one," he said.

"But you know well and good that lying for your friend and lying to Miz Clampert about her playing ain't the same, don't you?"

"Yes, sir."

We talked some more. I convinced myself—and explained to Daddy—that C.W. was scared enough, and maybe sorry enough, that he'd not do something like that again. I convinced myself that Uncle Frank had gotten back the rifle that had been stolen from his store, and other than the broken lock, no harm had been done. I convinced myself that C.W. didn't have a family that showed him what was right and wrong, so he should get a break. I convinced Daddy that I shouldn't tell on C.W.

I didn't convince Daddy that I shouldn't be punished, though. It took a couple of weeks for him to come up with what he thought was the right punishment. He told Deacon Clement that I'd dig the pit for the new necessary at the church. The digging wasn't too bad. But then I had to fill in the old one.

While I was doing all that, I thought a lot about truth and consequences and about what's really right and wrong. C.W.'s brother didn't tell on him, and C.W. got away with it. C.W. and I were friends for a while, but we drifted apart. I guess a lie wasn't a good reason for a friendship. Still, I cried when I heard he'd died in the war.

Induction Center

After Pearl Harbor, Daddy and I talked about what I should do when I turned eighteen and could enlist. Then, we found out that if he signed for me, I could enlist early. We went to the Selective Service office in Tifton, and did all the papers. Two weeks later, I got the letter when to report: Wednesday, April Fools Day, 1942.

There was only one streetlight burning when we reached the square. The others had been turned off to save energy for the war effort. Coal that didn't get burned in the electric plants could be used for the Navy, and the hydroelectric power from Tennessee had stopped coming to Georgia. The bus that pulled into the pool of light was painted olive drab, but if you looked closely, you could see the old letters under the paint: *Tifton Transit Company* and *Trailways*. The boys in the first couple of rows of seats were asleep. It had been 3:30 AM when the bus had left Tifton. It was 4:00 AM when the bus reached the square in Ty Ty where five boys and five sets of parents waited.

Daniel was there. He used to drive the school bus. His two little brothers were there, too. One was asleep in his daddy's arms. The other was holding his mother's hand and yawning like he wanted to be asleep, too. C.W. was there. His older brother was already in the Army, sent there by the judge after his third trip to the youth detention center in Waycross. Bert, one of C.W.'s buddies, and Melvin were there, too. I was there with Mama and Daddy. Calvin was asleep in the pickup.

270

Mama cried softly. She cried often and easily since my little brother Joey had died just a year and a half ago.

A spare figure in a black suit stepped from the darkness into the pool of light cast by the streetlight. Deacon Clement put his hand on my shoulder and spoke quietly.

"David, I know you don't think much of God, but that doesn't mean you're a bad person. You don't have to believe in God to be good, you know."

The deacon caught my eye. "I'd be obliged if you didn't tell folks I said that. Not everybody would understand."

" 'Course not," I said. "I'm not sure I understand."

"Do you mind if I pray for your safe return?"

I looked around. I knew all the boys from school. Three of them attended the Berea Baptist Church, which stood behind us on the square. Rather than answer the deacon's question I pointed to the three boys. "Their pastor isn't here."

"No," Deacon Clement said.

"Will he be?"

The deacon looked at the line of boys preparing to board the bus and understood my question. "Never has, before."

"No, Deacon," I said. "I don't mind if you pray for me. If you have any prayin' time left over, pray for them, too, huh?" The deacon nodded, and stepped back into the darkness. I kissed Mama once more, shook Daddy's hand, and joined the line to board the bus.

§ § § § §

271

We slept mostly, waking briefly when the bus stopped in Sumner, Poulan, and Sylvester. We all woke up when the bus jolted across the railroad tracks outside of Albany, and again when it stopped abruptly at the induction center. If anyone were still the least bit sleepy, he woke quickly when a man in a wilted khaki uniform stepped onto the bus and yelled. "Wake up, meatheads. You're in the Army now. Step off the bus and form a rank with your toes on the white line painted in the parking lot. If you leave anything on the bus, it's lost forever. Now move it!"

"Um, we ain't had breakfast yet," a voice came from the back of the bus. It was Bert, one of the boys from Ty Ty.

"You won't be gettin' breakfast, either. Don't want you pukin'. You'll get fed lunch—later." The uniformed sergeant stepped off the bus and immediately began blowing a whistle and yelling. "Come on, come on, Hitler and Tojo ain't gonna wait, and neither am I, and I'm meaner than the two of 'em put together."

The induction station had once been a Catholic high school. There were crucifixes on the walls. For the first two hours, we were herded—some would have said, "marched," but they'd have been wrong—from one classroom to another. In the first, our name, height and weight were written onto a form that looked like a manila folder. In the next room, soldiers sitting at desks asked us questions like who was our next of kin and what color were our hair and eyes—like they couldn't look up and see that much for themselves. The third man was asking everybody what was their religion. I had a couple of minutes to think before I got to him. I thought about Joey. I thought about the things Grampa Yount had told me. I thought about my talks with Deacon Clement and Granny Meeks, and what Sam Brown had taught me. When I stood in front of the third soldier, I was ready.

"Religion?" the man asked.

272

"Ain't got one," I said.

The soldier looked up. "Are you sure that's what you want me to put down?"

"Yeah," I said. "I'm sure."

The sergeant who had met us on the bus took us into a hallway lined with lockers. Uniformed soldiers, a few wearing white coats over their khakis and stethoscopes around their necks, walked through the hallway. At the far end of the hall, a group of young men wearing only skin walked somewhat gingerly around a corner and disappeared. . "Holy shit," one of the boys whispered. "They's naked!"

"Find a locker that ain't full, strip, put your stuff in it, and remember the number," the sergeant ordered.

"Huh?" one of the boys said.

"I ain't gonna walk around nekkid!" Another said loudly enough for his voice to echo down the hallway.

"Shut your pie holes, and do what you're told," the sergeant ordered. "You ain't the first bunch of recruits and you won't be the last. This is an Army post, now. Do what you're told."

He relented. "This is the medical wing. Everybody here's a medic—doctor or corpsman. There's hundreds of guys come through here every month. You ain't got nothing nobody ain't seen before. Come on, make it easy on yourself."

Awkward, red-faced, goose-bumped, and nervous, we shucked our clothes and stuffed them in lockers. Most of us had been naked in front of other boys before—in the locker room at school, at a creek or lake where we skinny-dipped. But here, in the middle of a hallway, surrounded by strangers, it was different. Daniel blushed until his neck was redder than his hair. C.W. dropped his shirt and started to bend over to pick it

273

up before thinking better of it. He bent his knees and stretched his arm so he could grab the collar.

We sat in a classroom that had been turned into a waiting room. There were two groups of boys ahead of us, and already another one behind us. The room was supervised, if that was the right word, by a uniformed boy scarcely older than we were. He maintained control through a loud voice and the fact that he had clothes on.

"I am Private Williamson," he informed us when we had found seats. It was the same speech he would use to the group that followed us, and the one he'd said to the group that preceded us. "I am a medical corpsman. You will sit. You may talk quietly. You will be called one at a time into the doctor's office. You will stand on the white X on the floor and remain silent until the doctor tells you what to do. You will do what the doctor says. When he dismisses you, you will return to your seat here. When your group . . . ." the boy's voice droned on. I figured I'd have at least two more chances to hear what the boy had to say, so I let my eyes close.

"Hisst!" C.W. whispered to the boy from another group who'd come back from the doctor's office. "What did he do?" We'd already had someone look at our feet, check our eyes and teeth, and half-a-dozen other things.

"Listens to your heart and thumps your tummy. Looks into your eyes and ears, down your throat and up your nose. An' then—an' then, he grabs your balls and tells ya' to cough."

"Somebody grabs my balls an I'm gonna do more than cough," someone said.

"Wh'ch ya gonna do, kiss 'em?" another said.

"What if you ain't got balls?" Melvin asked quietly. Melvin was one of the boys from Ty Ty.

"Huh? Whadda you mean?" C.W. asked.

274

"Um, I ain't got any balls," Melvin said. "Doc Winter said they never descended. Said they was working, though, seein' as how I started shavin' last year."

"Holy shit," Bert said. "Let's see."

"At ease, people!" the corpsman's voice boomed. "You." He pointed to Melvin. "Your testicles ain't descended?"

"Uh, no, sir."

"You're Four F," the corpsman said. "Come with me."

Melvin stood on the white X in the doctor's office. The doctor had listened to Williamson, then dismissed him. Now, the doctor looked at Melvin. He saw a skinny young man with little spare flesh anywhere on his body. His ribs could be counted by looking at them. Arms and legs were thin, but muscled; the boy was accustomed to hard work. Most of them were. Feet were well formed but the toenails were ragged, like they'd been cut off with a pocketknife or torn off when they got too long. Hair on his legs and trunk was sparse, that on his arms thick. The hair pretty much followed the lines of his farmer's suntan. Nervous tension, the strangeness of the situation, and the chill of the air had shriveled his penis; the doctor didn't need to push it aside to see that the scrotum was empty. Nevertheless, he wheeled his chair toward the boy and reached out his hand. Melvin flinched. *Good reflexes*, thought the doctor.

"Son, I'm sorry, but you're Four F. That means you can't be in the Army. Don't worry, there'll be plenty for you to do to support the war effort. Go tell the corpsman I said to get you dressed, get you some food, and get you on the next bus back to . . ." the doctor looked at the manila folder. "Back to Ty Ty."

It was my turn with the doctor. I stood on the white X wearing nothing but goose bumps. The doctor looked over the manila folder that was the beginning of my 201 File, and frowned. "The religion block's empty," he said.

"Yes, sir, it's empty all right," I said.

The doctor looked up sharply. I knew what he must have been thinking. *Another farm* boy. I returned the doctor's gaze, and then shivered as the man's eyes swept down my body. "Let's see your navel, boy," the doctor said.

I looked down. "Um, it's right there, sir," I said.

The doctor took a cardboard stick with a little cotton on the end of it, stuck it in a jar, and then stuck it in my belly-button. I smelled the alcohol and shivered with the cold touch. "You ever clean this thing, boy?" the doctor asked.

"Uh, yes sir," I said. I was lying. Who ever thought to clean their belly-button?

"Your naval has a pocket in it. You must clean it every day. I don't know how you haven't gotten infected, before."

I jumped. The doctor had grabbed my scrotum.

"Turn your head and cough," the doctor said.

I did what I was told.

"You're done," the doctor said. "Don't forget what I said about your navel."

§ § § § §

Melvin appealed the Four F ruling and the Army sent him for an operation at the Finney General Hospital in Thomasville, Georgia. He became a medical corpsman,

276

spending the war traveling on troop trains that transported wounded soldiers from the New York port of entry to Army hospitals around the country. Bert was assigned to the infantry. He served in North Africa then in the invasion of Italy under General Mark Clark. He was wounded once. I got tapped for the Marine Corps and spent the next three years in the South Pacific. Daniel, the boy who had driven a school bus, got assigned to a transportation unit and lived until the Battle of the Bulge, when his truck rolled over a land mine. Of the two little brothers he left behind, one was killed in Korea, the other in Indochina.

C.W. became a chaplain's assistant—must have been all the Bible verses he knew. People said that was an easy job, just putting out hymnbooks and Bibles for services. C.W. was on the troop ship, the *Dorchester*, which got torpedoed in the North Atlantic less than a year later. Four Army chaplains on board gave up their lifejackets, and got famous for it. In 1948, they were on a commemorative stamp, and were posthumously awarded the Purple Heart and the Distinguished Service Cross. There weren't many survivors. Most of the men froze to death before they could be rescued. One of them wrote C.W.'s mama that C.W. gave his life jacket to a soldier, too, but he didn't get on a stamp, and nobody ever heard of him.

Sugar Rationing

Even after Prohibition was over, making moonshine was a big thing in Tift County. It was partly tradition, partly mistrust of the federal government, partly because it was a way to turn corn into cash, and partly—at least I always thought—partly the thrill folks got out of fooling the sheriff and getting away with something. My daddy did it because there was no way honest farming could give us everything Daddy thought we ought to have.

The best moonshine was made with one-quarter malted white corn and three-quarters cracked yellow corn. Some folks ran a second batch by adding a few hundred pounds of sugar to the left-over mash and cooking it again. My daddy never did. "The second batch? It's the stuff you give to your brother-in-law," he'd say. And laugh. I never understood why that was funny. All of Daddy's brother-in-laws, except my Uncle Neal, were Baptists, and teetotalers. I knew that Uncle Neal drank bourbon, 'cause he offered me some when I turned sixteen.

Calvin wrote and told me about the time Mama had sent him to the Piggly Wiggly one Wednesday during the war. Aunt Helen wrote me the same story. I was pretty lucky to get both their letters, being that I was on some island in the Pacific that was too little to have a name.

§ § § § §

278

"Hiram Wilkes, don't you be a'blowin' your automobile horn at me!" Miss Clampert stood, arms akimbo, and a frown on her lips. Her face was tight, drawn back by the bun that held her hair. "That's a stop sign over there. In fact, it's a four-way stop sign."

Progress, in the form of sixteen stop signs at the four corners of the square, had come to Ty Ty. Miss Clampert had waited in front of the Piggly Wiggly, tapping her foot on the concrete, until Mr. Wilkes had parked his car.

"Miz Clampert, that don't mean you gotta' wait until four people are stopped afore you can go," Hiram said. He tipped his hat as he spoke. "Can I hold that door for you?"

The woman stepped aside. "Thank you, Mr. Wilkes— but don't you be makin' fun of me. Yesterday somebody didn't stop and put a dent in the fender of Deputy Donaldson's car. I think the deputy enjoyed writing that ticket."

Wednesday was a busy day at the Piggly Wiggly. The weekly delivery came in on the five AM train. By six o'clock, while most folks were still asleep, Mr. Jackson and the two colored men who stocked the shelves had delivered it to the store. Even with ration stamps, there wasn't always enough sugar and coffee to go around, and people who could afford sugar and coffee tended to shop early. Plenty of folks had to do without. They'd learned to use sorghum and honey instead of sugar, and roasted acorns, ground up, for coffee. At the diner, Edna was stretching out the coffee with chicory, and she wasn't telling where she got her chicory.

By the time Miss Clampert arrived, a line had formed. She joined the line in time to hear Mr. Jackson speak. "It don't matter if you got twenty thousand ration stamps, I ain't sellin' you two hundred pounds of sugar." Mr. Jackson's voice carried throughout the store, like he'd planned. The folks in the line, mostly housewives, surged toward the single cash register.

"I got the stamps and I got the money and the law says you gotta sell—" John Pressley said.

"This is my store, and right now, this is my sugar," Mr. Jackson replied. His voice dropped slightly, but the women all heard it. "Law says I can't sell without a stamp. Law doesn't say I gotta sell."

Pressley opened his mouth, but before he could say anything, Jackson added, "If'n you don't leave, now, I'll tell the sheriff you was trying to buy two hundred pounds of sugar, and he'll find your still, no matter where you got it hid."

Pressley blanched, then stalked out of the store. "Very well, ladies," Mr. Jackson said. "I've got forty, five-pound bags of sugar ready to sell. One to a customer."

§ § § § §

Somebody must have told the sheriff about Pressley and the sugar. It wasn't three days later that the sheriff found the still. Pressley had a rifle, but the sheriff had two deputies with shotguns. Pressley died when a load of buckshot hit his chest.

Ty Ty 1999

"Easter Sunday, April 1, 1945. It was April Fools' Day, and we were fooled, all right. Members of the New 4th Marine Regiment easily walked ashore on Okinawa, and then we found ourselves in a hornet's nest as the real fighting began."

That's as far as I got in my first writing assignment. In September of 1945, after I was discharged from the Marine Corps, I enrolled in the University of Georgia on the GI Bill. The first writing assignment was a college freshman version of "What I Did Last Summer." We were to write five pages about something memorable in our life. I knew Okinawa was something I'd never forget, but I found that I couldn't write about it. I had a hard time just thinking about it. So, I wrote about Ty Ty, Georgia, the town where I'd lived until I joined the Marine Corps. Except for Paris Island and Camp Pendleton and a bunch of jungle islands in the South Pacific, it was the only place I had ever lived.

For most of the kids I grew up with, Ty Ty was the biggest town they'd ever seen. The farthest most got from home was the County Agricultural Fair on the other side of Tifton. The cities of Albany, Athens, and Atlanta were just crackly voices on the radio. A telegram or a long distance call meant that someone had been born or had died. Nothing of lesser importance was worth the cost.

For a long time, I believed that nothing changed but the seasons. The occasional baptism, wedding, or funeral seemed part of the cycle of things. My story cannot be separated from

Ty Ty and its cycles, even though I left as a young man and seldom returned . I wrote about Ty Ty for the next fifty years, in between assignments.

Before I even graduated from journalism school I was hired by a New York newspaper that needed a war correspondent in Korea. The wars in Indochina—Cambodia, Laos, and Viet Nam—followed Korea. For the next four decades, there was never a lack of wars to keep me away from Ty Ty and the USA.

§ § § § §

It is the eve of the millennium. It has been fifty years since we'd buried Mama next to Daddy and Joey, and I haven't been back since then. Now I am driving from New York to another cancer clinic, this one in Jacksonville, Florida. I'm on I-75, and seeing signs for Tifton. When they built the Interstate Highway, they'd made one exit for both Tifton and Ty Ty. I turn toward Ty Ty. It takes a while to get out of Tifton— they've moved the city limits quite a way to the west, and the road is lined with gas stations, fast food places, and title pawn stores. There isn't much country any more. The old highway is now four lanes but it's still called the Jefferson Davis Highway.

A little green sign on a pole beside the road tells me I've reached Ty Ty. Leaning against it is a piece of wallboard advertising a permanent yard sale at the house by the road. Just past the house with the yard sale is a house that's missing a bunch of siding, and which has a blue tarp covering half of the roof. There are three colored folks in the front yard—two men in shirts and blue jeans, and a bare-chested boy in gym shorts that hang off his hips and below his knees. Today is Sunday, almost noon. Back when, they'd have been in church. Back when, everybody would have been in church.

282

It's hard to pick out anything. They'd ripped the town apart when they ran the four-lane through the town square. There hadn't been much left to tear down though. The WPA-built City Hall had been demolished after the fire in 1948. The new one looks more like somebody's house than an official building, except that it has a drive-in window like a bank so folks could pay their light and water bills without having to get out of their car. It's made of cinder block instead of Jasper marble. It's fancy cinder block, but that's what it is.

The bank building is still there, looking solid, but with its windows and doors boarded up with plywood and *No Trespassing* signs plastered all over it. I guess people do their banking in Tifton now; although from the looks of things, the only banking most of the folks need to do is cash a welfare check.

There is still a Railroad Avenue, but the tracks were taken up a long time ago. I have a hard time figuring out where they'd been. The tracks had been important, back when it made a difference on which side of them you lived.

Ty Ty Creek is so overgrown with the Ironwood and Buckwheat trees—the ti ti trees that gave the creek and the town their names—that I hardly notice it. A mile or so up the creek is where my daddy's farm had been. This is home, the place I've carried in my stories and in my mind. I turn north on what had been the Ty Ty—Sledge road. It's a fire road, now, and the land is planted in pine trees. There are signs saying it belongs to one of the big paper companies. I pull off at a wide place in the road.

The air is cool under the ti ti trees, and smells strongly of the earth. I wonder where the time has gone. No, if I am to be honest with myself, I should wonder what I did with the time. I take off my shoes and socks and stand barefoot for the first time in decades in the black earth of the bottomland. Years of frost have heaved up rocks, scattered like knucklebones thrown by a careless child. To my left is the creek that ran between us and the Moss farm. I still call it that, even though

Daddy had bought it for taxes not long after Mr. Moss was killed. I didn't learn until later that for years he'd sent money to Mrs. Moss until he'd paid her a fair purchase price for it.

The swimming hole where Calvin, Joshua, Luke, and I swam is gone, scoured away by a flood like the one that created it. My imagination wanders up the creek to the cave where my daddy and Mr. Moss made moonshine. I cannot see it, but I know it's there. Way over to my right is where our house stood. There is no sign of it. Not even the bricks of the chimney. The locust trees Daddy planted when I was five are gone, but the oaks remain. Their branches touch the ground and lift again to the sky. I curl my toes, as if to draw memories from the ground. They come—bad and good.

I remember running across the bottom through the white corn to find the Moss home burned to the ground by the Klan, but I also remember walking across the creek, defying my daddy, to make friends with a black boy. *Whatever happened to Joshua?* He left Ty Ty when I was fourteen. He'd come back during the war and stayed at least until his mama's funeral in 1947.

I remember the scarecrow Calvin and I built, the straw sticking from holes in its shirts and the bandana Mama told me to tie around its neck. I remember the slingshots we made to chase away the redwing blackbirds that weren't afraid of the scarecrow and, after my fifteenth birthday, shooting a few with the shotgun my grampa had given me. I sigh and walk back to the car.

According to the auto club map, I have plenty of time to get to Jacksonville, so I decide to go to Edna's. I'd had breakfast at a truck stop on the north side of Atlanta and figure that a burger and a cola would make a fine lunch. I guess my brain was playing tricks on me. I should have known that Edna's wouldn't be there. At least not like I remembered it. After I left for college, Edna's daughter had turned it into a drive-in with carhops on roller skates. I guess it did pretty well in the 1950s and 60s. Now, it is dead—closed and falling down.

Neither of the schools is there, not since about 1970, when they'd built the consolidated county school and started bussing the kids an hour or so to get there. Some evangelicals had bought the school the WPA built and tried to run a Christian Academy. After about four years, that had been absorbed by a bigger Christian school in Tifton.

Ty Ty Produce is closed and looks like it has been for years. I know that Sam and Mrs. Brown are dead. I had waited until they were dead before I wrote the story about Sam being inducted into the KKK. I smile at that thought.

The grain elevator still stands by the railroad tracks. It had been run by the Farmers Co-op. By putting everybody's corn together, the co-op was able to get better prices and freight rates. Peanuts were another matter. There was a big processing plant in Savannah, and the co-op shipped peanuts to them, but the freight for unshelled peanuts got too high, so the co-op built a peanut processing plant, and pressed peanut oil.

Freight rates kept going up, and in 1936, the co-op went bust. The president of the co-op wasn't even a farmer. He had taken out a loan using the grain elevator and peanut oil plant as collateral. He said that all the money went back into the co-op, but the books were in such a mess that nobody knew for sure. Everybody took his word for it, though, since he was a deacon at the Berea Baptist Church.

The Superior Court judge in Tifton gave the peanut plant to some people in Macon who held the loan, and they ran it for about a year before they missed the payroll one Friday. On Monday, the folks who showed up for work found the doors shut and chain-locked. During World War II, somebody re-opened the peanut processing plant to make peanut butter for the government. A lot of our military ration packs had a can of peanut butter in them. Every time I opened one, I wondered if it came from Ty Ty.

One thing hasn't changed. The Baptist Church is the biggest and most expensive building in town. They call it the First Baptist Church, but I'll bet none of them know it wasn't the first. The first was the Big Baptist Church on the Square. It had lost most of its congregation after the race riots in the spring of 1968, after Dr. King had been killed, and all the white folks who could afford it had moved out of town. The folks who were left tried to keep it open. They'd even rented it out to a Unitarian congregation on Sunday afternoons, but it hadn't worked. They sold the steeple bell to some huge fundamentalist church in Griffin. The pews went to an antique dealer. There wasn't even a sign anymore, and the white cemetery was becoming overgrown with thistle, like the old slave cemetery always had been.

I see the sign for Horton's barbershop and turn toward it. I am surprised that it is still there, until I get closer and realize it isn't. The windows are brown with dust, and the red and white candy cane pole is gone. I get out of the car and press my face against the window. Empty. There are white circles on the floor where the old fashioned barber's chairs had sat, and littler ones above where the ceiling fans shaped like ship's sails had been. The only thing left is a tool company calendar from which a blonde woman in a bathing suit surveys the room. I remember that the calendar women in the 1930s wore a lot less clothes than this one has on. The calendar page is August 1970.

I get back in the car and drive west toward the church. Among the poor and illiterate, Baptist was the church of choice. Among the affluent and politically inclined, Baptist was the church of choice. Since these two groups did not mingle, Ty Ty, like most towns, had at least two Baptist churches. Rich folks and politicians attended the Berea Baptist Church on the square; the poor folks attended the Gospel Truth Church. That had been my family's church.

The door is gone and all the glass has been broken from the windows. The cemetery is overgrown. Most of the

286

gravestones have been knocked over. I don't try to find where Mamma and Daddy and Joey are buried. It doesn't matter, anyway. Whoever they had been was gone even before they were buried. Where are they? Is Mama with Jesus? Is Joey really in hell? I guess I'll find out pretty soon. My doctors said the cancer has spread and that I will be dead before February.

I get in the car and drive back into town. My palms are sweating and my stomach churns. I drive down street after street, circling each block three or four times, looking for anything that is the same. I run a stop sign and nearly hit another car before I realize I am being irrational. I slam on the brakes and hit my head on the steering wheel.

I pull over in front of the old bank building and rub my head. This is the first time since Joey died that I wanted to pray, but I didn't know who to pray to.

I didn't know how long I sat there, and I may have fallen asleep. I hear a tap on the window. An old woman in a poke bonnet stands beside the car. I roll down the window.

"You all right?" she asks.

"Yes, ma'am," I say. "I just . . . I just can't find anything, anymore. It's changed so much."

"Grew up here," she says. It is a statement made in surety, not a question.

"Yes, ma'am," I say. "But I guess you can't go home again."

"Sometimes you can," she says. "But that's a secret, and some secrets are best kept."

She walks away, pausing for a moment to light a corncob pipe before turning the corner and disappearing.

I jump from the car and follow her around the corner, but she's not there. Across the street, behind the barbershop, is a group of boys I hadn't seen earlier. Two of them run toward me.

"Where you been Davie?" Calvin calls.

"Yeah, where you been?" The second one asks.

Joey.

Disclaimer

These stories were inspired by scenes in the American south—from Sledge and Tupelo, Mississippi to Concord, North Carolina to Waldo, Alabama and miles and miles on back roads in these and other states.

The fictional town of Ty Ty, Georgia was first created when I lived in Tupelo. I named the town for Ty Ty Walden, the dystrophic antihero of Erskine Caldwell's *God's Little Acre*.

After moving to Georgia, I discovered the real town of Ty Ty which was named for the Ironwood and Buckwheat Trees, also called White and Black Ti Ti trees, much as Tupelo was named after the Tupelo Gum Tree. After a visit to Ty Ty, I decided to incorporate into these stories some of its features including its location in Tift County, the "line creek" on the western edge, and a few street names. However, the town and all of its inhabitants and institutions as they appear in this book are fictional, and there is intended to be no resemblance to any person, living or dead or to any institution, present or past.

On the other hand, some characters are real people.

Sergeant Matthew Goodson (also spelled Gutson), a member of a North Carolina regiment during the Civil War, was my maternal great-great grandfather. He was wounded at Gettysburg; died shortly after; was buried in a churchyard; and, along with other Confederate Soldiers, was dug up by members of the church and buried in unknown graves. There is a cenotaph bearing his name at Gettysburg, and another in his hometown of Concord, North Carolina.

The Reverend James Read "Leather Lungs" Jones was my paternal great-grandfather. He had been a lieutenant in an Indiana regiment during the Civil War before becoming a Quaker and a Temperance preacher. He ran for Governor of North Carolina on the Prohibition Ticket, and received 223 votes. In later years, he accompanied the President of the WCTU on a Temperance preaching mission. He traveled extensively throughout the South and Midwest preaching and evangelizing. He died in 1925.

David's Uncle Neal is patterned after my own Great Uncle Amzi Nealy Goodson who graduated from North Carolina College of Agriculture and Mechanic [sic] Arts on May 28 through May 30, 1916 with a degree in Electrical Engineering. Graduation took three days, including the commencement sermon. He served in the artillery in World War I, and later became Vice President for Signals for the Southern Railroad.

J. Frank Goodson was my maternal great-grandfather. His father (Sergeant Matthew Goodson) was killed at Gettysburg. Frank was educated at the Boy's Academy of Concord, North Carolina, and became President of Yorke and Wadsworth Hardware Company.

Aunt Helen is an amalgam of my Aunt Helen Marsh and my aunts Lydia Hearne and Elizabeth Floyd, all of whom were grand southern ladies—in their own way.

Historical and Chapter Notes

Funeral Casseroles

Deacon Clement's Biblical references were to Matthew 19:14, *Suffer little children, and forbid them not, to come unto me: for of such is the Kingdom of Heaven*; and Matthew 18:3, *Verily I say unto you, Except ye . . . become as little children, ye shall not enter into the Kingdom of Heaven.* There are similar verses elsewhere.

Midwives were often called "granny women" regardless of age.

Little Money, Little Dreams

"Hooverville" was the name given to shantytowns built by homeless persons during the Farm Crisis and later the Great Depression. They were everywhere in the USA: from Portland, Oregon to Central Park, New York City. Some of the shelters were little more than holes in the ground with cardboard roofs that, of course, could not withstand rain.

Franklin D. Roosevelt contracted polio in 1921. In 1926, he purchased a resort near Warm Springs, Georgia, where he received hydrotherapy in an attempt to alleviate the resulting paralysis.

The flea market was surrounded by a barbed-wire fence, often called bob-wire.

Dr. Justin claimed his elixir could cure the "sugar," which still is a colloquial name for diabetes. "The grip" was, for a long time, a nickname for influenza. "Cramp colic" is what people called appendicitis.

There are probably as many recipes for Brunswick stew as there are cooks. This one is for the fancy folks; country folks might have used squirrel or 'possum in place of beef, pork, and chicken.

Brunswick Stew

bacon drippings

1-2 onions to taste, chopped

celery, chopped

1 ½—3 lb. ground pork

Optional same amount ground beef

1 ½—3 lb. shredded cooked chicken

3, 14.5 oz cans chopped tomatoes, drained

Optional: 1—3 C diced potatoes

1 cup ketchup or more to taste

1-2 t ground black pepper

hot sauce to taste

Worcestershire sauce to taste

3 (total) 14.5 oz. cans creamed corn and lima beans

Sautee onion in bacon grease. Add celery and continue to cook until the celery is softened. Add ground pork (and beef, if using it) and brown the meat. Put in crock-pot. Add chicken, and remaining ingredients except corn and beans. Simmer. Add corn and beans about an hour before serving and heat through.

Crayons, as we know them today, were invented in 1903.

Waldo, Alabama is a real town. I don't know if it existed at the time of this story, but it did exist in 2009.

Widow Alice's Shotgun

Frances Perkins, Secretary of Labor (1933—1945) was the first woman appointed to the Cabinet. She was instrumental in co-opting the labor movement into Roosevelt's "New Deal" coalition. She shares responsibility for the Social Security Act, the Fair Labor Standards Act, and laws restricting child labor.

The Bible verse Mrs. Smart quoted is: *For I was hungry, and ye gave me meat: I was thirsty, and ye gave me drink; I was a stranger, and ye took me in.*—Matthew 25:35

Brothers' Keeper

The rabbit tobacco Granny Meeks smoked is not a tobacco, but an herb of the sunflower family, *Gnaphalium obtusifollum*, also called Life-Everlasting, Catsfoot, and other names. It has a long folk history as a medicinal plant, whether smoked or brewed as a tea.

A New Slavery

"Debt slavery" or "peonage" was a time-tested method of keeping people tied to their jobs whether they were sharecroppers or tenants on a farm, or miners and factory workers who lived in a company house and shopped at the company store. It persisted in Georgia into the 1930s. In 1930, about 60% of the state's farm population were tenants.

Convict leasing began in the south after the Civil War. Georgia stopped leasing state felons to private interests in 1908, and the practice officially ended in most of the USA by 1928. There were isolated instances where it was practiced until the beginning of World War II. State governments, large corporations, and landowners benefitted. The official justification was that while the Thirteenth Amendment to the Constitution abolished slavery and involuntary servitude, it permits involuntary servitude as a punishment for crime.

See especially Holmes, William F., Ed., "Struggling to Shake Off Old Shackles," Beehive Press, 1995.

The Great Panic

"Good" moonshine was (still is) made with corn. After the first batch was run, some folks added a bunch of sugar to the mash, and made a second run. Alcohol is alcohol, but the second run is never quite as good as the first.

The Agricultural Adjustment Act was passed two months after the "bank holiday" mentioned in this story. The act required processing facilities (mills, packing houses, etc.) to pay a tax, which was supposed to be returned to farmers to "adjust" the inequity between farm and urban income. It expanded federal powers to back farm mortgages, and gave the president the power to reduce the number of acres under production. Farm associations (such as the Grange) were exempted from anti-trust laws. And, the president was authorized to "issue paper money" and to determine the value of the dollar in gold or silver.

In the first year of the act, because crops had already been planted, the Agricultural Adjustment Administration offered between $7 and $20 an acre to farmers to plow under their cotton. The act prohibited landowners who accepted payment from evicting their tenant farmers. However, the federal government did little to enforce this, and during the 1930s, one-third of sharecroppers were forced off the land. See James Bell, *Not What We Were: The Changed and Changing South,* iUniverse 2012 (Kindle Edition).

The Ponzi Scheme wasn't invented by Mr. Ponzi; however, his was the first such fraud to be massive enough to attract a lot of attention. Charles Dickens wrote about such a scheme in *Martin Chuzzlewitt* (1844) as well as in *Little Dorrit* (1857).

Thanksgiving Day had been declared by President Lincoln to be the final Thursday in November, and would have been November 30, in 1933. The change to the fourth Thursday was made by President Roosevelt, allegedly at the behest of merchants who wanted to expand the Christmas shopping season.

The "Fifteen Percent Account" and its victims are described in a press release by the Maryland Attorney General. The link is http://www.oag.state.md.us/Press/2000/pr345.htm.

Saturday Market

The expression, "poor as Job's turkey," is not biblical. After all, the turkey is native to Mexico, and Job never saw one. The notion is that if Job were poor, his turkey would have been poorer. The expression dates from the 1880s, perhaps earlier, and appears in Tennessee Williams's play, *Cat on a Hot Tin Roof* set in the 1950s.

Martha Sasq sells honey made from pollen of the black and white ti ti trees. The "white ti ti tree" is *Cyrilla racemiflora*, also known as the he-huckleberry. The "black ti ti tree" is in an entirely separate genus. It's *Cliftonia monophylla*, also known as the buckwheat tree or ironwood tree. Both are technically shrubs, which may, however, grow to a height of more than 12 feet and resemble trees. They are both known as sources of pollen for honey production.

A shoofly is an elevated, wooden contraption that looks like a bandstand with a tree—frequently a huge liveoak—growing through the middle. It's high enough off the ground to discourage many biting insects including mosquitoes and no-see-ums.

"Drummer" was a popular term for a traveling salesman.

For where your treasure is, there will your heart be also. —Matthew 6:21

Vagrants

Laudanum is a mixture of cocaine and alcohol, once used as an anesthetic.

The girls' jump-rope verse refers to cotton flowers (white and red), and is also a comment on the high rate of infant mortality at the time.

"Ridin' the blinds" was a term used to describe one way of hitching a ride on a train, in this case, a passenger train. The technique seems to have been lost to history.

Bank Robbery

Bonnie Parker and Clyde Barrow were killed in a shootout with law enforcement officers in Louisiana on May 23, 1934.

The Earth Cries Out

Rachael's verse about pride is: *Pride goeth before destruction, and an [sic] haughty spirit before a fall.* — Proverbs 16:18. Interestingly (or not), one electronic version of the Bible refers to a "naughty spirit."

Calcium hydroxide, a type of lime commonly available at the time of this story, was often used to reduce the odor of "pit" outhouses. Wood ash from the stove was also used, but was not nearly as effective.

Boilin' Sorghum

Sorghum (*Sorghum bicolor*) is used as fodder, the production of a sweet syrup (sorghum molasses), and to create biofuel. It is technically a grain. From a distance, a mature field of sorghum cane looks a lot like corn.

David's recollection of what Deacon Clement had said about "jots and tittles" likely refers to Luke 16:17, *. . . it is easier for heaven and earth to pass, than one tittle of the law to fall.*

Chit'lins (or chitterlings) are intestines, usually of a pig, used worldwide as food. They are usually boiled (often with onion) and then may be battered and fried.

"Lightered pine," sometimes called "lighter pine" or "fatwood" is a resin-impregnated pine heartwood used as kindling.

The Klan to which Granny Meeks refers is, of course, the Ku Klux Klan (KKK). The first Klan was established in 1865 in Pulaski, Tennessee by Confederate veterans, alleged to have been lawyers. This Klan was suppressed by the Federal Government in the late 1800s, and was largely replaced by other organizations including the White League.

D. W. Griffith's 1915 movie, "Birth of a Nation," was credited—if that's the right word—with the creation of a new KKK at Stone Mountain, Georgia, less than 200 miles north of the real town of Ty Ty.

Christmas

The poem is, of course, "A Visit from St. Nicholas," more commonly known as " 'Twas the Night Before Christmas," by Clement Clarke Moore.

Decoration Day

Memorial Day was proclaimed on May 5, 1868 by General John Logan, national commander of the Grand Army of the Republic, in his General Order No. 11, and was first observed on May 30, 1868, when flowers were placed on the graves of Union and Confederate soldiers at Arlington National Cemetery.

Macon and Columbus, Georgia and Columbus, Mississippi are among the several towns that claim to have originated Decoration Day or Memorial Day, some even before the end of the war. In Georgia, April 26th was (still is) Confederate Memorial Day. Decoration Day in Ty Ty was May 10.

The Sons of Confederate Veterans claims descent from the United Confederate Veterans, and was organized in Richmond, Virginia, in 1896.

The United Daughters of the Confederacy is an amalgam of many groups, most notably the Daughters of the Confederacy, established in 1890 in Mississippi, and the Ladies' Auxiliary of the Confederate Soldiers Home in Tennessee. It was formally organized in Nashville, Tennessee, in 1894.

The American Legion was established in 1919.

Kudzu, that grew wild in the old slave cemetery, was originally imported from Japan in 1876 to landscape a garden at the Japanese Pavilion at the Philadelphia Centennial Exposition. By the early 1900s, it had been planted throughout the South as forage for cows, pigs and goats as well as for erosion control. It thrived in the acidic soil common to the South and during drought. And thrived. And thrived.

Death and Retribution

Debeaking chickens (and other fowl) is done to prevent injuries in close quarters caused by pecking and cannibalism. Yes, cannibalism. It wouldn't be done at a processing plant; however, in the vernacular, killing, plucking, and preparing chickens is sometimes referred to as "debeaking."

A "shank" is a homemade knife.

Haunted House

The worldwide influenza pandemic (1918—1919)
killed between 20 and 40 million people. As recently as 2011,
some scientists believed they had isolated the virus responsible.

Klan Revival

There are probably as many Klan hierarchies as there
are Klans. The one David knew was this:

1. Exalted Cyclops (assistants: 12 Terrors)

2. Great Titan (assistants: 12 Furies)

3. Grand Dragon (leader of a Klavern) (assistants: 9
Hydras)

4. Imperial Wizard (assistants: 16 Genis)

Much of the terrorism conducted by the Klan was
carried out by the "Klavaliers," a strong-arm group whose
Captain was nicknamed the "Chief Ass Terror."

The Tuskegee Institute records more than four hundred
lynchings of Blacks between 1920 and 1950. Not all of the
lynchings were in the South, nor was the South the exclusive
stompin' grounds of the Ku Klux Klan.

Many Klan secrets were revealed on the "Superman"
radio show in the 1940s after Stetson Kennedy infiltrated the
Klan but was unable to get help from state officials in
countering its activities. He turned his information over to the
writers of the radio show who revealed the secret handshakes
and passwords to children throughout the USA.

Civilian Conservation Corps Camp Oglethorp

Civilian Conservation Corps camps were run by the
Army and the US Forestry Service. There was a Commanding
officer and Barracks Leaders, many of whom would have been
veterans of World War I. "Enrollees" were ages eighteen

through twenty-five. Later, the age limit was dropped to seventeen. Older men who trained the enrollees were called LEMs—Local Experienced Men. They were work crew supervisors, and usually World War I veterans in their thirties and forties.

A *mohel* is a Jewish person trained in the practice of ritual circumcision, or *"brit milah."*

There were attempts at racial integration of the camps, but it didn't work anywhere in the USA, not just the South.

Influenza

Aunt Helen's thoughts were based on Epicurus (341—270 BCE): "Is God willing to prevent evil, but not able? Then he is not omnipotent. Is he able, but not willing? Then he is malevolent. Is he both able and willing? Then whence cometh evil? Is he is neither able nor willing? Then why call him God?"

"If God is good, then he is not all powerful. If God is all powerful, then he is not all good. I am a disbeliever in the omnipotence of God because of the Holocaust. But for thirty-five years or so, I have been believing that he is doing the best he can."—Norman Mailer, *The Gospel According to the Son*, Random House 1987.

David's reference to angels, Lot, and Sodom and Gomorrah is from Genesis 8:1—15. Two angels came to visit Lot, who lived in Sodom. Lot entreated them to sojourn in his home. When the men of the town came to Lot's house and demanded he turn the angels over to them so that the men might "know them" (i.e., have sex with them), Lot instead offered his virgin daughters. The men refused; the angels struck them blind.

Women's Christian Temperance Union (WCTU)

Prohibition began on January 16, 1920; it officially ended on December 5, 1933. The Georgia legislature had

300

passed a prohibition against alcohol in 1907. Blockadin' or making 'shine was important (still is, in places) not only as a tradition, but also as an essential part of rural economies.

The WCTU was established in 1873.

Cotton candy, originally called "Fairy Floss" and still called that in Australia, was invented in the late 1800s and was a feature of the 1904 World's Fair.

Boarding House Fire

The radio program David wanted to hear, *Jack Armstrong, the All American Boy*, began on WBBM radio, a "clear channel" station, in Chicago. It would not have been difficult to pick it up in Ty Ty on a winter evening. The program ran from 1933 until 1951.

Barbershop

Field and Stream magazine began publication in 1895.

The verse David was thinking of is: And Jesus saith unto them, "Yea; have ye never read, 'Out of the mouth of babes and sucklings thou hast perfected praise?' " Matthew 21:16

"I didn't mean anything by callin' Art a *retard*. It was just the way people talked back then."—David Sasq

Old Man Moss

One reason the "40 acres and a mule" paradigm didn't work was that most land was too hard to plow with only one mule.

"Denigration of blacks under the curse of Ham was an old and eminently functional standby." Stephen J. Gould, *The Mismeasure of Man*, W. W. Norton & Company, 1981.

Big David Sasq attributes the command, "raise not thy hand in anger" to the Bible. The phrase does not appear in the

King James version; however, there are warnings against anger. Here's one: *A man of wrath stirs up strife, and one given to anger causes much transgression.* Proverbs 29:22. Big David also misquotes the second phrase, which reads, *He who spareth the rod hateth his son: but he that loveth him correcteth him betimes.* Proverbs 13:24. Deuteronomy 25:3 limits the number of lashes given to a guilty man to 40; there appears not to be a limit on the number of times a child may be hit. Of course, flogging isn't the only punishment specified for recalcitrant children. Stoning to death is specifically called for in Deuteronomy 21:18—21.

The verse David was thinking of as he looked at the picture of the white Jesus and the white children is: *Jesus . . . said unto them, Suffer the little children to come unto me, and forbid them not: for of such is the kingdom of God.* Mark 10:14, Matthew 19:4

And, *Thou shalt not kill* comes from Exodus 20:13, Deuteronomy 5:17, and elsewhere.

The Golden Rule (usually quoted as "Do unto others as you would have them do unto you") appears in Matthew 7:12 (*Therefore all things whatsoever ye would that men should do to you, do ye even so to them . . .*) and Luke 6:31 (*And as ye would that men should do to you, do ye also to them likewise.*). It appears in earlier writings (those of Confucius, for example) and in other religions including Hinduism, Buddhism, Taoism, and Zoroastrianism.

"Guano" was a term for fertilizer, often required in fields whose nutrients had been depleted by repeated crops of cotton.

Blockadin' and Raidin'

The arrangement by which a person who was arrested for making or selling moonshine could buy his freedom (and buy back his car) from the sheriff was common, and an important source of income for sheriffs.

The Worth of a Man

The complete verse (I Timothy 5:18) reads, "For the scripture saith, *Thou shalt not muzzle the ox that treadeth out the corn. And, the labourer is worthy of his reward.*" Where the scripture sayeth this is open to question. The first part is from Deuteronomy 25:4. The second part appears to have been made up by the author of I Timothy who was almost certainly not the Apostle Paul. See Bart D. Ehrman's *Forged: Writing in the Name of God*, Harper Collins, 2011 (Kindle Edition).

In 1938, *Time Magazine* used the terms "World War I" and "World War II."

The Sword in the Stone, now contained in *Once and Future King,* was published as a stand-alone story in 1938.

A brief discussion of De Tocqueville's thoughts on slavery, and some speculation about what effect they had on US history, are at http://www.c-spanvideo.org/program/81239-1.

Party Line

The "Blue tick" or "Bluetick" hound is bred to be an athletic hunting dog, highly prized for coon hunting.

Coming of Age

On June 21, 1939, Wednesday, the New York Yankees announced Lou Gehrig's retirement after doctors revealed he had amyotrophic lateral sclerosis.

A "snipe hunt" is an excuse to take a boy out in the woods, usually at night, and leave him alone on the pretext of hunting snipes.

Paid God

There are many biblical references to something done seven times. A specific reference to "seven times seven" is at

Leviticus 25:8 ff. when a year of jubilee is to be declared in seven times seven, or forty nine years.

In the 1930s, fewer than 10% of rural homes had electricity. The Rural Electrification Administration (REA) was established in May of 1935, and helped create more than four hundred rural electrical cooperatives, which provided electricity to nearly 300,000 homes.

At its heart, Hoppin' John is blackeyed peas (or field peas), chopped smoked pork, and rice. Many cooks will add onion; some will add crushed red pepper; some will serve it with hot sauce.

Deacon Clement's scriptural theme for his first sermon was from Job 1:21.

The story of Jesus driving the money-changers out of the Temple in Jerusalem is at Matthew 21:12, Mark 11:15, and John 2:14. The story of Jonah and the people of Nineveh is told in Jonah 3.

Sinkhole

DDT is not soluble in water; however, given the limestone underlying the fictional Tift County and Ty Ty, it could have percolated through the soil and been carried to the wells. It is now known not to be a carcinogen, although it was suspected to be at one time.

Granny Meeks's description of dreams is paraphrased from one of Uncle Remus's rhymes by Joel Chandler Harris. The last copyright date found was 1903, putting it in the public domain.

The notion that the gates of heaven and hell are close together, and without signage, paraphrases something Carl Sagan said in "Cosmos." I do not believe he was speaking in a religious context, but metaphorically.

304

Funeral Casseroles: Part II

Matthew speaks of two sparrows for a farthing. The comparable verse from Luke (12:6) reads, "Are not five sparrows sold for two farthings, and not one of them is forgotten before God."

The poem Granny Meeks quotes is a piece of "It's Good to be Old if You Know How to Do," from the rhymes of Uncle Remus, cited above.

Charles Robert Darwin

The "Christian fiction" genre is a recent phenomenon. It would have been unlikely in 1940, even in this fictional town, that library books would be so designated. On the other hand, it's not entirely impossible.

The title of Darwin's book was initially, *On the Origin of Species by Means of Natural Selection, or the Preservation of Favoured Races in the Struggle for Life.* By 1872, the title had been shortened to "The Origin of Species." Neither Darwin nor any reputable scientist has ever suggested that humankind is descended from apes.

The "Scopes Monkey Trial" was in 1925, fifteen years before the events in Ty Ty. Science was using index fossils to show the relative ages of rock in the early 1800s. By 1921, radiometric dating had shown the Earth to be from 1.6—3.0 billion years old. More recently, the age of the Earth has been established at about 4.5 billion years.

In condemning "science," Reverend Fletcher paraphrases and quotes (a translation of) the works of Augustine, co-Bishop of Hippo, and later canonized by the Catholic Church, who wrote that there is no need to be "dismayed if Christians are ignorant about the properties and the number of the basic elements of nature, or about the motion, order, and deviations of the stars, the map of the heavens, the kinds and nature of animals, plants, stones, springs, rivers, mountains . . . For the Christian, it is enough to believe that the cause of all created things is the goodness of the Creator." See Luis Granados, *Damned Good Company*, Humanist Press, 2011, Chapter 2.

When Reverend Fletcher speaks of Peter as the rock of the church, he badly misquotes Matthew 16:19, and embellishes quite a bit on his alleged powers. Fletcher's command to Mrs. Simmons paraphrases and misquotes slightly this verse: *Let the women learn in silence with all subjection. But I suffer not a woman to teach, nor to usurp authority over the man, but to be in silence. For Adam was first formed, then Eve. And Adam was not deceived, but the woman being deceived was in the transgression.* I Timothy 2:11-14. The authorship of I and II Timothy is questioned by some scholars. See *Forged, Writing in the Name of God*, by Bart D. Ehrman, Chapter 3.

Mrs. Simmons's response is from 1 Corinthians 13:13, "And now abideth faith, hope, charity, these three; but the greatest of these *is* charity." Some more recent versions of the Bible replace 'charity' with 'love.'

Deacon Clement's Visit

The Hobbit was published in September, 1937.

Airplane

"Sweet milk" was milk straight from the cow, as opposed to buttermilk (what is left in the churn after making butter).

Ushabti

For in the resurrection they neither marry, nor are given in marriage, but are as the angels of God in heaven. — Matthew 22:30

A whip for the horse, a bridle for the donkey, and a rod for the fool's back.—Proverbs 26:3

Buggy Jugs and Other Mistaken Identities

Granny Meeks's misquotation of the Bible is a common mistake. There are two versions:

"Ye shall know them by their fruits. Do men gather grapes [from] thorns, or figs [from] thistles?" Matthew 7:16

"Wherefore by their fruits ye shall know them." Matthew 7:20

In the Book of Mormon, published in 1830, Moroni 7:5 reads, "For I remember the word of God which saith by their works ye shall know them, for if their works be good, then they are good also." This references 3 Nephi 14:16, which is almost identical with Matthew 7:16.

Mrs. Fletcher was guilty of another common misquotation, that the sins of the father will be visited upon the children unto the seventh generation. The relevant verses are:

Exodus 20:5, "I the Lord thy God am a jealous God, visiting the iniquity of the fathers upon the children unto the third and fourth generation of them that hate me . . . ." and Deuteronomy 5:9 which is a copy of the verse in Exodus.

This is contradicted in Ezekiel 18:20, which reads, "The soul that sinneth, it shall die. The son shall not bear the iniquity of the father, neither shall the father bear the iniquity of the son: the righteousness of the righteous shall be upon him, and the wickedness of the wicked shall be upon him."

No wonder David was confused.

Truth or Consequences

The "lying spirit" to which David refers is described in I Kings 22:20—22: " . . .and the Lord said, 'Who will entice Ahab, that he may go up and fall at Ramoth-gilead?' And one said one thing, and another said another. Then a spirit came forward and stood before the Lord, saying, 'I will entice him.' And the Lord said to him, 'By what means?' And he said, 'I will go out, and will be a lying spirit in the mouth of all his prophets.' And He said, 'You are to entice him, and you shall succeed; go out and do so'."

Ty Ty 1999

The description of the US Marines landing on Okinawa was written by my father, Paul W. Lentz, Major, USMC. He was there.

The Serviceman's Readjustment Act of 1944, also known as the G. I. Bill of Rights, became law on June 22, 1944. Colleges across the nation quickly ramped up for the anticipated wave of veterans whose living expenses and education were funded by this act. Many colleges erected pre-fabricated housing (nicknamed "the pre-fabs").

Knucklebones, or "jacks" is an ancient game first played with small bones from an animal and now with six-pointed, metal pieces.

Acknowledgements

The manuscript was edited by Charlotte Robinson, Pat Butler, Lani Clancy, Sara DeLuca, Sharon Kling, Ellen Ulken, Jerry Watts, Rebecca Watts, Michael Weinstock, and Ann Wright. I appreciate their many suggestions and corrections. Where I have failed to incorporate them, the fault is mine.

The Writers' Circle which as of this writing meets at the Peachtree City, Georgia, Public Library suffered through early drafts of many of these stories, unstintingly sharing their talents and knowledge. The composition of the group changed over the years, and I cannot name everyone, but I thank them all.

Everything I know about blockadin', hog boilin', and a great deal more came from the *Foxfire Books*, created by Eliot Wigginton and his students beginning in 1966.

Trademarks

Trademarks herein, which may include Dixie (as in "Dixie cup"), Mason jars, Piggly Wiggly, Sterno, Trailways, Wells Fargo, Western Union, Sears-Roebuck, and World Series, are the property of their owners.

Bible Verses

Most Bible verses are quoted from the Oxford King James version.

Internet Links

Internet links were correct at the time of the writing.

Made in the USA
San Bernardino, CA
26 March 2016